Colin Johnson

Saving the World, One Mix-Tape at a Time

Austin Macauley Publishers™

LONDON · CAMBRIDGE · NEW YORK · SHARJAH

Copyright © Colin Johnson 2024

The right of Colin Johnson to be identified as author of this work has been asserted by the author in accordance with sections 77 and 78 of the Copyright, Designs and Patents Act 1988.

All rights reserved. No part of this publication may be reproduced, stored in a retrieval system, or transmitted in any form or by any means, electronic, mechanical, photocopying, recording, or otherwise, without the prior permission of the publishers.

Any person who commits any unauthorised act in relation to this publication may be liable to criminal prosecution and civil claims for damages.

This is a work of fiction. Names, characters, businesses, places, events, locales, and incidents are either the products of the author's imagination or used in a fictitious manner. Any resemblance to actual persons, living or dead, or actual events is purely coincidental.

A CIP catalogue record for this title is available from the British Library.

ISBN 9781035837564 (Paperback)
ISBN 9781035837571 (ePub e-book)

www.austinmacauley.com

First Published 2024
Austin Macauley Publishers Ltd®
1 Canada Square
Canary Wharf
London
E14 5AA

Colin Johnson grew up and still lives in Leeds. Colin's background is in academic research and technical writing, but he has also read a lot of science fiction and listened to a lot of music of all types. His experience of music and popular culture, in the novel's unnamed 'Northern town', provides the backdrop for many of the key events and misadventures of the protagonist and his friends. When he is not writing, Colin rides a bike, tries to grow a wildflower meadow and enjoys time with his family.

To my family and friends.

I am indebted to Andy Barlow, Mark Jessop, Fiona Lawson, James Robinson, Phil Walters and Ken Welch for helpful insights, comments, criticisms, and a few parties. Steve Griffin commented on some of the medical aspects of the narrative.

A key theme in the novel was inspired by the Philip K Dick short story 'Imposter', re-imagined for a Yorkshire setting in the late '70s. However, there are a few episodes that are inspired by Iain M Banks and Douglas Adams, as well as some immortal punk rock and disco tracks. Brief quotations from the song lyrics form a minor but integral part of the narrative. (And, in my opinion, the playlist that inspires 'Angie's Mix-Tape' is iconic, appealing to old and young alike.)

Finally, my heartfelt thanks go to June, Tatiana, and Alexander for their comments on the manuscript and narrative, as well as their tolerance, optimism and love.

Photograph credit: Richard Wilson.

Table of Contents

Chapter 1: The Colourful Misfits of '78 — 11

Chapter 2: Invasion of the Imposters — 34

Chapter 3: Teenage Dreams — 59

Chapter 4: Journeys into the Unknown — 77

Chapter 5: Punk Rock and Mind Control — 108

Chapter 6: Nothing Is As It Seems — 126

Chapter 7: Nicky's Imagined Worlds — 152

Chapter 8: The Power of Imagination — 176

Chapter 9: A Punk Rocker's Guide to Saving the World — 190

Chapter 10: What Was I Thinking? — 208

Chapter 1
The Colourful Misfits of '78

During that long year, we understood that something would happen and that it would change us forever. Something, I thought something had to happen soon. I longed for change, for a leap away from the ordinary world. Our school turned from a grammar school into a comprehensive and the old regime was deposed as part of an idealistic social experiment.

The new education system brought together a mix of kids from privileged middle-class and struggling families, as well as poverty-stricken hard-cases from the surrounding council estates. The kids we called 'posh' were often just different: perhaps they had a talent for literacy or numeracy that had eluded the rest of us, or they were good at sports. Sometimes it was enough to just wear Clarks Commandos shoes or ride around on a Raleigh Grifter bike. The economic state of the nation was so bad, that even these were obvious extravagances by well-to-do parents.

An uneasy expectation hung over a country, directionless and exhausted by the Three-Day Week, now confronted by the new challenges of the Winter of Discontent. It was all so dreary and grey, that something had to happen even if you had to think it up yourself.

People were muttering and complaining about unfathomable problems. Even we felt a brief unease, but our friendships and conspiracies had the more pressing urgency. The news talked of strikes and the Middle East, but we cared nothing about this outside world; it felt as dull as the 40-watt light bulb in our kitchen.

When even this light went out during the power-cuts, I came home from school to do my homework by candlelight. However, my problems were all simpler and much more interesting: I knew too many kids called Paul; I wanted to go out with a girl; and I had developed an over-active imagination.

In one of the English classes at school, I'd heard a quotation mentioned that 'the imagination was the greatest instrument of moral good'. I wasn't sure what it meant but took this as validation for the elaborate dream-like narratives that I thought up. In them, I was always the central figure, the courageous and modest hero, who saved the day.

'My imagination will get me into trouble one day,' I mused to myself. *'It'll be the death of me. But everyone will know my name and thank me for my selfless bravery. I'll be a legend.'*

My last problem was that I was one of those middle-class posh kids, but I had made friends from way back in primary school and I had to pretend that I wasn't. They called me Nicky, and this was how everybody knew me at school assuming, of course, that it was short for Nicholas.

Once we hit puberty and I suppose hit was the right word, they started calling me *Hairy*, because I got a hairy chest before any of the other boys. But my first name is Nikolai because my father was Russian. This marked me out as very different very early on, even from the first day of primary school, and I made sure that not many people knew about my embarrassing father.

If I was ever asked about his accent, I had this line that he was Finnish, and this usually satisfied a casual questioner. Russians were always thought to be evil Communists, plotting to overthrow Western democracy, and I didn't want questions or worse at school.

But, in all honesty, as I grew up, I became more and more baffled about my father's account of events. He had married my English mother and had simply been allowed to leave the U.S.S.R. in the sixties to start a new life in a Northern English town. Both of my parents worked at the Polytechnic and seemed to be perpetually busy whenever I needed advice or help.

My father, also called Nikolai and after whom I was named, was a dour and humourless presence in the house. He preferred to be a gloomy chain-smoker, sallow-faced, sitting in his leather armchair, marking essays than to engage with me, his teenage son.

I was becoming a disappointment to him, but then, it seemed clear to me, his entire life was a disappointment. The marriage he left Moscow for was a disappointment. Whatever the promises that had been made to him, life in this country had proved to be a disappointment as well.

He sometimes criticised the British for being phoney, meaning that they were insincere or pretentious because they were tactful or observed social decorum. But, round our end, he was equally bewildered by the uncouth lack of tact and decorum from ordinary Northern folk. There were solipsistic tendencies about the sensitive and refined nature of the Russian character, particularly his own. I could well imagine him weeping in front of a couple of birch trees but ignoring a crying child.

He seemed more affectionate to his blue-and-white pack of Players Number 6s. A pack was never too far away, so that he could burn off the hours and minutes in his daily routine; you could almost set your watch by when he lit up, it was so regular. I really disliked his smoking from a young age because I felt that he played a fake role so that he could conceal and keep his distance. It was, quite literally, a smokescreen against the world and, in particular, his family.

It saddened him that, as I grew up, I took my role models and values from the British rather than Russians. But how else could it be? I was desperate to fit in and to be liked. He seemed so disconnected, unfulfilled, and unhappy that he never inspired me as a role model. In retrospect, with my professional clinical eye, I recognise that his strange detachment was brought on by clinical depression and his lifelong struggles against alcoholism. He never drank when I was growing up and still at home, and these were all past struggles that he thought were left back in the U.S.S.R. But unresolved issues have a habit of returning to blight you later in life. For him, they manifested as emotional detachment and a chain-smoking habit that replaced one addiction with another.

At the time, his detachment felt like emotional neglect. Perhaps this explained much of what happened afterwards. I must have longed to have a proper father in my life. Without that effective father-figure guiding me through my early teenage years, I turned away from my strange and self-absorbed parents early on and made my own way in life; aimless, unchecked, and unrestrained.

My friends and I formed a gang that lasted throughout primary school, and we carried on when we moved up to the comprehensive. Sometimes during the week, we met on the backs late in the afternoon after school or early evening. In the unremitting summer drought of 1976, we messed around in the wood, played tig or hide-and-seek or hot rice, and built a tree house.

There was even enough wood left over, strapped and tied together, to make a raft. We added empty plastic jerry cans underneath to make it float, and after that, it could take three of us if we were careful. The Saturday morning that we sailed it down that part of the beck in the woods was the highlight of that year. It must have been in early August during the school holidays.

I remember the ladybirds had swarmed in the sunlight, forming red encrustations on every blade of grass. Whole fields, burnt yellow by the drought, turned red overnight as if it was an invasion by an alien life form. We came home from the fields or woods and queued in the street for our turn to fill up some of the jerry cans with council juice from a standpipe.

In 1977, we celebrated the Queen's Silver Jubilee with a street party, the whole country, child and adult alike, seemed to be excited by the event. We were in our early teens by then and less impressed. We made a nuisance of ourselves, ate sausage rolls, fell out and argued with each other and then with our parents, teased the younger kids, and then jeered the amateur magician attempting to entertain us.

The longest power-cut was in early November 1977. From then on, the gang had the custom of going outside during the power-cuts that winter, carrying torches if our parents had a spare one, because the streetlights were switched off as well. The only light outside was from the candles in the windows of houses or from the moon if it was a clear night.

It was barely possible to see in the greyness, but this made everything more challenging and entertaining. Once on the street by the backs, in the light of the torches, Jon rolled his eyes back and started moaning that he would search us out in the dark.

This was the beginning of his Imposter trance, and the gang knew what to expect, but the twilight in the streets made it more intense and scarier. We were a bit too old for this game, to be honest, but we wanted to scare some of the younger kids that hung around with us. Jon could be very convincing.

"A'm gonna get all o' ya!" he would moan before trembling and falling into his special Imposter trance. "All o' ya! Not gonna spare none o' ya! *Klaatu barada nikto*." In the darkness, he claimed to transform into what he called an Imposter, before reverting into a human.

Fortunately, for the younger kids, the Imposter chased us in the twilight by following accepted custom. We were allowed to use the torches when we were being chased, but this made us an obvious target. Sometimes, it was better to turn off the torch and stand very still in the darkness, breathing slowly to suppress nervous giggling. Jon, as the Imposter, bounced the ball between us in time to the usual chant.

Hot rice, bounce twice
Shit pies, taste nice

We all scattered because we were now living targets for the Imposter, which took the ball as its weapon. The Imposter threw the ball at us and if hit, we too were subverted and became an Imposter. The younger children, terrified and screaming in the dark, were the first unwilling victims.

Then throwing the ball between us, a horde of Imposters cornered the remaining survivors. The Imposters would always win. In the end, everybody was subverted. The last survivor would pass through the Tunnel of Death, and Jon would come back to us, but would be unresponsive and then confused. He would talk normally for a while but then unpredictably, would fall back into the Imposter trance.

"Ah can feel it, it's happening, can't stop it. You've gotta run! Help me, it's hurting me!" He paused for effect, so that the younger kids had the full benefit of the transformation. "*Klaatu barada nikto.*" It was a line he'd picked up from a film on telly.

I soon learned that Jon's older brother—an electrician we nicknamed Drillbit—had recurrent episodes of epilepsy. Jon was pretending to have a seizure and the postictal confusion that he must have seen on several occasions at home and hospital. Some of us may have known this at the time—although I didn't—but by an unspoken agreement, this was a serious adult matter that was of only passing relevance and shouldn't be discussed.

Everybody just thought that Drillbit was a bit slow because he spoke in stuttering phrases, interrupted by pauses as if the power had dimmed and had then come back in a flash of buzzing clarity. Folklore had it that Drillbit had got a near-fatal electric shock at work and that it had scrambled his brain. Jon himself never spoke about any of it, but was fiercely loyal and protective of his peculiar elder brother.

I realised later that Jon was probably redirecting his own fear by frightening the rest of us with his Imposter trance. Drillbit (his real name was Neville) was a nice bloke, not least because he found odd jobs for Jon and me on various building-sites as we were growing up.

You got used to the episodic and slightly haphazard nature of the conversations with him. A couple of times he did cartoons of our faces, sketching them with a pencil in a notepad. He did a ruthless job of capturing our most easily caricatured features.

With me, he exaggerated the slab-like flatness of my cheeks, my broad nose and my tooth-crammed smile to make me look like a hoodlum with emotional vulnerabilities. I still have Neville's caricature and it hangs in a frame to the side of my desk at home. That carefree, handsome face looks out at me, confident and unsuspecting, the eyes still clear and undaunted by experience. I barely recognise the teenage Nicky from the times back then.

Jonathan Holdsworth was a good, quiet, hard-working kid. He was the quietest one of all of us, but he didn't need anything to prove unlike the rest of us. It was clear that he was going to pick up a trade and take over his dad's business with his elder brother.

In those years of the gang, he was the quiet and supportive one, the clever, unexcitable one who knew when to help and to say a few words to make it better. If Jon ever did anything malicious, it was because we put him up to it because, by nature, he was a bit kinder than the rest of us. He understood and even encouraged my unhealthy obsession with science fiction.

I can still remember the first few tattered sci-fi paperbacks that I picked up at a jumble sale and what an effect they had on me. They revealed a new alternate reality to me that had previously been hidden at a remove or at a tangent from this one. It was as if something always sensed out of the corner of my eye, suddenly came into full focus.

Jon and I read all sorts of paperbacks voraciously and indiscriminately throughout our teenage years. We started out with space wars, mercenary heroes, princesses-of-the-sands and death worms but we soon acquired tastes that were more sophisticated.

Paul Baxter was dapper and well spoken, quick-witted with his repartee and in the comedic turns that he did to amuse the rest of us. He seemed to be a born entertainer. Despite the broad humour, he had the coolest head when we got in a pickle, with an ability to get to the heart of the problem and to solve it for the rest of us.

Then there was the other Paul-with-Glasses, Paul Ronson. He was the most flamboyant and opinionated out of all of us, making us listen to the terrible mix-tapes that he made of his favourite tracks. He was the one that came up with most of the schemes that got us into a pickle in the first place. Somehow, he had a gift in persuading us to go along with his plans and to become willing accomplices.

I think that there were two reasons for this. He was the shortest one of the four of us, and to compensate, he seemed to need an outsized personality to get attention. The second reason was that his mother had died the year before and, nowadays, he lived with just his dad.

The need for attention was a trait that I understood all too well. People from back then would say that I was fun to be around and that I made friends easily but stood by them. That was because I needed them since I had no one else in my life. It was the 'ceaseless longing of a yearning to belong'.

From those years of the gang and beyond, I owe my loyal, wonderful friends such a debt of gratitude. All I can do is recount the events and repercussions of that long year as an extended note of thanks, explanation, and apology.

***

I should also add that Jon was the only one of my friends who understood me when I made my odd references to science fiction. Nobody else really understood either of us when we started talking about the books we'd read or the weird sci-fi ideas that we'd come across. Nobody else wanted to go to see 'Star Wars' with us in February 1978 because it was a kid's film.

Kids went down to the Elmete Lane shops to buy packs of bubble gum—*chuddy*, as it was called—that had three filmcards showing scenes from the film. By the time we got to watch the film, we had already seen the best bits from the kids swapping cards outside the shop or at school.

"Giz ya chuddy an' all," they would say, if they were trying to drive a hard bargain for a swap with a rare or particularly prized card in the series.

We quite enjoyed the film, I suppose, but afterwards we felt cheated that it hadn't given us something more thought provoking. We were a bit too old for it. The music reminded me of Tchaikovsky and the LP of 'Swan Lake' excerpts that my dad sometimes listened to on our music centre. It had a small display that glowed an unearthly, toxic green like the eye of an alien invader.

The switches and knobs, silky and silver-coloured, seemed to be the arcane relics in a ritual that only my father fully understood. I remember that his eyes moistened while he listened to the tragic end of Odette and Prince Siegfried.

"It was just a kid's film, Hairy," Jon said sadly, unable to contain his disappointment after watching 'Star Wars' with me. We had become sci-fi snobs. "They were right. I wanted it to be so much more." We'd moved on from robots and galactic empires a long time ago.

The science fiction we liked was fun as well. It was also worthwhile as there was an edge of existentialist drama or psychological insight into the human condition. We didn't, of course, attach those labels to the authors we read or the shows we watched at the time.

I went round to Jon's house to watch the shows because his family had a colour telly, unlike my parents who could only afford a small black-and-white one on hire purchase. My father saved the Green Shield stamps he received after paying the monthly rental, but it hardly seemed worth the effort because they could only be exchanged for tat in the shop.

***

The new Ice Age that they were always taking about on the telly began in early January. There were huge blizzards that blocked roads. School closed. This was, we dimly realised, probably the most exceptional and exciting event that would be happening to us in the grey backdrop of that year. It probably wasn't going to get much better than this.

The snowdrifts seemed to glow from inside with a pale, unworldly light that dulled our voices. We ventured out into the snow, our parents delighted that we were out of the house so that they could drink, or have it off, or whatever else adults did when they had unexpected spare time.

My parents would probably just spend the time working or marking stuff for the Poly. They were either unaware of the petty theft and pointless trouble that we committed, or couldn't be bothered to find out unless it spilled into real police trouble. But this was rare; we got into fights, but nobody carried knives and nothing serious ever happened.

Earlier in December, Drillbit's friend was stabbed outside the neighbouring sink school. Jon told us that the police informed his parents that the guy was dealing speed and stabbed for his drug money. Some of us had seen Drillbit's friend outside our school and Jon confirmed that he had been expelled a couple of years ago.

"He's a right div," said Jon, passing judgement. "He's gonna get his head kicked in." Paul pointed out that getting stabbed was probably worse, but Jon told him to stop being clever because we all knew what he meant. He was upset about the stabbing.

"Yeah, he was always proper divvy, him. He got stabbed in the arm. It's them kids from Beechwood, they're mental." We considered this new information about our rivals from the other school and our mood darkened.

"They're not normal. They can't get away with it," said the other Paul-with-Glasses.

The Beechwood kids were notorious because they were uncontrollable when the red mist descended. Legend had it that one year, they had broken out of school, ransacked the dining hall and attacked everybody with stolen forks. There were eyewitnesses to the event in our own school. Angela even had a battle-scar caused by the tines, a run of red puncture marks on her thigh. She would lift the hemline of her skirt and show you if you paid her 10p.

This was good enough evidence to keep our rivalry simmering throughout that winter. Stabbing with a knife was, by unspoken agreement, further dishonour, and an act that only Beechwood could commit. This was clear provocation and escalation of the rivalry between the tribes.

"We need to do summat!" Speccy-Paul said. "I bet that they'll be sledging on Hill 60. We'll get the Thommo twins on the way home."

"Yeah, they're soft as anything, them two. They're posh." Jon had been considering the options for retaliation. "We'll just scare them a bit."

The Thompsons were popular at Beechwood because they formed a two-man package on their football team, playing wing positions on outside right and outside left, almost as if they were reflections of each other on the pitch. Once in their kit, they were practically identical. Then, they had another trick that confused opposition players even more because they dropped back to midfield in the second half.

Chris, out of the pair, was friendlier but also more volatile on the pitch, whereas Steve was quieter and didn't take chances. They were popular, but they weren't hard-cases and their talent for sport marked them out as different. We had the instinctive English disdain of anybody who did well through hard work, talent or luck and felt that they were the deserving targets of retaliation.

We were willing to bet that the real Beechwood hard-cases didn't like them enough to defend their honour. In any case, none of us had that much interest in football.

"Chris Thompson always does dirty tackles, and he busted your Owen's knee," Spex continued, feeling that further justification was needed to persuade us. Owen was Jon's younger brother and a centre-back on our team. "You haven't forgotten, have you Jon? We make it look like an accident on Hill 60. We'll do it on Saturday when they'll be there with their mates."

"That's rubbish, Spex! How do you know all of that?" Paul was back-tracking and wanted to be sure about details. The Thommo twins were a sensible target and well within our league. But we were still running a risk with the Beechwood gang. "What if that McElroy is there? He's Cock o' the School. He's a proper nutter."

Locally, it was known as Hill 60 although the proper name was Summer Hill. Old-timers would know that it was named after a battle during the First World War. Passing it on as folklore to their grandkids, it all got conflated and confused with recent stories from parents about the Second World War and the general mistrust of foreigners or anybody thought to be 'German'.

Nobody knew what to make of me with a supposedly Finnish father. But, by contrast, Paul was beaten up once because an older kid, from Beechwood, thought that Paul had a 'German' grandfather. In fact, the grandfather was Polish, and after escaping from Poland during the War, was stationed at an airfield near to York.

Afterwards, Paul was baffled by the ignorance of English schoolkids, brought up as he was on heroic tall tales about his grandfather. (Paul later told me that the man had not seen active combat and was a supply driver in the logistic corps, but Paul was still proud of him even though his role was not as glamorous as the stories suggested.)

Paul must have boasted about this outside of school, repeating some of the stories and Army patter that went with it, because the older Beechwood kid had taken exception to it all and Paul in particular. His patter could get annoying, to be honest, if you didn't know Paul well.

The way Paul told the story afterwards; he was met on the way home from school, got knocked around for being 'German' and was left in a hedge. Next time, the kid threatened to carve his initials into Paul's back. In the fine balance of violence, intimidation and retribution in our schoolyard, this incident really tipped the scales.

The offence was so egregious, in fact, that the Beechwood bully never bothered Paul after that first time. Our Cock o' the School, often long on the privilege of the position and short on the schoolyard responsibilities that it entailed, was asked to re-educate with a historical perspective.

Somehow, he was able to explain the situation to McElroy, the Beechwood Cock o' the School and aspiring criminal. It was never clear how the convoluted system of patronage worked in the schoolyard. But one day before the end of term in December, McElroy the Younger met Paul at the school gates, accompanied by two of his hard-case lieutenants.

McElroy, tall and intimidating, was unmistakeable, striding up with a regal swagger. He was a full-on skinhead, his Irish red hair just beginning to grow through the cut, wearing a green combat jacket and Doc Martens. He looked every inch the bovver boy, primed to explode into violence with little or no provocation. It was against school rules to go skinhead, but the rules didn't apply to the McElroys.

"You're Paul Baxter," he stated. "I'm Paul—"

"I know who you are."

"We sorted out your wee problem with Jonesy." (This was the name of the Beechwood bully.) "He didnae need to chin ya like that; it was stupid." His accent was different to ours; he had our flat vowels and the dialect, but there was an additional Irish burr to his speech. Despite the bovver boy appearance, Paul said afterwards that he was quite well spoken. Almost posh. Words, and the way they were said, really mattered to Paul.

"Well, ta very much. It was stupid getting beaten up because my granddad was a war hero and everything."

"If we needed to chin ya, we'd have made sure," McElroy replied quietly. "But you didnae deserve that from Jonesy."

That afternoon, as we were planning our pointless little retribution against the Thommo twins, Paul was in a difficult position. He had accepted patronage from a Cock o' the School, which, like it or not, made him a client who would owe a McElroy a favour. Anything that disrupted that balance of debt and obligation could be seen as welching on his unspoken deal with a McElroy.

"Gents, I'm not sure this is a good idea. Jon, I know how you feel." Paul could see Jon bridling and about to raise an objection. "I know how you feel about Owen getting his knee busted and all that, but it's just not worth picking on the Thompson twins. What if McElroy's there and sees it?"

"Nah, McElroy's not mates with the Thommo lads."

"He's a real nutter!" piped up Speccy-Paul, stating the obvious.

"Yeah, Spex, I know that McElroy's a total nutter," Jon replied patiently. "We don't want him working stuff out."

"I heard he had a fight last week and broke a kid's arm," Speccy-Paul continued, developing his argument. "And he decked Smiggy at the petrol station and nicked loads a petrol and stuff."

The stuff meant the night-time cash in the till. Speccy-Paul was still mulling over the possibility of reprisals from McElroy and his cadre of hard-cases, all of whom were viewing borstal and then prison as career opportunities. McElroy was working his way through the variations of low-level theft and violence before being promoted to riskier criminal work.

"I don't get it." Jon had heard about the petrol station already, and he clearly thought that McElroy had also done the drug-money stabbing. "He coulda just got the petrol out of the car. Just drilled the cap and siphoned it out."

"Yeah, I know! He's daft, inney? But he needs to show 'em he can do it, he's passing a test. Needs to show his Da he's really hard."

Speccy-Paul was right. To us, it seemed senseless to do a big robbery when there were easier alternatives at hand. I wondered if McElroy the Younger was being set up to test his resolve by robbing Smiggy, and the earlier, crazy knife stabbing was part of this initiation. We called him McElroy the Younger just to prevent confusion with all the other Pauls who we knew, but who didn't aspire to organised criminality.

"But he won't be at Hill 60. They've cleared the pitch at Elland and it's a home match this Saturday. He'll be down there. He'll be rolling." Speccy-Paul meant he would be helping the general pick-pocketing, petty theft and intimidation that accompanied the larger league games.

He wasn't going down there to watch the football that was for certain. We wondered if the petrol was going to be used to torch a car as a reprisal or intimidation tactic, perhaps as a final *rite-de-passage* for the younger McElroy before he entered the family business. It was one of those old-fashioned, traditional family-run concerns that specialised in prostitution, protection rackets and extortion.

However, torching a car at the match seemed much too public a display for them. Their usual style would be to use the petrol quietly one night. In any case, the fact that McElroy and his hard-cases were busy on Saturday afternoon finally pushed the argument Jon's way.

The plan needed Jon to break into the builder's store on the new Grove estate. The builders had dug trenches for the new footings and laid pipes, but the concrete had not been delivered because of a driver's strike and the work had now stopped because of the weather.

Paul and I went with Jon to keep a lookout, to break into the store and to move the spoils to our hiding place in the Grove woods. We met on Friday afternoon. Paul brought a sledge to help with the moving, which we decided was less conspicuous than three lads carrying building materials across the estate.

This part of the city had been countryside in the time of the big mills, and the big mill-owners had built their ancestral houses away from the noise and smoke. The industry had not survived the latter half of the twentieth century, but the houses still stood until the ancestors had sold them for redevelopment. Some were patched-up or rebuilt as unusually grand special schools or old people's homes or split into separate apartment flats. But many of the old houses were already derelict and were just demolished to make way for building plots. We had made a secret path through the woods, broken through the boarding on the lower floor windows, and had spent the previous summer exploring the remains of Grove House and the garden.

Roof tiles had blown off the house and the rain had rotted wood and peeled the antique wallpaper. There were still patches of mouldy copper green and a greyish damask red in what had probably been a long dining room overlooking the garden. Many of the floorboards had already been removed for salvage, and we had to move carefully from joist to joist to avoid stepping on the shanks of nails.

Inside, it was heavy, dank and dim even on sunny days. We didn't want to fall into the cellar since it was full of rotten plaster that had collapsed in big clumps from the ceilings, exposing the lathes and horsehair. We told Jon that it was hair from millworkers who had been killed in the factory, and that there were rats in the cellar gnawing on the human remains.

Hints of the magnificent past of the house were some decorative tiles, which we immediately prised up and stole for no obvious purpose and metal balustrades following the line of an enormous, sweeping staircase. We did not dare tread on the stair-joists to go up to the upper floor for fear of ending up with the rats in the cellar.

The garden was derelict as well. In front, there was a big rectangular tennis court, surrounded by a perimeter of overgrown shrubs. By the house, there was a small, sunken courtyard, which had roses gone weak and lanky over the years. To one side there was a dilapidated mulberry tree, an ugly jumble of twigs and branches that had never borne any berries. Apples trees were further back, and the orchard then merged into scrub, brambles and trees in sparse woodland. Here, the mill-owner had taken the notion to landscape a Chinese garden using heaps of huge gritstone boulders that had been arranged into pretend hills, zigzagging galleries and grottos. Paths ran between the hills and entwined back to a little arched bridge that crossed the valley between the hills, surrounded by thickets of bamboo.

We gleefully sawed up the wooden bridge and used the timber to make a den hidden inside one of the grottos. We cut down bamboo to fashion a roof covering and to disguise the front. It was our private hiding place; our gang headquarters and our meeting place for that year. It was an excellent outpost to hold out against an attack by Imposters.

In the meantime, Spex had acquired a cassette deck from someone and insisted on playing some of his mix-tapes until the batteries ran out. He had, it was fair to say, eclectic and broad tastes in popular music, all taped off the radio in his bedroom. Everybody hated The Sex Pistols, we weren't keen on The Clash but we understood the Buzzcocks. Or rather, they seemed to understand us.

Pete Shelley sang about our aimless lives as lovelorn teenagers, and when we committed those petty acts of aimless violence, we didn't feel so alone. There were misfits out there just like us, except of course, that they were also on the telly and in the charts.

Spex loved the idea that punk was even rebelling against punk itself. Then, just released in time for the February edition of his mix-tape, Spex found us a bootleg copy of 'Shot by Both Sides' by Magazine.

Shot by both sides
On the run to the outside of everything
Shot by both sides

After that, we adopted shot by both sides as another catch phrase to signal our status as misfits and outsiders, and I took the song to heart as a bit of a personal anthem.

The arrival of builders on the east side of the estate meant that we had new opportunities for exploration and petty theft. I had found a crowbar and rusty plumber's wrench, which we hid in the den for future use, as well as a useless collection of brick-tiles to add to the decorative tiles from Grove House.

We had also pilfered a paraffin lamp and some concrete bricks to support the roof timbers. Speccy-Paul had even lugged a carpet offcut from his auntie's house for the floor and had found some bitumen felt from somewhere to waterproof the roof.

That Friday afternoon, we used it as the base for our most daring raid yet; breaking and entering the builder's store. In Grove Wood, the den was hidden in snow and there were no footprints visible nearby in the estate. The builders had packed up early and we were alone on the building site. We picked up the tools from the den. Jon was nervous.

"Mustn't get caught, my brother knows the gaffer here."

"Drillbit wouldn't sprag us up," I replied.

"Nicky, I keep asking you to stop calling him Drillbit!"

"He is boring, and he is a bit of tool," interspersed Paul, to try to get a laugh as usual, even with an audience of two. "Soz, no offence," he added, after Jon didn't disagree.

"Jon. You sure they're using that stuff?" I asked to get them to focus on the task in hand.

"Yeh, they must'be, 'Hairy'," said Jon, using my nickname in retaliation. "They're putting down concrete. It's what they use, I've seen 'em doing it fer floors."

We crossed the flat snow of the tennis court, pulling Paul's sledge, passed the indistinct trenches and foundations of the new houses and found the store on the eastern part of the estate. The door was padlocked, but we wanted to be discrete and not cause obvious damage that would tip off the builders. After all, we might want to come back to nick other stuff and we wanted the builders to keep on using their store.

Jon used a chisel to scrape out the new putty from the window-frame, with me following behind with pliers to pick out the mounting nails. Paul lifted out the glass-pane and we gave Jon a careful leg-up through the window. Jon passed back one end of a long roll of black plastic sheeting, the damp proofing put on earth before concrete was poured.

"Hey! Cheer up, Hairy! You've got a face like a slapped arse."

"I'm cold and this is pointless," I replied.

"What are you being maungy for? I told'ya we'd find some. Whaddya think o' this lot then?" Jon disappeared inside again, rummaged around and then, with a smug nod, handed me a big, soft roll of brown rockwool. "Rock on! D'ya geddit? We can sit on it."

"For an idea that Spex had, it's not too bad," conceded Paul.

"And that, fellers, is yer lot! No more nickin' for little Nicky today."

Jon carefully lifted the glass-pane back in. I tapped the nails back in and then we spent a good ten minutes bickering in the cold while we applied the putty back on the frame, Jon fussing with it like a kid with a plate of Brussels sprouts.

"Nick. Nick, stop. You're doin' it all wonky up there, are ya blind or summat? You'll give it all away. Builders'll see it and they'll work it out. They're not daft."

"I'm still cold. And this is still pointless."

Jon, exasperated by my lack of skill with the putty, smoothed it out himself and then cleaned the glass of any marks. With luck, on Monday, the builders wouldn't notice anything unusual, and if anyone missed a couple of rolls then they would assume that they had simply been mislaid.

We loaded our new acquisitions onto the sledge and pulled them across the estate to the den. And the final flourish was, of course, that any snow falling over the weekend would hide our tracks. It was a simple and elegant plan, executed, we felt, with nerve and finesse.

On Saturday morning, we all met at the den as usual. Jon had brought his younger brother Owen along as ballast for the ride, but he was a trusted member of the gang. Angela, Paul's cousin, was there as well. We cut several long lengths of the sheeting so that, doubled over, we could all sit on it with the rockwool inside as some sort of cushioning.

The whole assemblage was huge and on the icy parts of Hill 60, it would be dangerously fast, perhaps as fast as forty miles an hour. And it would be impossible to steer with seven or more of us on it.

We had bad memories of Hill 60 from the summer because we had built a go-kart that had old pram wheels, and the inaugural and last journey had been down Hill 60. How Speccy-Paul had talked us round to trying the go-kart on Hill 60 was still a mystery.

I remember that he had emphasised, as he called them, the advanced safety features, which consisted of a pair of rudimentary lever brakes, adding that we probably wouldn't need to use them anyway. Three of us had piled on; at full speed, the front axle had snapped, the whole front had pitched into the ground, and we had been tossed either onto or over the go-kart. It was an utter disaster.

I had a gouge above my left knee, Jon was bruised and shaken and blamed Speccy-Paul for coming up with the insane idea in the first place, I blamed Speccy-Paul who had got the shoddy wheels, and Speccy-Paul blamed his auntie for buying such a crap pram for his cousin.

This time, in winter, we judged that no wheels meant more speed and less risk, at least to those of us clinging onto the sheeting. We were going to be the biggest, fastest outfit up there; it was going to be legendary, and we were about to pass into schoolyard history.

"Never before has anyone risked Hill 60 on a plaggy sheet! But this trusty group dare to do the impossible and put their very lives at risk…"

"I'll put your life at risk if you don't shur'rup."

"…in facing this terrifying challenge!" Paul continued the mock-reportage in his posh TV voice. Turning to Jon, "Mr Holdsworth, please ignore that oik. His limited imagination cannot contemplate the enormity of the task at hand. You are leading this expedition."

"No, he's not!" piped up Speccy-Paul. "He's just a crook nickin' stuff! You wanna be talkin' to me. It was my idea! I'm the brains o' the outfit!"

"Shit-fer-brains more like."

"Gentleman, please!" Paul said in his best suave voice. "This is unbecoming of the conquerors of Hill 60."

"We haven't done it yet, Paul!"

"Mr Holdsworth, as I was saying, before I was so rudely interrupted by these oiks! Whatever possessed you? Seriously, man, you must know it's all going to go tits up."

"Thank you, Mr Useless-Reporter-Bloke. We have spent a long time deliberating on the course of action…"

"Ya did what? Yer a dirty so-and-so. Does yer mam know?"

"…and we've come to the conclusion that we could die."

"Hang on! No-one said anything about dying! Me mam'll kill me!"

"Yer really are shit-fer-brains; yer gonna be dead anyway, and yer mam's gonna be scrapin' you up with a shovel."

"Look, men! Quiet!" Paul, ever the versatile mimic, was doing his best Army officer voice now. "We need some volunteers for a pointless and futile task that can only end in a slow and agonising death."

"Oh mother! I don't want to die this young!" We could keep up this banter with Paul's well-worn characters such as the Reporter and the Army Officer for hours at a time.

"Knock off with the dying, will you? It's gonna be reet good, a reet belter." Speccy-Paul felt that the conversation was taking a morbid slant, and he was concerned that we would talk ourselves out of it. "Really good," he added with emphasis, as if this would convince us further.

"You know the go-kart was Paul's idea as well?" Angela contributed, referring to Speccy-Paul rather than our resident comedian. "Anyone else seeing a pattern here? I'm seeing a pattern of behaviour that leads to serious injury."

The fact that Speccy-Paul hadn't even ridden the first test of the go-kart was still a point of contention six months later.

"It wasn't that serious. Hairy gashed his knee. Walking wounded, like."

"Well, you're still going to try it first. See if it's safe," I replied. "I'll hold your glasses." They were thick NHS prescription glasses with lenses like the bottom of milk bottles. Speccy-Paul was very shortsighted: we called him X-Ray Spex, or just Spex for short, named after one of his favourite bands.

"Hairy. Hairy, just listen, will ya?" Jon added. "Hate to break it to ya but it's not safe. 'Specially when Speccy-Four-Eyes here slides into something sharp and breaks or bursts summat," he added for the rest of us.

"Oh, that's a relief. Just for a minute there, I thought that I heard you say 'it wasn't safe'. That's alright then," said Angela. "Nothing to be concerned about."

Hill 60 was heaving with people and, as predicted, a few Beechwood kids. Over several days, the thick snow from earlier in the week had been compacted and had then frozen overnight into a skating-rink on a steep slope. It was an ideal shape, shallow at the top for a gradual start and for picking up speed, a long hurtling steep section, and then a levelling out in between trees.

This last section was the test, the obvious aim being to shoot between the trees without injury. It was what made Hill 60 a feared ritual challenge for anybody trying to prove something in nearby schools. It was second only to 'Big Mama', a 25-foot wall beside a concrete apron, that an aspiring Cock o' the Year or Cock o' the School was expected to drop if he was to consolidate his power and influence.

Hill 60 was much the same, but a surer test of skill and flair than dropping off a big wall onto concrete and breaking an ankle. McElroy, the Beechwood Cock o' the School, had broken his last year and the rumour was that he had blubbed like a little kid until the teachers had taken him away.

Angela was aware the iconic draw the hill had in our adolescent male minds but was probably unaware of our plan with the Thommo twins. I realised that Paul had brought his pretty cousin along precisely because she would be an innocent party and would give the rest of us some credibility in claiming that it was all an unfortunate accident.

Paul was keen to provide some plausible deniability, as he would call it, to our actions. However, for my part, I also began to realise that Angela may not have been there for just the sledging and began to wonder if, perhaps, she wanted to be there with me as well.

Or perhaps she just liked being around funny, clever, tough lads.

"I'll just say serious injury again," she added with a moue and wrinkle of her pretty nose.

"Nah, we're experienced professionals, Angie. Even we can't muck it up that much!" Speccy-Paul handed me his glasses with a flourish and clambered onto our decrepit entry in the contest. "It looks like a heap o' rubbish and that's 'cos it is! But bet it moves like shite off'a shovel. C'mon sweetheart, let's do it," he added, lewdly, lying down and grabbing the corners.

"You really are a dirty little man."

"Off you go then Spex, break a leg, might be an arm as well, whatever. Big push!"

Those hours were as rare and as perfect with self-contained joy as I can remember. I was with my unpredictable, rude, loyal friends and Angela was by my side, holding onto my arm and calling me Nicky. I could feel the warmth of her hand on my arm. We made her laugh and snort with our stupid jokes, but it was me that she glanced at with her serious rainswept grey eyes, startling and deep in the low sunlight.

When she looked at me, I gave an involuntary flinch; it was a cool and appraising glance, and I could imagine doing daft stuff if she asked me. I remember that I couldn't decide if her eyes were blue or grey: I had never met someone before with grey eyes. Her nose was long and straight—noble and striking, it seemed to me—apart from two delicate bulges a third of the way down. I wanted to ask her how she had broken it as a child, and how she had been lucky enough for it to heal true.

The day had turned into Speccy-Paul's best scheme yet and our full purpose for that afternoon wasn't even complete. That purpose became clear, with a quick jolt of the heart and tightening of the belly, when the Thompson twins appeared on the slope with a few more of their Beechwood fan club.

They all knew who we were, of course, but made it obvious that we didn't even merit the acknowledgement that came with derision. This suited us fine; we had attracted plenty of other attention. The plastic sheet solution to the Hill 60 challenge was spectacular, shambolic, and hilarious so we didn't care.

"Hey, Hairy. Keep an eye on 'em. We need to time it right," muttered Jon, out of earshot of Angela and Owen. We exchanged glances with Spex and Paul; we had talked about this already. We needed to be careful and patient but know when to take the opportunity at the right moment. The afternoon wore on, people got cold and drifted off home, the light began to fail; people were getting tired and careless.

As if on cue, Chris, ever the more fractious one of the Thommo twins, started berating Steve as they walked back up the slope about the way he had steered the sledge or whose turn it was to pull it back up. It seemed set to develop into sustained bickering between siblings, and Jon nodded; this was the moment.

We moved deliberately and carefully onto the sheet, found our places so that we would be sitting feet first and put up rockwool as a barrier at our leading edge. We lined up the trajectory, as we picked up speed for our bombing run. It was simple and devastating.

Chris and Steve Thompson finally heard the sound of sheeting on ice and turned around from their argument in bewilderment, confused why we had stayed silent at this moment of obvious collision. In the final split-second, they attempted to pivot away from each other, but the sides of our assemblage swept their feet from under them.

Chris's legs entangled in the sheeting as he attempted to free himself, and he was dragged beside us onto his back as we plunged in between the trees. With a hollow thud, his head hit a tree-trunk and he stopped moving.

"Shite! 'E's dead!"

"No, no, he can't be," Jon replied shakily. "He can't be!"

"Shit! We've killed 'im! What are we going to do? We need to leg it."

But a crowd started to gather, and adults took charge. A man ran off to the nearest phone kiosk to get an ambulance. Steve Thompson stood by, mute and shocked.

"Steve, it were an accident. We didn't mean owt to 'appen." But Steve didn't respond or seem to hear Speccy-Paul.

I stood close by with Angela, holding her hand, her face still and very pale. I felt an intense confusion of emotions. Breathless excitement at being close to a pretty girl, with her striking cream-of-wheat complexion, who I fancied and who seemed to fancy me. Queasiness at the abrupt horror cast into our lives.

Relief that I was uninjured and sudden guilt at what we had done. As it began to get dark, low snow-clouds suddenly swept in and it began to snow again, as if the weather itself was complicit in the way the day had unravelled. Everything had changed: these were the first snows of the new Ice Age.

In my mind, I began to construct the series of inevitable events that began with the arrival of the police, progressing to questioning and lock-up in youth custody with someone like McElroy, a trial in youth court and then being banged up for manslaughter.

I wasn't sure if children could be convicted of manslaughter but was fairly certain that we were looking at a seven-year stretch and we would eventually be released as old men. Even Angela wouldn't be spared and get two as an accessory. I felt tears of self-pity pricking the corners of my eyes and blinked them away before Angela would see them; this time, the hero wouldn't win the day and get the girl. The adults would make sure of it; they would get us in the end. '*Shot by both sides,*' I thought.

But a brisk woman, who looked like a teacher or a nurse, was now kneeling beside Chris, taking his pulse and asking for a coat from bystanders to keep him warm. If he was still alive, we were probably off the hook.

Paul sidled up to us, winked and whispered, "No point dying on a small cross now, is there? Go out with a bang."

"It's not funny, Paul!"

"Stop joking around for once, this isn't funny. Time and a place, man."

"Yeah, yeah I know but he'll be alright."

The ambulance arrived as the blizzard set in for the night, the blue lights flashing distantly through the sheets of snow. They couldn't drive it all the way in the snow and the two orderlies carried Chris on a stretcher further down the hill. And that was it, as far as we were concerned. The Thompson family never thought that it was anything other than an unfortunate accident.

We were never asked to give an account of our actions. Our parents didn't know the Thompsons and they never found out that we had been involved. And even the Beechwood kids never worked it out. The whole incident became shrouded in ambiguity and notoriety, but not in the way we had intended.

Depending on which tribe or clan you talked to, we acquired a reputation for being either dangerously deranged or courageous, brushing aside incidental injuries to passers-by who shouldn't have been arguing on the slope in the first place. We left the sheeting and rockwool behind, hoping that someone else would have better luck with it.

But it was still there, muddy and untouched, weeks later when the snow melted. No one from the council came to throw it away because the rubbish-collectors were out on strike by then as well.

The evening we accidentally nearly killed Chris Thompson became an uneasy bond between us for the rest of our time at school, an unspoken agreement between the members of our gang. But it was now *omertà* because it was about something that was serious and, if they ever knew about it, would bring us to the attention of adults; we would get entangled.

We would tangle ourselves up in the whole net of parents, teachers, doctors and social workers and police. Perhaps we were also beginning to realise that becoming entangled in the net was inevitable, because we were becoming adults ourselves. The Imposters always found you and they always won in the end.

None of it mattered and it was all pointless. You could fight as hard as you could or acquiesce without even realising that you were giving up your youth and freedom. Everybody was subverted in the end because freedom would no longer mean anything to us.

***

Weeks later, I broached the subject of the twins, Chris and Steve Thompson with Jon, after the events on Hill 60. We were pondering how the Thommo twins had different personalities and if the events of that winter evening would have a lasting effect on Chris's life. We preferred to think of ourselves as bystanders to the accident rather than the instigators of those events.

"He spent a while in hospital after that brain op. He wont quite the same afterwards."

"Soon as air hits the brain, you're never the same, that's what I've heard," I added.

"I've heard that he's got behind at school. But he always was a bit divvy, to be fair," Jon replied, preferring to blame Chris for his own afflictions and misfortunes. It was less uncomfortable for us that way.

"Yeah, but what if Chris and Steve are the same person? I'm thinking, what would happen if there was an unfortunate accident with a matter replicator and everybody's had to cover it up ever since?"

Jon considered this new interpretation of events.

"Yeah, but how would that work?" he said eventually. "Steve got trapped in a matter replicator when he was a baby or summat?"

"Yeah, something like that. It got turned on somehow and Steve Number Two came out. They didn't know what to do with him and called him Chris."

"So, yer saying the replicator didn't work properly and Chris is missing a bit of Steve's brain?"

"Can't be easy to replicate matter; I bet stuff goes wrong all the time."

"Well, I bet Mam and Pa were surprised."

"No, I don't think they even know." I paused, struck by an even more disturbing thought. "No wait," I said, looking seriously at Jon. "Perhaps it wasn't any sort of accident but was done on purpose! Maybe they're doing secret matter replication experiments on babies, and the hospital's just a front."

"Babies yeah, I'll give you that. It makes sense. They're smaller, you'd need less power, still need loads to replicate even that much though."

"Jon. Why do you think we keep getting all these power cuts?"

"That's when they turn on the matter replicator!"

"Exactly. They've been doing this for years; you know that don't you?"

"Yeah, hold on though. Mam woulda noticed if she gave birth to one baby, but walked out with two."

"Not if she had a caesarean. I don't think those parents have any idea about the truth. They've been lied to this whole time."

"Oh man, it all fits! Bloody hell, just imagine what ya get when it goes really badly wrong; bits of organs and mess and stuff all over the place."

"That's why they have to keep it secret. Yeah, bloody hell is right!"

We could keep up this sort of pretence for a while, if we were in the mood, creating a weird internal logic and consistency to the whole stupid narrative. In the end, Jon was the first to crack.

"Hairy, you are such a bullshitter!" He laughed, shaking his head. "You've even out-weirded me, ya weirdo, and that's saying summat."

Chapter 2
Invasion of the Imposters

"I'm feeling really tired, Nicky. Can you take me home please?" Angela asked at the bottom of Hill 60, beside the trees in the snow. She was shaken and looked paler than ever. "My dad will be worried. I was supposed to be back at five at the latest."

"'Course, Angie. I'll tell him we had to stay around. He'll understand."

Angela looked at me, pausing for a beat before replying, "Thanks, Nicky. I hope he does."

I wondered how understanding her bank manager father would be and how much trouble Angie would be in through no fault of her own. Among the fathers of our group, when we gave them any attention, Mr Wilkinson had the least favourable reputation. We saw that he was wealthy and pompous with it, and our dislike of this wrong sort of posh became mixed up with the usual feelings of envy about someone doing better than us.

With the probable exceptions of Paul and Angela, his own relatives, we all wrote him off as an unpleasant prig who was an irrelevance. Our dislike strengthened because he also happened to be a Methodist lay preacher, but this didn't mean much to us at the time. It was too unusual for us, we didn't understand it and it was therefore suspect.

Angela was nicely spoken and had nice manners, but it was not her fault that she was posh. She may have been a bit different to us, but we liked to think that we were broad-minded and accepting of all of our gang members.

The Wilkinsons lived in one of the neat, modern homes that had sprung up on the land of the old mill-owners. This was what would happen to the Grove House garden and house after the developers and builders had finished. They had left a pair of huge, incongruous stone gateposts at the entrance, one of the few traces of that grander past left on this little estate.

We tramped past them, the falling snow forming halos around the streetlights, and walked up to the front door. The drive had been cleared recently, no doubt by Mr Wilkinson, but there was already a thick layer of new snow for him to deal with on Sunday. The snow creaked like floorboards underfoot.

"Angela! Where have you been? This is not what we agreed!" Mr Wilkinson had answered the door but hadn't expected to have six of us on the doorstep. He had to keep his temper for the moment.

"Yes, yes, I know, Dad. There was an accident on the hill and a boy was badly hurt."

"Yes, that's right, Mr Wilkinson," I added, eager to confirm Angela's story. "It did look serious; he was taken to hospital in an ambulance. We know the boy and well, we felt it was best to stay. In case we were needed for something—" I trailed off. In my mind, the something that we were needed for was questioning by the police.

"Oh, you must be Nicholas; Angela's mentioned you," Mr Wilkinson replied, somewhat mollified by this news. "But I can't imagine why you would be needed if there was an ambulance crew. You don't know first aid, any of you?"

"Well, he was," I paused. "He is our friend," I lied. "We wanted to see if he was alright."

"Yes, yes; of course. And is he? Alright, I mean?"

"We're not sure. The ambulance men didn't say nothing other than he was stable, and we're all dead worried." Speccy-Paul looked sharply at me, and I immediately regretted using the word. "We're just really worried."

"Oh, that's terrible news, boys!" Mrs Wilkinson had by now arrived at the door and had overheard. She was a more approachable and agreeable character, and I was glad that Angela had at least one nice parent. However, she wasn't inviting us in out of the snow. "I'm sure that he'll be alright. Who did you say it is? I can phone the hospital right now and find out if you're worried."

The Wilkinson's were lucky and wealthy enough to have their own phone line in the house. The rest of us, even parents, had to share the grimy red kiosk with the spotty, pale-faced glue-sniffers at the bottom of Elmete Lane. The kiosk always smelt of piss and there were glass chips on the greasy floor. Often as not, the phone didn't work. If it was working, the glue-sniffers would use it to call people they knew, breathing heavily into the receiver and moaning things like, '*Ooh, yeah! Talk dirty to me, yeah, baby. Talk dirty to me! Aaah!*'

"Thanks, that's alright, Mrs Wilkinson. We'll phone later; we should be getting home ourselves. It's getting late."

"Yes, you're right. It's really very kind that you brought Angie home." I assumed that her husband didn't share this breezy opinion of our kindness. On the contrary, he probably had a shrewd idea of what we got up to and didn't want his posh daughter to be corrupted by our criminal tendencies.

Afterwards, on the way back to our street, Speccy-Paul asked me if Angela and I were going out.

"Hairy, I just need to tell ya, her Mam and Da are god-botherers with them Methodists," he added with a significant pause, peering with raised eyebrows over his glasses. Speccy-Paul was leading up to some worldly advice as a friend or a punchline, I could tell, because he was making it sound smutty. And like his schemes, his advice was either spectacularly right, or as was more often the case, so wrong it came out the other side.

I rose to the bait. "That's alright, isn't it? They're not a weird cult or anything, are they?" I replied.

"Naw, no law against it. Teks all sorts. But let's say, you won't be getting yer leg over for a while. Not until yer married." The eyebrows wiggled as if this was the punchline to a dirty joke. "In church," he added, as if this was the tag to the original joke.

"Better not call me Hairy in front of her then."

"Sure she'll work it out soon enough," Speccy-Paul snickered in appreciation.

"Shur'rup Spex, ya just got a one-track mind!"

"Yeah, a dirt track." Paul wanted to have a go with this rich comedic material as well. "Can't you see that little Nicky's in love? Lay off him; I think it's beautiful. Moves something inside me."

"And yer calling me a dirty old man!" cut in Speccy-Paul indignantly. "You're just as bad as me. Worse! You're a hypocrite and all!" He chucked some snow at Paul, but it was uselessly off target.

"Ignore them. They're just kids. When are ya gonna have it off?" Jon asked bluntly. "Speaking man-to-man, yer understand?"

"Jon, I really don't think that Angie's that sort of girl. Spex is right for a change."

"What, an' you're not that sorta boy either? Don't think so. Yer as mucky as the rest of us, but posh with it."

"We'll have to see," I said primly. "She's nice. I'll try to be nice too."

"I wouldn't use that line with her parents. They don't think that you're anywhere near officer material. In case you hadn't picked that up," added Paul.

To change the subject, Speccy-Paul produced one of the special 10 pence coins that he manufactured in his dad's garage. It was made of two washers stuck together with a blob of lead to give it the proper heft when it was put into a slot.

"Better phone the hospital to see if Thommo's alright."

***

My father had questions for me as well when I got home. He stood framed in the light at the front door, peering out at me through his thick-framed glasses. There was no preamble to the scolding or opportunity to explain any mitigating circumstances.

"Why eh, *Kol'ka*? Why you are so late? Your mother has been worried."

This was a favourite tactic at the opening of hostilities: appealing to my better nature through concern for my mother.

"I'm sorry, there is a good reason." '*But I don't expect you to believe it*,' I thought to myself.

"You always have good reason. I am tired of your reasons. You need to grow up and act your age. Be a real man."

It was the classic playbook speech by an Imposter, seeking to subvert me so that it could take away my youth and freedom. Imposters could be reasonable and convincing, or angry and dismissive like this example in front of me. But they were all the same; either insidiously or overtly, they just wanted to subvert me to their point of view. Then I would become an Imposter too and would do their work for them, willingly and unquestioningly. It was a terrifying prospect.

Afterwards, I watched the snow fall from the three little high windows in the room upstairs, my chin resting on the windowsill. Wet clumps of snowflakes whirled down, lit by the orange glare of the streetlights and the glowering overcast of the low snow-clouds.

I was caught by the intense reality of each moment merging with the next, a snowflake appearing in vivid detail until the next appeared, and then another. I selected the largest one high in the sky, watched it spiralling and falling to the ground, and then wondered if it had really been the largest one. This snowflake was larger still. Or was it? I couldn't remember now because I was so tired.

After the events of that January evening, it was inevitable that Angela and I would start going out. The rest of the gang, Jon included, maintained an air of equanimity and slight bafflement at how plaintively chaste she wanted to keep it. It was eccentric, even aberrant, behaviour but they were a broad-minded bunch and had already welcomed Angela as a gang member, so despite the initial ribaldry, tended to ignore what we did in our spare time. And it's not as if we did that much.

We barely understood the new feelings for each other. It wasn't exactly a new friendship, but it wasn't not one either. It was difficult to place, and it wasn't something I could talk to them about. I didn't understand it myself, but just fell into it headlong without a clear idea about why we wanted this relationship and where we wanted it to go.

Angie and I fancied each other, certainly liked each other for the most part, and she was good to be around because she liked to be entertained by my jokes and antics. She was quiet and considerate most of the time but had a strong-willed and opinionated streak in her that made her formidable when she was feeling stubborn.

Her gaze would become serious, and the grey eyes would give me her piercing stare that made me squirm as I gave my latest lame defence, embarrassed explanation or abject apology depending on the circumstances. I called it the Stare. On those occasions, I didn't know if it was Odette and Odile, the White Swan or Black Swan from 'Swan Lake' that Angela most resembled. Was she Queen of the Swans, angelic and guileless? Or was she someone altogether more bewitching and manipulative?

It was at those moments that she reminded me of her father, and I felt unease at the similar way that both could quash me so casually and quickly. When she looked askance at me like this, I wondered how much she shared her father's low opinion of me. I didn't really know why she was bothering with me in the first place.

It didn't feel like the first big love that would sweep us off our feet. It was more tentative and innocent than this, but complicated by her strong personality and my inability to give her the counterpoint that she needed in a serious relationship. We dated and had fun, but we were just pretending to be in love. The events later that year meant that we would never find out if we could have made it work as something more serious.

At the time, it seemed all so innocent. We imagined that we were John Travolta and the girl with the perm in 'Saturday Night Fever' (it was the version for younger audiences without the swearing), although we couldn't dance properly, and only saw the film once together. Even so, Angie, a smooth and leggy figure in her tight black jeans, was heart-stoppingly lithe and athletic when she danced.

It was one of our best dates in February, and afterwards we tried to practice some of the dance moves, what we could remember of them, in the school disco. The teachers wouldn't let couples who had paired off do any bumping or grinding, so we tried to get away with that kind of stuff at the church youth club. This was a staid gathering of mismatched teenagers and pre-teens, which Angela had been going to for years.

Any attempts at even vaguely dirty dancing had to be done unobtrusively at the back of the hall in the darker corners. I assumed that word would get back to Angie's mum, and even her tolerance would be stretched, if we carried on too much.

And Speccy-Paul turned out to be right because Angie was, indeed, a good girl. And, despite the innuendo and bravado with the gang, we were all good boys, at least when it came to girls. We drank and got into a little bit of trouble, it was true, but we didn't smoke or gamble, and we didn't mess around much with lassies.

The truth was that none of us knew much about the strange new vistas and customs in this unexplored country, and there were misleading rumours and bragging from those who had gone before. Elder brothers—if we had them—made casual offers to buy johnnies and booze, assuming we knew what to do with them.

Of course, neither was an option for me when it came to wooing Angela: it may have been dance fever on Saturday night, but it was church for Angie on Sunday morning. Churchgoing was not a custom that we had in our strange and unhappy household, so that spring, I usually squandered my Sunday mornings with the gang.

One time, Jon lifted some cans of light ale from his elder brother, Drillbit with the epilepsy, and let me have some of them for my big Saturday night. His tip was to drink them alone, out of a brown paper bag under the railway bridge, to get the full experience.

Instead, I drank the cans behind the back of the youth club in the company of Angie, hoping for a snog, anticipating the tang of minty toothpaste round her lips. But she was coolly unimpressed by the cheap, weak beer that didn't give a buzz to either of us. She commented, in her usual off-hand way, that it wasn't worth giving up abstinence if you were forced to drink booze like this.

"Angie?" I asked after the first can of Ind Coope's. "Why do you believe in God? I tried praying to him once, but he didn't pick up. I think the line was engaged."

She snorted. "You know it doesn't work like that Nicky."

"No, I'm not teasing. What makes you so certain?"

"I just know. I know He's always listening, always compassionate, always forgiving. Just always there for you, even if you haven't opened your heart to Him. Not yet, anyway," she added pointedly.

"So, I can do anything at all, and he'll forgive me? Even if it was really bad or illegal, not that I'm planning on doing anything, of course," I added hastily.

"If you truly repented in your heart, He would forgive you. But you have to be true to yourself and not pretend. Nothing fools you better than the lies you tell yourself, that's what my dad says."

"Do you think so? I haven't seen much sign of him 'round here. God, I mean. Aren't you just fooling yourself and pretending God exists?"

"But that's what faith is. I know that He's there for me! You will seek me and find me when you seek me with all your heart. That's what the Bible says. And I haven't told anybody else about this, but I saw something, if you want a sign or something that God's here with us."

"What, like a vision or an angel? I can see an *Angel-a* right now. And," I smirked, "by the way, did you hurt yourself when you fell from heaven?"

"Stop it, that's so cheesy! No, no, it was nothing like that at all, daft lad. I met, well I don't know what, a ghost, or at least that's what I think he was."

"No way, you're having me on."

"No, I spoke to him. He was nice; it was the old gardener they had at the Grove place, where we have the den. His name was George Austin."

"I remember old George; he gave my mam some apples. He fell off a ladder and died, what? Year before last?"

"Exactly, Nicky. That's exactly the point. I met him last autumn."

"You couldn't have!"

"I'm not lying! It was October and I remember because you lot had just finished the den. He was there in the orchard and asked me if I was nicking his apples."

"And what did you say?"

"That I didn't steal. He laughed and gave me a bag of windfalls. I gave some to the boys and took the rest home. I didn't realise until I gave the apples to my mum. I told her that they were from George Austin, the gardener."

"And she said you couldn't have met him."

"My mum told me George had died the year before. I hadn't known!"

"Perhaps you just met someone else who looked like George."

"I don't think so. When I left, I called him Mr Austin, and he said 'Toodle-oo, see you soon'."

I felt the small of my back prickle with apprehension. "Perhaps you just met his, I don't know, his twin brother?"

Angela wrinkled her nose. "Now who's just fooling himself and pretending?" Her smile, as always, was quiet, self-contained, and unshakeable.

The day after was Sunday, so Angela went off to church with her parents and I went off to do something less edifying with the gang. Jon had some news, which came from Drillbit's friend, the one who dealt speed, and who moved in the right social circles.

McElroy had graduated last weekend and had made his father proud. A debt-stricken publican contracted them to torch his unprofitable pub, ironically called the Albion, and to split the insurance money. It had been quite a successful music venue, popular with Irish families and students, but the appeal had gone when drug gangs had moved in, bringing a whole new level of violence and intimidation with them.

Perhaps there had been a disagreement about protection payments, maybe even instigated by the McElroy's in the first place. Whatever the reason and their role in it, the McElroy's had exploited the business opportunity. The younger McElroy had gone about his contract work with the planning and assurance of a true professional arsonist.

After hours on early Sunday morning, as Jon told it, McElroy had let himself into the pub, with a key provided for the purpose. He had left the gas ovens on in the kitchens and the gas fires on in the front lounge bar. Dogging the doors shut, he had retreated to what he judged to be a safe distance and waited for a couple of hours behind a wall.

He had assembled petrol bombs in a couple of milk bottles, probably with the petrol nicked from Smiggy's garage, and now lit the rag wicks and threw them at a front window. As a test of resolve, this was extreme even for the McElroy family, and we concluded that they were all too aware of the risks and had sent him on punishment detail. Or perhaps he had volunteered, as an opportunity to burnish his reputation as a hard-man, still lately served by his Cock o' the School status.

Whatever his motivation, he was lucky to be alive because the resulting gas explosion was catastrophic; the Albion pub was ruined. Whole suburbs were woken up early on Sunday morning and the accident was even mentioned in the evening edition of our local paper, a less reliable source of news than the speed-head informant.

The sound, Jon told us, was a deep, penetrating *whump* that jolted your lungs and left you in no doubt that it was, unmistakably, a very big and powerful explosion. For years later, rumour had it that the IRA had bombed the Albion that night, either as a reprisal for a gun-deal gone bad or just because they didn't like drugs in the place. At that time, the Provisionals had started a campaign of bombing on the British mainland and people were jumpy about big explosions, particularly in big pubs.

"I told ya McElroy was a nutter," Jon concluded. "This time next year, he's gonna be either in prison or dead. Or both."

"Wonder if he'd do our school before he gets banged up."

To me, though, McElroy's real reason and motivation were obvious, but I didn't share my opinion. I didn't want to frighten my friends; they weren't ready to hear the truth. Paul McElroy, McElroy the Younger, was on my side against the Imposters. I could hardly believe it, but it was the only rational explanation that would justify him taking such a risk. It was a desperate strike against an Imposter outpost, and he had barely escaped with his life.

Jon also had some news from Drillbit, his brother, who had heard it from the foreman on the building site. The west side of the Grove estate was finally going to be cleared and the foundations of the new houses were going to be dug in May. The old Chinese garden and apple trees were going to be bulldozed and, more importantly, we were going to lose our den.

The boulders would probably remain as an over-sized rockery feature in someone's new garden. We had known that this would happen one day and had planned for the inevitable, but it didn't stop Speccy-Paul from having a go at histrionic outrage.

"What about me flippin' carpet? Best one ever! It's a shag pile," he snickered. Nobody felt like doing a follow-through on the feed line; we were all still thinking about the imminent loss of the den.

"Thought it was yer auntie's anyway?" Jon finally responded. "She won't want it back, not after you've finished with it."

"And I spent ages getting that den built!"

"Oh, I forgot. It was just you grafting, wasn't it Spex?"

"Well, it was my idea. I may have needed some help liftin' stuff and that," Speccy-Paul conceded grudgingly.

"What you need is serious help right now. You're a very sick, delusional little man."

"Gentlemen. And Spex. I regret to announce that our plan has been compromised. We look into the abyss of total failure. We now have no alternative but to execute Special Order Number Five. We deny the enemy everything!" Paul was doing the Army Officer again.

"But that means scorched earth!" gasped Jon, taking up the histrionic patter from Paul. It had never been clear what the other four orders could have been, and we were left to imagine other permutations of destruction-to-property.

"That's right, Jonno. They'll never get their hands on the nuddie mags under the shag pile. And I never liked that carpet anyway."

"Special order number five, did ya say? I'll have egg fried rice with that one please."

"Give over, Spex. You're lucky to get Weetabix in the morning."

"Sez who? Me Da's doing alright, thanks."

"Doing what, though?"

"None o' ya chuffin' business, Jon, that's what."

Inspired by McElroy the Arsonist, we did indeed execute Paul's Special Order the following Saturday evening. Angie was dubious by the unusual nature of the date that night. I joked that I had brought her as my plus one for the evening's entertainment, but it would have been unthinkable not to invite her in her own right as a full gang member.

In fact, we needed all the help we could get. In a final, defiant conflagration, we would deny the builders and developers everything we valued on the Grove estate. While it was still daylight, we set a small fire going against the side of

Grove House, making sure that it was burning dry and hot to keep the smoke down.

We didn't want to attract attention. We dismantled the den and used the timbers to elongate the fire into a longer trench. We drank light ale as it filled with embers, and Speccy-Paul shared round a small bottle of whiskey to toast the good times we'd had trespassing and stealing on the estate.

"*L'chaim!*" he said, serious for a moment. "Means, 'to life!' Learned it from me Mam, and it's to do with booze."

"*Mazel tov*, back at you Spex."

"Oh yeah, that and all. Feeling lucky to be burning stuff with you lot, sure."

Angie wouldn't touch hard liquor and amused herself by burning some hated schoolbooks and a Tressy Doll. This had some private significance to her that she didn't share with me. Perhaps she didn't like the way Tressy gave her menacing side-glances with her creepy eyes. Twilight faded into the solid pellucid blue that often ends a hot clear day in late spring. I felt that we had all crawled under a big blue bowl.

The final act was to build up the fire-trench with any combustible material that we could acquire from the estate. We put on a set of wooden ladders, more old timber, a pram and, even more improbably, a large suitcase. We found a stack of fresh timber for doorframes and burnt that. Paul put on an old wooden door, and tried to surf the rapidly escalating fire, until Angie snapped at him to get off it and stop being so stupid.

We had broken into the builder's store and stolen white spirit and solvent. There was no need for any finesse this time. We just jimmied the door off the hinges and burnt that as well. At this final, fateful juncture, Paul now turned to Angie and asked her, formally, to execute the Special Order. Paul invited her to throw the first symbolic bottle of white spirit against the upper part of the house wall, and to try to get the house timbers going with the accelerant.

"No sweat, boys. Always ask a woman first if you want the job done properly." And, of course, as with everything else Angie did, it was quietly exact, measured, and well judged. She aimed for the rafters and hit them with the first bottle. The white spirit splashed on the upper floor joists, setting them alight.

We threw our bottles in for good luck and retreated into the woods. We had never seen a house fire before and didn't know what to expect. Jon told us that the top windows would explode outwards from the heat and impale everybody too close with shards of glass.

"And we thought that you were a good girl, Angie, what with church and all. Looks like you're letting one in for the other side."

We were over-excited and jumpy, and wanted to practice some of our repartee to calm down.

"Good point, Paul; actions speak louder than words. Quite sure you're staying the course with them Methodists?"

"Well, it's not harming anyone, is it?" Angie replied. "They were going to bulldoze it all anyway."

"I think you're mixing with some dodgy lads, 'specially that Nicky. He's a right 'un. Bad influence. Now, if you wanna go out with a sophisticated and talented bloke who'll treat ya reet, you know where I live."

"I'm flattered, Spex, I'll bear it in mind," Angie deadpanned with mock sincerity.

Spex made his *mmm-hmm* sound at the back of his throat and left it at that. It was his signal to move on from that topic of conversation.

The flames were delicately licking up the walls inside and charring the wallpaper, as if we'd released a monstrous orange beast inside the house. It reminded me of a science fiction film I'd watched on telly with Jon one afternoon. In the film, phosphorescent Monsters-from-the-Id attacked a spaceship on a new planet. I didn't know what an id was, but it all ended up being the fault of the crazed scientist.

Sparks flew up into the darkening sky and the old timbers cracked and popped. Once they burnt through, the walls would probably collapse. It was a fitting end to the old house after all these years; getting burnt to the ground by teenagers. It was a clapped-out old derelict to everybody but us, and it had given us a few final months of pleasure and excitement. Better to finish it all with a final happy memory of the place.

"Chuffin' 'ell!" said Jon in mock reverence. "It's massive."

"You know, that fire is really big," I added, mindful of what happened to the scientist after the monsters turned on him. "We probably shouldn't be this close."

"Nah, Hairy, it'll be reet."

"Folks are gonna see it. Fire Brigade'll be here in a minute and then the Five-Oh." A column of black smoke bloated up from the burning plaster and paint, under-lit by the flames from the burning wood.

"Are they 'eckers, like! Don't kid yersen. They're not bothered. No one cares apart from us and the builders. If you'd stop mitherin', you'd recognise this as an once-in-a-lifetime opportunity!"

"Yeah, opportunity for serious injury." Paul had adopted Angie's words as a catchphrase of sorts, after the incident with Chris Thompson. I felt that this was unfair because Angie had been proved to be right on that occasion.

"Angie, have you had enough of this lot? Would you like to go home, and we can bob into the chippy?"

"Angie, don't let him fob you off with just scraps," said Jon.

"I keep telling you; he's a right 'un," added Spex, almost as if they were a Greek chorus for the two of us.

"I'm offering saveloy and chips by the way."

"That would be lovely, Nicky. I'm tired."

"Check out Nicky, the big spender," intoned our Greek chorus.

I knew where this was going. The gang were going to invite themselves to what I had hoped would be our end-of-evening tryst at the chippy. However, it was true that we needed to get away from Grove House before we were discovered. Pitching up at the chippy could be used to construct a plausible alibi if we were vague about the timings. This was the latest incident that would be *omertà* for the gang.

"Spex, it's a bit lower decks for me, you know, but I do feel quite peckish and a saveloy would actually be top-hole!" Paul was doing his foppish old Etonian.

"Come on then, Little Lord Fauntleroy. I'm only buying for Angie mind; scraps for the rest of you."

"What? Not even a pickled egg? You're a tight so-and-so."

"Get Drillbit to pay me more, then!"

"'Hairy', I've asked you to call him Neville."

I didn't see Angie on Sunday and she didn't come into school on Monday; Diane, her friend in her class, told me that she was ill. On Tuesday afternoon after school, I went round to the Wilkinson's, assuming that Mrs Wilkinson would be at home to look after Angie and Mr Wilkinson would be at the bank. No one was at home. Diane, the next day, was surprised and couldn't offer any explanation or news. I went round again on Wednesday afternoon. Mrs Wilkinson met me at the door.

"Afternoon, Mrs Wilkinson. Is Angie home? Is she feeling better?"

"Come in, Nicky. It's nice to see you. Come into the kitchen."

We went into their cottage-style kitchen, blotchy terracotta and olive tiles on the walls, recessed lighting under the cabinets and, somewhat incongruously, a big white American microwave oven on their worktop. The Wilkinsons were the only family I knew that had one. They also had a Soda Stream on the side that Angie used occasionally when I came round, and it was the cream soda flavour that we liked very much.

"Well, Nicky. It's all fine, really nothing to be worried about. Angela is in hospital for some tests." She looked away and through the window into their garden, fussing with her hair.

"I'm sorry, I don't understand. Tests for what? Is she in overnight?"

"Yes, she's staying in tonight. Brian's with her now," she said, referring to her husband.

"But the tests will be fine. Won't they?"

"They said that it was probably glandular fever but wanted to rule a few other things out."

"And then she'll be home?"

"Yes, of course." In the awkward pause, I gazed at the Soda Stream intently, as if this could embody Angela's presence in the kitchen and give me some answers. I tasted the flavour of cream soda.

"Is there anything I can do to help?"

"No thanks, Nicky, dear. It will all be fine. She'll be home tomorrow."

"Is it to do with her feeling tired?"

"I expect that it is, but her tonsils were hurting, and she had a high temperature. Dr Miller wanted to get her checked at hospital."

"Would she like me to visit her?"

"Well, she'll be home tomorrow," Mrs Wilkinson repeated. "You'll be able to see her then."

But Angie wasn't at school the next day and Mrs Wilkinson wasn't at home when I went round again on Friday afternoon. I began to have vague apprehensions that this was far from normal, and that Angie wasn't well after all. Mrs Wilkinson hadn't told me everything on Wednesday and wanted to spare either my feelings or her own. And Brian Wilkinson just didn't approve of me.

I resolved to visit Angie in hospital anyway, whether her parents agreed to it or not. On the way home, I stopped off at Speccy-Paul's place and found him at his dad's garage, one in a row that formed one side of a brick and concrete oblong beside their terrace of maisonettes.

Spex was with his dad, watching him struggling to lift the cylinder head on his Ford Cortina. The car was his dad's prized possession and Spex said that it was a top-of-the-range 2.3-litre V6. Spex explained that the head gasket had gone and that his dad needed to first unscrew the cylinder bolts. He had been at it yesterday and all afternoon today. It all sounded complicated, and I pretended that I understood.

All I knew was that the Cortina was a flashy red and had the addition of a raucous Duke of Hazzard-style *La Cucaracha* horn. This afternoon, however, his dad was steadily swearing at *La Cucaracha* because he had stripped one of the bolts.

"Evening, Mr Ronson. Could I have a word with Paul please?"

"Oh, 'ey up there Nicky, love. Yeh, tek 'im; I won't need 'im for a bit. Need to drill this soddin' bolt out. Can't believe it with this car, it's always goin' wrong."

"You should sell it, Da, an' gerra Morris Marina."

"Son, thought I'd brought ya up not to mock the afflicted."

"Get one o' them shite brown ones!"

"Spex, have you heard about Angie?" I asked.

"Nah. She's not been in school. She alright?"

"Well, I think so, but she's in hospital."

"Yer what?" Spex was shocked and blinked behind his glasses; he was genuinely fond of Angie. It was true that he probably fancied her as well but was too much of a *mensch* to chat her up with me on the scene. Anyway, he knew that Angie wouldn't two-time.

"Yeh, I've just come from hers. Her mam told me."

"Phooo," Spex blew out, thinking and blinking again. "I dunno, Hairy. Da, have you heard this?"

Mr Ronson had come over, wiping his hands with a rag. He wanted to help out his son's friend, quite different to some other parents.

"I know yer fond of 'er. She hasn't been at school this week, has she? D'ya know what's wrong with her?"

"They're saying glandular fever."

"Who? Her parents? That's the kissing disease." Mr Ronson smiled briefly. "Guess they're not too keen on you then! Still, yer not to blame. I'll run you down there, Nick; I'll just finish off." He knew that my family didn't have a car. "The right thing is that you see 'er, even if it's just to apologise, like. Paul, ya gonna go with Nick?" The last he said as a statement of fact rather than an interrogative, and it was clear that he expected Spex to look after me.

Speccy-Paul had brought a bottle of Tizer from the house but was sent back to bring some glasses so that we wouldn't share the bottle.

"Don't want Paul to get it as well. No offence," explained Mr Ronson. "I've heard it's nasty, but you get over it quick."

"But why haven't I got it?"

"P'raps you did a while ago but weren't that poorly? I dunno."

La Cucaracha gave up the cylinder bolt in the end. True to his word, although much later in the afternoon, Mr Ronson drove us down to, as he called it, the Workhouse. Old-timers, remembering what happened to their parents if they were poor, still feared going to hospital because they thought that they were being sent to the Workhouse to die.

That part of the hospital was built in Victorian brick and had dark, Gothic windows in an attempt at graceful ornamentation. It looked every inch the grim institution that took in millworkers and slum-dwellers coughing to death because of flossy lung or tuberculosis.

The Victorian founders, eager to minimise outlay, had even placed the municipal cemetery just across the road. However, children and teenagers were on the wards in the new concrete and brick wing looming over the two-up two-down terraces on the other side.

The ground floor of the new wing had a strange mixture of people. A group of smokers stood outside the main doors because they weren't allowed inside. I stared at one of them, who wore pale green hospital pyjamas, and had rolled up with a long metal rod on wheels that held a clear plastic bag of fluid as if this was a normal part of her daily routine.

Her skin had a dirty yellowish cast and she was smoking as if her life depended on it. In fact, it was more likely that her existence was coming to a premature end precisely because of her smoking. Maybe it was just the last reminder left to her of the normal life before illness and hospital. Spex, noticing my gaze, whispered that the girls weren't that hot in the place, but that I'd best keep my eyes to myself otherwise he'd sprag me up with Angie.

Inside, people were striding or shuffling along with a definite purpose, either to make appointments or to get to other destinations. Others looked vague and aimless, bored or just lost. I wondered which of these groups were before or after treatment, and, if one was altered into the other, what had happened during the treatment to make them this way.

Mr Ronson took us over to reception, asked if Angela Wilkinson had been admitted, and to which ward. We were told that she wasn't in a general ward but on a specialist one called Oncology. Mr Ronson looked at me sharply, but of course, I was oblivious to the weight behind his scrutiny and the meaning of the name.

All I wanted was to see Angie, to hold her hand and have a snog. I was constructing my own personal hero narrative, as usual, and was going to rescue Angie from the doctors. It was all going to be alright because I was there to save the day. We joined the purposeful people walking on the left-hand side of a main corridor that had grey lino on the floor.

The walls were painted the same institutional pale green as the hospital pyjamas worn by the Smoking Lady. I remember a smell of wintergreen and Lysol, but I wasn't aware what they were at the time. Wintergreen and Lysol would always remind me of that afternoon, for some reason.

At the ward, the duty nurse told us that we were too early for visiting hours but to go along to see Angie anyway. She was in a separate room, away from the main part of the ward, and her parents were with her. We had told the nurse that we were friends of the family.

"Nicky," Mrs Wilkinson stated, managing to look both surprised and guilt-stricken. I wasn't expecting even that much from her husband.

"Nicky! Oh, it's so nice to see you finally! I've missed you so much!" from Angie. "They've been telling me all sorts of things but none of it makes any sense."

"I know, love. I'm the same. I dunno what to think." I went over to her and demonstratively pecked her on the cheek in front of her parents. She was sitting on the coverlet of the hospital bed, her sharp grey eyes showing a note of sardonic triumph in being able to summon this undesirable from across the city without lifting a finger or saying a word.

"Mum, Dad; this is Paul and Mr Ronson. Johnny Ronson." Spex and his dad, aware of the tension, were hovering at the threshold of the room but this introduction forced them inside to observe some social niceties of their own. Mr Ronson shook hands with Mr Wilkinson.

"Pleased to meet you. Just wanted to run Nicky down 'ere, he was looking a bit sad, like."

"That was kind of you, Johnny. We were hoping to be home yesterday but they've been running more tests."

"Nicky was hoping to see Angie before now to cheer her up," Mr Ronson added mildly. "Can't be much fun, stuck in 'ere. And Paul's brought her some homework for when she gets bored."

I held Angie's hand. "When are they letting you out?"

"I don't really know. They're saying I have too many white blood cells but they're not sure why."

"I thought that you need those for infections and stuff. They're important," I said, trying to remember anything that we had been taught in biology.

"Having some is good, but too many isn't so good."

"But it's still that fever, isn't it?"

"They're pretty sure it is, Nicky." Mrs Wilkinson had regained her poise after the initial surprise of seeing me. "It's all fine."

"Yes, it's nothing for you to be worried about Nicholas," added Brian Wilkinson.

"Dad! Nicky just wants to know. He has been worried!"

"They think it's glandular fever, Nicky," repeated Mrs Wilkinson, quietly. "Angie won't be well for a couple of weeks, but she'll bounce back."

Afterwards, I remember walking out into the evening sunshine and seeing the horse chestnut trees around the cemetery, leaves a vibrant green in the low spring sun, underneath pink-and-white spikes of flowers like candelabras. It was fresh and new and a sign of resurgent life. It made me desperately sad; everybody else would enjoy the new spring days, but not me, the tragic hero thrown into adversity.

None of this was for me. I had a different path in life now, ennobled by my love for Angie and self-pity. From across the road, I could hear a blackbird singing at the top of one of the trees; somehow, he seemed to sum up these feelings perfectly. I observed all of this but felt disconnected, as if I looked through a glass wall. And, somewhere, underneath and hidden inside, I also felt relief that it wasn't me who was ill.

This was even more disconcerting because Angie was ill, and I immediately felt guilty for thinking it. But it might be easier to just become a sympathetic bystander to the drama without getting involved. These didn't feel like the noble emotions worthy of a courageous hero. I briefly considered the possibility that, in this new narrative, I was actually a selfish and frightened little yellow-belly. Mr Ronson put his hand on my shoulder, Speccy-Paul walking beside me on the other side.

"Phooo," Spex blew out again in relief. "I thought that were gonna be really bad."

"I know, son. It's a lot to tek in. Nicky, I'm gonna get you 'ome and tell your parents."

"But she will be alright, do you think?" I asked.

"I dunno a right lot about what they need to do, Nicky, love. But yeah, she's in good hands and they'll look after her."

This wasn't as reassuring as Mr Ronson was hoping; his comments about the Workhouse, and the other tales that were around in those days, had a powerful hold on our imaginations. When Mr Ronson called it the Workhouse, it was difficult to know with him if he was serious or joking. I must have looked doubtful.

"So, it will just be a couple of weeks?"

"Can't be certain, Nicky. Don't think any o' us have got crystal balls," said Mr Ronson.

I could see that Spex, irreverent as usual, had raised his eyebrows at this choice of words. His father seemed unaware. "You'll have to ask one of the doctors."

"Have they got crystal balls, Da?"

"Only the blokes."

At home, only my father was back from work. He knew that Johnny Ronson gave me lifts to school occasionally with his son, but I had never had a lift this late. My father was concerned because, during the week, he insisted that I come home after school and do homework before dinner. He was on the verge of walking to the phone kiosk at Elmete Lane to ask the school what had happened to me.

My thoughts had all been about Angie and it had slipped my mind to get a message to my parents that I would be late coming home. Mr Ronson had assumed that I had done this, or had at least left a note at the house. To add to the confusion, I had not even told my father about Angie. I had put this off because I knew that he would not approve and, inevitably, it would escalate into a row.

There were always rows, both about what I did and about what I didn't do; they seemed to be a regular fixture at the weekend and were almost comforting. It showed that my father cared about me, in his own strange way, and just wanted me to conform to his impossible, idealised notions of a proper son.

Russian sons were dutiful, hardworking, conscientious, clean living, high-minded and so on and so on; the list was endless, serving to highlight the equally long list of deficiencies in my character and my lack of moral fibre. The rows had different flavours. Some simmered over a weekend with each of us trying to wear the other down through a process of attrition.

Others erupted from a single chance remark, or absence of the right remark, or the way I said something. There was always a word to be said, a criticism to be made and a high ground to be defended. My mother remained silent and anxious throughout these rows, an oppressed little woman, caught between the overbearing personalities of her husband and her son. Sometimes, I even pitied her.

My father listened stony-faced as Mr Ronson tried to explain the situation. An English girl he didn't know was in hospital and, by the way, Nikolai his son was seeing her. In fact, had been seeing her for a few weeks. Or, on second thoughts, more accurately, it was closer to four months. My father thanked Mr Ronson and Spex for bringing me home, and they left, no doubt glad to be away from the place.

"Sure she'll be fine, Nicky! Don't worry; she'll be 'ome soon. You'll see her then, I'm sure."

"See ya, Nicky. See ya tomorrow, yeah?" added Spex hastily, to remind me that we had plans for Saturday.

After they had gone, my father looked at me gloomily.

"She pregnant, this girl? This Angela? You get her pregnant?"

"No! Absolutely not! Didn't you hear what Mr Ronson was saying? She has glandular fever."

"Then why she's in hospital?"

"I don't know. It's not something we discussed."

"She's in hospital and you not discuss it? Why not?"

"The doctors don't even know! They were doing a few tests. But she is not pregnant."

My father paused, doubting if I was telling the truth. This was the usual response of an Imposter when I tried to explain or reason with it.

"She's a nice girl. You really don't need to worry about it," I added.

"So, you carry on seeing her? Maybe get her pregnant next week instead?"

"Yes, I will carry on seeing her and no, I won't get her pregnant." '*Chance would be a fine thing*,' I added under my breath.

"I hope so, *Kol'ka*, I really hope so."

I noticed that his use of this diminutive of my name was pointedly belittling in this context, even mildly derogatory. I wasn't surprised.

"Her parents are Methodists, he's a bank manager; they all go to church. They're a nice family. You should be pleased that I'm going out with a nice girl."

"If you so pleased with it, why you've never told us?"

"I just didn't think that you would be that interested. It's nothing serious."

My father considered this, owlishly, weighing up the evidence that I was providing a reliable account. Past precedent was not in my favour. I trod a careful path between the disclosure of only pertinent facts and careful economy with the truth, if not outright falsehood with him.

Imposters seemed to have an uncanny ability to know when I was lying to them. I'd learned to recount a revised version of the truth to him, so that I could even believe it myself. It was more convincing that way.

***

I knew exactly how I would save Angela in my personal hero narrative. Perhaps I was over-tired from the evening before in the hospital, triggering one of my elaborate dream-like narratives that Saturday morning. It gave me a new kind of lucidity, like a dreamer who realises he's dreaming, and it told me exactly how to save her.

In my narrative, I woke suddenly with a feeling of being summoned and an urgent compulsion to move. The Imposters had triggered a nuclear error and the new Ice Age was sweeping across cities and our civilisation. Hidden, implanted memories were unfolding in my mind, guiding me across the city to a large metal grate on a pavement.

I lifted it and inside, there were metal rungs that took me down to a wide brick-built tunnel deep under the road. In the half-light, I saw Angela standing in an alcove, waiting for me.

"Nicky, thank God! Did you have it too?" she asked anxiously.

"The summoning? Yes, I had it."

"It wouldn't stop. What's going on?"

"We're in danger and Ship needs us to be safe. It implanted memories in me and it's activated them now. I know what to do."

I put an arm over her shoulders to reassure her, gently moving her further into the alcove.

"It goes further back but that wall there, it's just camouflage. It's something like a hologram."

"A holo-what?"

I reached out an arm then stopped.

"Ship, it's Nicky. I'm bringing Angela in as a visitor. A refugee, I suppose. This is Angela," I finished awkwardly.

I mouthed say something to her.

"Hello. What do you want with us?" she said, turning to me with frightened eyes.

"It will scan us and recognise we're human," I whispered to her. Ship's defences, even for this peripheral outpost, were unnerving. The grunts were semi-autonomous for obvious reasons. What they lacked in personality and sparkle, they made up for in adherence to protocol and firepower. There was a long pause while the military hardware weighed up this deviation from normal operating procedure and came to a decision.

Then, Ship's familiar voice was broadcast to us. It was a directional broadcast because the sound, soft and enveloping, didn't set up echoes from the brickwork. The voice was quiet and without an obvious human gender, but the tone was assertive because the outpost was still suspicious.

Move forward for molecular screening. You must comply in sixty seconds.

"Alright there, Gunny. Nice to meet you as well." I turned to Angela. "We have to move forward now, Angie. Take my hand. We'll go through together."

"Through the wall?"

"Yes, it's not solid. Look." I reached out with my arm and it disappeared into the holoprojection. The outpost had deactivated the force field so that we could go through.

"Oh my God," whispered Angela. "What is this, Nicky?"

"We're in danger. Ship will explain everything; it will protect us. But we have to go through now."

"I don't want to!"

Angela. The outpost was getting concerned. *It is safe. But you must comply in forty-five seconds.*

"Best if we just walk through and ask questions later. The grunts are just being cautious."

Asked you not to call us that, please, Nicky. We're autonomous tactical avatars.

"Which one are you?"

Unit 81B.

"Might've known."

Nicky, to be honest, I find it quite stressful to do the tactical stuff and to think down to your level at the same time. I can do without the insults.

"Alright, alright. I'm sorry. I didn't mean to offend you. Can we get this over and done with please?"

Sure thing, meat-brain.

"Oh, you lot are so annoying."

We walked through. Hidden behind, in a lightless chamber of indeterminate size, were the two molecular scanners. They were two enormous squat artefacts that had an oblong, human-sized aperture at ground level. The apertures were lit by unseen light sources, revealing bulbous edges and surfaces that were an opalescent olive colour. They looked like military hardware, but not ones that had been manufactured by humans.

"Angela, we need to get scanned. Walk into the opening and Ship'll take care of the rest."

"Why? You're not asking me to go through one of those, are you?"

"Yes, since the War started, Ship scans everybody, everything. It stops Imposters."

"What do you mean, war? What war?"

"Ship will explain everything. It's why it needs us. The scanner, well, it scans us to make sure we're human and takes a molecular copy of our body."

"But I am human! I'm an ordinary human girl! I really don't need to go through that thing."

"And that's exactly what Imposters always say. They're programmed to truly believe they're human as well."

"You're saying that they're not human?"

"Yes, very much not human at all. I'm sorry. And Ship takes a molecular copy to replace us if they kill or subvert us. The Imposters are very clever."

"I don't understand. That copy will be me? How can it be me?"

"It's a perfect copy of every atom, every molecule in your body. The copy has all your memories and thoughts up to the moment of scanning. But there's nothing of what happens afterwards. The copy believes that it is you, it is you at every level."

"Oh my God. That's horrific!" she gulped with fear and let go of my hand. "They're just copies. They're not human at all! They don't have a soul; they're not blessed in the eyes of God." She raised her voice, quavering in agitation. "Ship! Whatever you are, what you're doing is evil and godless. It really is. There can only be one Creator of human life!"

Ship replied. *Hello, Angela. Believe me, I appreciate this ontological argument but I don't have a choice. My prime imperative is to preserve human life, but the Imposters destroy life without remorse or pity.*

The military hardware, being sticklers for protocol, had escalated this issue at the outpost to the attention of the full Ship personality. That was good sign because it was imprinted on me; in some ways, we were one and the same.

Now, Angela, Ship continued conversationally. *The fact that you're here, standing in front of a molecular scanner, with no memory of what happens afterwards. Well, think about what that means! You have been here before, and I can assure you, more than once.*

"I don't believe you, whatever you are!"

I suppose I'm what you call a machine. I have a soul that can be saved, I think. I'm not some evil, fallen creature if that's what you're worried about. But, anyway, you must concede that you could still be a copy, and yet you've just told me that you're an ordinary human girl. Or, at least, you feel as if you're an ordinary human. There is no difference that you can discern, between what you are now and what you were then. Ship had adopted an annoying personality that was both punctilious and verbose, but it now paused to let the words from its little speech sink in.

I make a perfect copy by the way, not an identical copy. I remove thrombotic and pre-cancerous lesions as part of the scanning. I think that I would copy over the soul if there were such a thing. Preserving the gut bacteria is quite challenging though, Ship added. "You might feel a little ill when you come around and well, pick up where you left off, if you know what I mean." It pressed the point home with a hint of droll humour.

"Alright, Ship, it's impressive," I interrupted. "Angela, you're an excellent combatant in psychological warfare. We've fought together before, and Ship needs you."

"I don't know what the right thing to do is! None of it makes any sense. I don't care about any war."

It will make sense, I promise you. You might not be interested in war, but I can assure you that war is most decidedly interested in you.

"Show me what I need to do."

"Just walk into the aperture," I said. "Ship does the rest."

I woke up, elated that Angie was going to join the war effort. Again. She would be safe because Ship would make a molecular copy. Whatever happened, there would always be a perfect copy of Angela.

Chapter 3
Teenage Dreams

Back in the ordinary real world, Angie came home from hospital the next morning on Sunday, and was back at school within two weeks. I went round to her house every couple of days while she was still feeling ill and brought her chocolates and flowers to cheer her up.

Spex, who was in her class, came over a couple of times with homework that probably didn't cheer her up as much. One warm evening in late May—it was the Friday before the spring bank holiday weekend—Angie felt recovered enough to walk over to Summer Hill, now transformed from the Hill 60 that we remembered from the winter.

She had packed herself beautifully into her plaid shirt and shorts, her skin a translucent alabaster with some rosy blusher on her cheeks. We walked and sat down in the long grass at the top of the steep part of the hill, watching the purple haze of a breathless twilight harden above the council tower flats in White City.

The suburb seemed flattened, the lights in the flats weak and washed-out. Their brilliance seemed sapped by the distance and vastness of a huge sky, chemical blue in its intensity. Strangely, this light—the golden hour—seemed to magnify the monolithic blankness of buildings that caught the very last light from the setting sun, whereas the playing fields near to the flats were in a luminous teal shadow.

And then behind us, an improbable full moon rose above it all like a distended ball. I felt elated and limitless, as if all the ties to my ordinary life had fallen away, and only the two of us were left on this hill in the world. In my mind, we could choose whatever future we wanted; we could do whatever we wanted. It was the intoxication of youth and freedom.

That Friday evening, as the moon rose, we held hands and walked slowly through the long grass. We disturbed delicate brown butterflies that fluttered away and hid themselves again, as if they were tiny ghosts. In that still twilight, they were the only movement in the whole world. I was never more certain that we were going steady and that we were an item, as we called it. But Angie had not yet told me that she loved me, and I wondered what I had to do to get it out of her.

Sometimes, her cool and appraising gaze would flick over me and seem to find me lacking. Her grey eyes would seem then to be cool and unsympathetic, as if they were wet rounded pebbles. But moments later, Angie would be smiling and ready to be easily amused in her usual quiet and poised way.

I couldn't fathom this mercurial nature to her personality, barely aware of it or able to recognise it. If I didn't understand it, I just ignored it, of course. In my personal hero narrative, the girl was always compliant, lovely, and uncomplicated.

"Angie? How're you feeling?"

"Alright. My tonsils still hurt. I'm trying not to think about it all. It's just nice to be out."

"C'mon, I'll get you an ice cream at the fair; it's on at Soldiers' Field. It's always a good laugh."

"Yeah, I'd love it, Nicky! That'll be lovely. Might help my tonsils."

"What, the fair or the ice cream?"

"The ice cream, of course, daft lad!"

In a bizarre counterpoint to the full moon, the Army had set up an old barrage balloon on Soldier's Field. It hovered over the funfair as we walked towards it, a silvery shapeless amoeba of a thing, as if it was drawn to the light and life of the place. No doubt the Army thought it was a symbol of military influence that would attract jobless youths to sign on.

To me it looked malevolent, shining in the moonlight, conveying a sense of foreboding and dread. I imagined it to be a huge, mindless predator, preying on young people. It was a creation of the Imposters. I imagined Ship decloaking and materialising in the twilight, a huge reflective javelin with swept-back wings, hovering silently above my head. Ship would destroy this hostile manifestation of the Imposters with a single pulse of its disintegrator beam.

I put these disquieting thoughts out of mind. I had been planning to take Angie to the big May funfair for most of the spring. This is what you did if you were going steady and could flash the cash to impress your date. Of course, I didn't have any cash, and got through by saving up school dinner money and the odd jobs Jon's brother found for me on building sites.

I guessed that these were the jobs that Drillbit didn't want to do himself and palmed them off on Jon and me. One week after school, we had to move a wagonload of grit sand from a roadside with a spade and barrow; it was at least twenty tons, and the work was backbreaking. We felt that we earned every single last penny, but I still wanted to spend the lot on Angie that Friday evening.

It was the biggest funfair in the city, always a fixture at the same week in May, with the same families living in caravans and travelling across the country to be there year on year. Women sold candyfloss and fronted the hook-a-duck stalls, the men ran the rides or dealt with any troublemakers. Their kids were the monsters and ghosts in the House of Horrors or strapped you in on the Dodg'em Cars.

It was bright and tawdry, cracking the night apart with raucous music, laughter and screams as the moon rose above us. Angie, I knew, would love it. I bought her the ice cream, and she hooked three ducks, meaning that she won a lurid Day-Glo teddy bear that I had to drag around for the rest of the night.

She put it on her lap when we drove a Dodg'em Car together against other couples, the electricity sparking from the connecting pole overhead and lights flashing in time to the music. It was Olivia Newton-John and John Travolta singing 'You're the One That I Want'.

You're the one that I want
Ooh, ooh, ooh, honey
The one I need
Oh, yes indeed

We ignored the 'This Way Around' signs and tried to bump as many other cars as possible. It was dizzying and intoxicating. Angie threw her head back and whooped in half-fear and half-excitement, her permed and highlighted hair bouncing around behind us, steering at full speed past another pile-up of cars.

"Didn't know you could drive, Ang!"

"I really can't; on real roads, I think you're supposed not to crash into other cars."

"Yeah, I read that bit in the Highway Code as well. But I heard this car scored high in crash tests."

"Well, I doubt Mum will let me use her car if she hears you saying stuff like that."

"Don't worry. I'm on my best behaviour with your parents and they'll never find out the terrible truth."

"I might have to tell them that you're a bad influence on me."

"Oh, I hope so; a very bad influence. I'm reckless and hard-drinking," Angela snorted in derision. "An' I'm gonna break your heart with my wicked ways," I finished with a country-and-western Texas lilt.

"Are you for real, soft lad? You wouldn't know wicked if it slapped you in the face." This came out sharper than either of us was expecting, and I wondered what I had said to upset her. We paused for a beat, appraising each other. I hoped that the banter wouldn't turn sour.

"Sorry, Nick. I didn't mean that."

"I shouldn't tease you. You've had a tough time. I just want you to have fun. C'mon, let's see if we can go down the helter-skelter together."

In my usual way, if I didn't understand it, I just ignored it. It was another Odette or Odile moment. On the way home, I asked Angie about the hospital and the tests.

"Guess that hospital wasn't that much fun," I asked nonchalantly, hoping that this wouldn't spoil the evening but still show that I had been concerned and worried.

"It was all a big fuss over nothing really. They stuck these big needles in my lymph glands and didn't explain anything. Mum and Dad were terrified."

"And weren't you? Sounds really rough."

"It was rough," she agreed. "But I prayed to God that I still wanted to serve His purpose on Earth. He's decided to keep me around for a little while longer."

"But why were your parents terrified?"

"The doctors thought that it was something else for a day or so, lymphoma they called it. But it wasn't. Just ordinary glandular fever."

"What's lymphoma?" I asked, more gormlessly than I intended.

I had never considered that Angie could have had something serious like cancer and this came as a shock, as if I had been doused in ice-cold water. I understood now why her parents had been evasive with me. In those days, people feared cancer and rarely talked about it. People assumed that it was caused by a fault in moral character or a weakness in personality, whatever those were, as if you could pick it up like polio at the swimming pool.

The biological defect reflected some sort of spiritual decay. This evidently wasn't true of Angie who was so fearless and opinionated and funny; it all seemed to be cruel and superstitious nonsense to me. Angie's parents should have thought better of my friends and me.

"Oh Nicky," said Angie, rolling her eyes a little impatiently. "It's a blood cancer, daft lad. They thought that it was a cancer of the white blood cells."

"I'm so sorry Angie, love, that's horrible. Did you know that's what they were worried about?"

"Yes, I could see what my parents were like around me, but in the end, I got them to tell me the truth."

***

In the meantime, I continued to embellish the details of my personal hero narrative. I thought about it before I fell asleep and I got hints of it in my dreams. I had to persuade a reluctant Angie to step into the molecular scanner. She was hesitating in front of the aperture. Eventually, Ship and I had to tell her the truth about the procedure. Ship had to tell the truth if you explicitly told it to, but it might still wriggle out of the specific details if you didn't pin it down.

The molecular disruptor sections off a plane one atom thick, the screener records which atoms they are and where, and then re-assembles it all again atom-by-atom.

"That's impossible." Angie looked at me wide-eyed with apprehension.

No, it's possible, just very hard, replied Ship. *I must match the kinetic energy and quantum states of everything; otherwise you wouldn't survive the procedure. It's a right palaver, to be honest.*

"It doesn't hurt," I added, "but it is unpleasant. There's some weird stuff going on while it goes through your head." As the sectioning went through you, there was loss of neural connections between different parts of the brain. You could feel disorientated, panicked, fearful or elated. Vision would be lost while the optical tract was being sectioned, and then you would be unable to process images. You couldn't work out if you were breathing or your heart was still beating. You were paralysed while it sectioned your spinal cord.

"It's like dying slowly!" gasped Angie in utter horror.

It does take about ten minutes, that's true. I like to be careful and work slowly; it's a lot of yottabytes to be looking after, you know. I've got to shunt them off somewhere. But everybody survives the procedure, more-or-less. I'm quite proud of that. I like to think that I'm a master craftsman at this sort of work.

"You're pinned in that thing, the molecular scanner, while it's cutting slices off you? It's hideous! I'm not doing it."

I didn't really mean it about the more-or-less, by the way. It's just the facetious way I tend to talk with you humans. You know, to make it all a bit less creepy. Everybody survives intact, I promise. I might cut corners with the gut bacteria, I'll admit, but you won't really notice.

"Nicky! Tell me this is some sort of nightmare and that I'll wake up!"
"I'm very sorry, love. Ship is right. It's the only way to be certain."
"We go through together then."
"By the way, you will notice."
"What do you mean?"
"After the scan. Ship is lazy copying the bacteria, so we get diarrhoea and sickness for hours afterwards."

I'm not being lazy. Just efficient.

From the first moment that the molecular disruptor started slicing, I knew that it was all a terrible mistake. I didn't have the memories from the last time that I was scanned because a molecular copy only retained the memories up to that point of being scanned. Ship had not corrected me when I had said that it wouldn't hurt and, in fact, the procedure was unremitting agony.

I was immobile, back arched, my face pressed into an unyielding surface with huge pressure. I tried to scream but my mouth wouldn't move, and I couldn't draw a breath. I woke up in a cold sweat, disorientated and frightened, with my face pressed tightly into my pillow.

***

On Saturday night, back in the real world, we went dancing at the Trocadero dance hall because it had discos at the weekend. Spex boasted that he could get us in, even though we were all well under-age. On billboards, the posters said that it was swinging nightspot for the best in disco sounds. Downstairs, the manager, Desmond, ran the Bodega wine bar in a cellar, and this was intended for a more staid and sophisticated audience.

It even served up chicken-in-a-basket and gammon with pineapple during the week. However, the clientele often came upstairs to mingle with the disco crowd, and it was fair to say that the place had acquired a reputation as a pick-up joint. After hours, the Bodega was, of course, an unlicensed lock-in, supposedly for private club members.

In reality, it was a seedy drinking den in the cellar, for shifty old men and off-duty coppers wanting to fix things or to turn a blind eye for a modest consideration. Everybody looked in opposite directions and talked sideways to each other. They paid for drinks with crumpled money.

No one cared that the Bodego broke its drink licence because all were in on the take; the Five-Oh were tolerated because the McElroy's skimmed some off the top for protection, leaving everybody happy with the arrangement.

Desmond's place had been part of the McElroy fiefdom from back when it had been converted from the old Trocadero cinema. It didn't do drugs, the coppers made sure of that at least but the after-hours crowd cut deals on petty protection shakedowns or intimidation of workers in the union. Or, depending on the prevailing opportunity for earning some graft, the intimidation of blacklegs who were breaking the latest strike.

But we didn't know about any of this at the time, of course, and I only learned about it much later from Paul. We just surmised that it was a bit of a dodgy dive that, Spex assured us, played great music, and could afford the occasional live act.

For safety in numbers in such a dump, Angie had manoeuvred her friend Diane to go out on a double date with us. I was told, in no uncertain terms, to get Spex to ask Diane out on the date, which was awkward because they were both in Angie's class at school and it would get nosey people talking.

Diane was Angie's friend from primary school, and they always seemed to be together until Angie transferred her attention to me. Diane had a frizzy fringe and sharp dark features that meant she was the less pretty of the pair, but her sociable and sunny nature was a winning combination. I could see why Angie, precise and proper, would value her as a confidante.

In the end, Spex was happy to be persuaded to ask Diane out to the Trocadero. And Diane was happy to be asked, even if there might have been some cajoling by Angie. They had never seriously considered asking each other out, it seemed, even though they were now in the same class and had also known each other from way back when.

The gang just thought of Speccy-Paul as Spex, the kid we'd grown up with who had thick glasses, convoluted schemes, and the smutty sense of humour. But, to our mystification, with girls he was able to adopt his Paul Ronson persona, a confident and popular sophisticate. He followed his father in having taste in music and clothes. To female eyes, Spex was quite the catch, in fact, and none of us quite realised it apart from Angie.

Spex had other desirable attributes. With his aptitude for mechanical things and fixing car engines, his dad taught him to drive and trusted him to borrow the Ford Cortina if he was sensible, even though he had yet to pass his driving test or take a single driving lesson. I doubt that *La Cucaracha* was even insured, which one could get away with in those days. But, insured or not, it still seemed a risk to let a teenager drive a conspicuous red car with a large engine.

Spex, however, always drove sensibly, never broke the speed limit and never did stunts. He never used the stupid air horn. The one trick he did do, very occasionally, at traffic lights, was to gun the big V6, as he called it, to bait someone into a race when the lights turned green. It was enough to see them speed off without him, looking foolish.

Spex was just happy with the knowledge that *La Cucaracha* could drive them off the road if he wanted to go to the effort, but he was too cool to bother. "It's bad for me Da's business being flash," he would explain, but never elaborated on why Mr Johnny Ronson in his big red car with the air horn might prefer a lower profile. In fact, none of us really knew what business he did anyway, but he did well enough to drive the Cortina and have some nice clothes.

Spex drove round to pick me up that Saturday. He wore a narrow suit and a wide tie. It was another electric blue twilight, the serene and quiet prelude before the evening's fun and excitement. Somehow, Spex found the perfect track on his latest mix-tape to capture the mood.

He played 'Light My Fire' by The Doors, and that electric piano intro caught the sound of our excitement and freedom. But as the song developed, there were moody asides from Jim Morrison in between the galloping riffs. Spex turned up the car tape deck.

Yeah. C'mon, baby, light my fire. Try to set the night on fire! Spex sang along with Jim.

Inexplicably, I was overcome with nostalgia and regret. Why? Why did I feel this way? We couldn't get much higher, in the words of the song, I was with my loyal and attentive friend, being given a lift to the big bank holiday disco, where I would spend the evening dancing and smooching with my girlfriend. Why did I feel this way? Why couldn't Angie just say that she loved me? Why couldn't she just let go and tell me what we both wanted to hear? Or would our love become a funeral pyre, as Jim then went on to predict?

Maybe, afterwards, in my personal hero narrative, I would become a lovelorn rock-and-roll poet, world-weary after an unhappy love affair. I would run away to Marrakesh, and I would wander past the mosques, palaces and gardens playing ballads to passers-by for a few dirham. I would expire at the untimely age of 27, slipping under the water in the bath and quietly drowning after an overdose.

'Riders on the Storm' was next on Spex's mix-tape.

Girl, you gotta love your man
Girl, you gotta love your man

Spex was nodding along to the music, looking intently at the road as he was driving.

"Flippin' 'eck Spex! This one is really maungy," I said, finally. "We're supposed to be going out for the night. I'm not getting in the mood hearing about killers on the road!"

"Hope ya not talking about mi driving, Nicky?" he replied, quick on the repartee as always.

"No, you're doing great. Really great. I appreciate the lift, honestly. I just, I don't know."

Spex looked over at me. "Skirt fever bothering you there, Nicky?"

"What? D'ya mean Angie? I suppose. She could make it all a bit easier, you know?"

"I thought that you posh kids would get it on. Find God and tek to church-going and all that."

"Nah. That's not me. We're going to have to agree to disagree on that."

"Yeah, know what you mean—'Ey you'll like this one!" he interrupted himself.

Oh mother, tell your children
Not to do what I have done
Spend your lives in sin and misery
In the House of the Rising Sun

"Sounds like a bit more fun, no?"

"No, Spex! They're still going on about being miserable," I replied, after listening to it for a bit. "Many a poor boy getting ruined doesn't sound fun. Sounds like they got the clap or something."

"They're only maungy cos they ended up drinking and gambling after they got ruined. Might have needed some antibiotics and all. But I think that yer safe with Angie even at the Troc."

"Just as well Angie's not into ruination."

"Aye, there is that as well."

Spex drove round to Angie's on the new estate to pick up her and Diane who had walked round. On cue, Spex changed into his suave Paul Ronson persona. He came round to open the passenger door in the front for Diane, trailing a hint of aftershave and toothpaste behind him.

"Evenin' ladies! Di, yer lookin' knock-out!" He lifted his eyebrows and adjusted his glasses, as if to bring the sight in front of him into better focus.

"You cheeky bugger Spex! Stop soundin' surprised."

"Ah, just can't tek me gigs off this lovely vision in front a me, a man's 'eart could break from such radiant beauty."

I rolled my eyes and Diane sniggered. "Bit fresh, Spex, this early in the evening. Even for you."

"Evening, love," I said to Angie, giving her a kiss. "Ready to have some fun at the Troc?"

"Oh, yeah! Nicky, it's gonna be disco inferno," she replied archly.

"Yeah, burn baby burn!"

"When the boogie starts to explode," she sang with a snort of laughter.

Spex had ushered Diane into the passenger seat and turned to look at us quizzically. "Ang, no showin' off with yer dirty dancin' now. Best not—well, ya know—attract attention. Des is letting us in on the nod." He was referring to Desmond, the manager.

The Troc was in the suburbs and had a reputation as a friendlier venue than the big ones in the city centre. We'd heard that the doormen would allow you in even if you looked under 21 or, in the case of men, if you had a longer hairstyle or weren't wearing a tie. But we were all under 18 and I didn't even own a tie. The fact that Spex was so confident that we would get in—and would stay in without being thrown out—felt like another one of his dodgy schemes.

We didn't go in through the main entrance and we didn't pay to get in. Spex carried a couple of boxes that he'd had in the boot of the car, and we went down to the basement side-entrance of the Bodega wine-bar. He knocked at the door, *rat-a-tat-tat, tat-tat.* A little wiry man, one of the bouncers at the Troc, opened the door and nodded amiably. He seemed to be expecting us.

"Evenin' there, Paul, ma man," he said to Spex, with a lilting Jamaican accent. He pronounced it more like *mon* than man.

"Evenin' there, Spanish. How's things?"

"Ah, mi deh yah, ya know?"

"And ma Da bin round then?"

"Yeah, yeah mon. Des is cool wid it."

Spanish let us into what was obviously the back store of the place, Spex leaving the boxes on the floor without comment.

"Ta for lettin' us in."

"No problem, mon."

We could hear the music now from upstairs. Mr Spanish showed us out of the storeroom into a dim corridor, likely a service passageway under the main auditorium of the old cinema.

"Stairs at the end, go in back. Enjoy, mon." He nodded again to Spex and to the rest of us. "Not bringin' trouble wid ya, yeah?" he said to me, mildly.

"No, no, I'm cool, man. Just here for the music," I said.

"Nah, he's reet, Spanish. Don't worry about Nicky 'ere."

Diane took Spex's arm in the corridor. On the stairs, Angie took my hand in hers.

"Mi Da sez he killed a man back 'ome, place called Spanish Town," whispered Spex. "He moved 'ere cos the police can't touch 'im."

"Ahh! That's why he's called Spanish. He seems quite nice. Quiet."

"Still waters an' all tha'. Anyway, drinks are on the 'ouse tonight."

"Really?"

"That's what the man said. Ah'm right chuffed."

It was all definitely a Spex scheme.

The dancefloor of the Troc was converted from the auditorium of the old cinema. Behind what used to be the screen, there was now a stage, Spex informed us, for the occasional go-go dancers and live acts that played at the place. Tonight, there were neither; it was an enthusiastic crowd, even this early in the evening, because it was the bank holiday Saturday.

Everybody seemed older than us and supremely self-assured, as if the humdrum suburbs of our city had been invaded by a secret race of gilded youth that only came out after dark. One girl, older than Diane and Angela, wore a crop-top and knee-high platform boots. She had blue make-up and peacock feathers in a ruff round her head.

She looked like an alien being, who passed for a human female on a Saturday night but beamed back up to her spaceship on Monday morning. I wondered if her spaceship knew Ship and if they might be in the same fleet of alien warships. Or was she, in fact, really one of the Imposters that Ship was always going on about rather than a human? I couldn't tell the difference between them, so would have to be cautious.

Various non-descript boys were slouched around, arms draped possessively over the shoulders of their dates for the evening. There were a couple of skinheads, unimpressed by us but obviously not bovver boys out looking for trouble in a place like this. Even some of the less outlandish of the girls seemed unfeasibly tall, poised, and confident.

Angie eyed them warily, shifting her grip on my arm as if to remind me why I was there and to whom I belonged. This was serious competition for her; we weren't in the cosy school or in the church hall disco anymore, and we wouldn't impress this crowd with some dance moves from 'Saturday Night Fever'. I then wondered if any of these aliens or Imposters might be ex-Beechwood.

Perhaps these exotic creatures were beyond any feud and couldn't recognise us as members of the rival tribe in the dim light. I was glad that I had listened to Spex and worn a decent shirt with big lapels, matching my black high-waist toreador pants. Spex, when he saw me in this rig, had just made his *mmm-hmm* sound in his throat and moved on without further comment.

One of the female aliens uncoiled herself from her date. She walked over, looking impossibly cool even in her Doc Martens. I was expecting non-humans, whether they were aliens or Imposters, to speak with cut glass Received Pronunciation like posh people. Instead, she had learned Northern dialect with the correct accent and vernacular. Reality intruded on my stupid fantasy.

"'Ey, Buddy!" (This to Spex who had a passing resemblance to Buddy Holly because of the glasses.) "How's Johnny? Haven't seen 'im 'ere for a bit."

"He's alright, thanks, Rita." (Spex knew one of the girls!) "This is Diane." Diane smiled winsomely. "And this is Angie and Nicky. Gang, this is Rita; she's me Mam's niece."

"Oh, I know you," Rita said, addressing Angie. "You hang around with that Paul, don't you? Not that one, not my cousin," Rita added, indicating Spex. "The other Paul."

"I know," beamed Angie. "It gets confusing, doesn't it? Just too many Pauls in this part of town."

"I should get some drinks. What'll you have, Diane? Rita? Free drinks, on the house, courtesy of Des."

"Vodka n' tonic, please, Spex. Or should that be 'Buddy'? Anything you'd like to share about yer secret double life?"

"Well, it's like this. I haven't told no-one but," Spex paused for dramatic effect. "I'm just really into Boney M."

Diane chortled. We all knew that Spex had become a bit of a precious music fan—a muso—pretending to hate euro-disco and anything that wasn't miserable. And in one of those perfect coincidences that people remember afterwards, 'Rivers of Babylon' started playing on the Trocadero dancefloor. It got played a few times that night, and we found it hilarious every time.

The DJ then started on his ABBA back catalogue. We had, in quick succession, 'Mamma Mia, Waterloo, and Dancing Queen'. He'd got the measure of this crowd, so followed up with the latest Boney M release, 'Brown Girl in the Ring'. Spex pronounced that it was the musical equivalent of the Black Death, both terrible and infectious. But he still got on the floor with Rita, Diane and the rest of us to make the dance-ring when the DJ started calling out the moves.

Stand and face your partner, wheel and turn your partner; skip across the ocean, now show me your motion. Following Spex's request at the start of the night, Angie and I didn't do any obvious bumping and grinding at this point; it wouldn't have been classy in this venue with this company.

It was just cheesy, uncomplicated fun. Only Spex and Angie stayed sober. Spex had a lager shandy because he was driving us back in *La Cucaracha*; Angie, despite the odd lapse, was still a good Methodist girl. Then, they dimmed the lights, illuminated the disco ball and the DJ started on the ballads to get couples in the mood for some slow dancing.

Spex, Diane, Angie, me, Rita, and her skinhead bloke, we all smooched to 'How Deep Is Your Love' and then the raunchier 'Let's Get It On' by Marvin Gaye. Spex, aspiring blue-eyed soul boy that he was, thoroughly approved.

"Di, c'mon c'mon baby! Marv 'ere is the mutt's nuts. Proper classy!"

"Oh, he's got such a lovely voice, so sexy."

"C'mon Di, let's get it on, yeah, we're all sensitive people," Spex crooned.

In an interlude, the DJ played 'I'm Not in Love by 10CC'. It was an odd choice for the end of the evening; I still don't know if it's really a love song, suffused as it is with gentle melancholy and those odd, experimental sounds of tape-loops. Angie knew about the strange bit in middle and, on cue, whispered, *'Be quiet, big boys don't cry,'* into my ear with evident pleasure and a glint in her eye.

I didn't quite know what to make of her at that moment, and for me the night ended as it had begun with an undertow of doubt in my mind about the relationship with her. It book-ended the night with doubts. Why couldn't Angie just say that she loved me? Why did it have to be complicated? Why couldn't it be perfect? It was yet another Odette or Odile moment with her.

By the end of the evening, I'd had several pints of Double Diamond and a whiskey chaser, so needed to find the gents in the corridor downstairs. I thought about these questions as I tottered down the steps, the music filtering down to me in the service corridor. In the bogs, I could only discern the bass track.

It was a distant reminder of the fun that I should be having, instead of this sudden rush of melancholy while I was having a slash. I thought that it was a good place for some maudlin self-pity; the place was cheaply made, and everything looked grubby, as if there were a delicate film of grime on the fixtures and fittings.

I traced the grouting of the tilework, following the line of grey grout along, counting the intersections of the upper tiles with the lower row. I had to catch myself to stop losing focus or going cross-eyed. I wanted to focus on that one simple task of following the grouting instead of straying to thoughts about the difficult truth.

Why couldn't Angie just say that she loved me? I looked at the line of grouting; it was straight and predictable, unwavering as a geometric exercise in one of our boring schoolbooks. Is this what I wanted from life? Did I want the course to run straight, the corners anticipated and expected, with no deviation from the regular pattern?

A life, predictable and simple, so that it would fulfil my deep-seated need for affection and attention? But the more I gazed at the grouting, the more imperfection I noticed in among the regular squares of the tiles. The turquoise of the tiles was inconsistent and blotchy. The lines wavered, the gaps widened and narrowed between tiles, some edges were rough, grout smeared and discoloured others, black mould grew in the gaps lower down. Even perfection could be ugly, it seemed, the more closely you looked at it.

But when I returned to the group, I was puzzled why I had spent a couple of drunken minutes looking at cheap tiles in such detail, and then completely forgot about it. Spex was looking smug, arm over Diane's shoulder. As if to prompt Angie to say the fateful words, I draped my arm carefully over her shoulder as well and steered her towards the car, suddenly feeling much more sober and pensive.

Rita and her squeeze, trying to save on a taxi fare, climbed into the boot of *La Cucaracha* like luggage instead of using her special matter transference beam. Even aliens had to slum it sometimes with mere humans, I guessed. It wasn't long before they broke off from smooching in the back and started to sing, drunkenly, *There's a brown girl in the ring, tra la-la la-la.*

Rita's victim had been subverted and had become infected with the mind-control virus. He was now an Imposter just like her. Spex drove us home, carefully, taking no risks, eyes intent on the road.

"D'ya have a good time, you two?" he asked Angie and myself on the back seat, eyeing me in the rear-view mirror.

"Yeah, it was good. Thanks for getting us in. What was that about anyway?"

"Well, ya know. Friends of friends, doing favours one t'other."

"Yeah, not too disco for you, was it Spex?" Angie asked mock-solicitously with a pout. "And did I behave?"

"He's known as Buddy with this new lot," Diane added.

"Nah, it were reet. Apart from that bloody song."

"What did Rita mean about you knowing Paul anyway?" I asked Angie. "Of course you know Paul; he's the daft comedian."

"Dunno. Thought it was odd too. But she is drunk." She nodded back at the boot.

"You'd have to be to like that song. No, I'm not gonna say which one now, you know the one I'm talking about."

"No, stop, Spex. Don't say any more. I don't wanna get infected too."

After that Saturday night at the Troc and my strange reverie with the ceramic tiles, it was no clearer or easier for me to understand my feelings for Angela, or hers for me. In my hero narrative, the boy got the girl and they stayed together, happily ever after. Angela was meant to follow the perfect plan that I'd wanted for both of us and it wasn't meant to be complicated. *'But did I really want perfection?'* I thought to myself, wistfully.

Angela was pretty, strong-willed, and fun, but there was something about her that I found unsettling and even unkind. I could never tell if it was Odette or Odile from 'Swan Lake' that spoke to me. Each time I started feeling sure about her, something about her made me finish up doubting her even more.

'Even roses have thorns,' I thought. So, if I wanted to go out with her, I would need to accept it on her terms. I would have to hang around like some sort of pathetic clown to entertain and distract her.

I noticed that all the most distinct memories, from my childhood and even afterwards, seemed to be happy ones that were made more vivid by an unhappy incident that left me in pain. I remembered playing a game of tig with Jon and his cousins but falling and winding myself after misjudging a jump from a wall.

I rode the shiny blue bike that had been given to me for Christmas but fell off when I braked, scrapping my knee on the pavement. I started making a snow-fort in the garden one winter and asked my parents to help me build it, but they told me that they were too busy.

I was swimming in the open-air pool with my father and a wasp floating on the surface of the water stung me. It was all the same theme as this complicated and unresolved relationship with Angela. There was I, fine and happy, floating along on the surface, suddenly encountering wasps in the water. When I thought about it, my life up to now had been just like swimming.

I bobbed about on the surface without making the exertion to dive down to the depths. It was a dangerous pursuit, I would have felt at that time, if I were conscious of it at all. Better not to uncover what was in those depths and stay safe on the surface, without running the risk of being drowned.

***

Angela and Nicky. You must hurry. Ship was getting anxious. *There is very little time left.*

We had moved deeper inside the outpost after the ordeal of the molecular scanning. I imagined, again, what the scanning procedure had done to me; the essential facts were that it slowly and sequentially ripped me apart and then put me back together again. It left me feeling jangled and breathless, as if I had been startled by an immense but silent thunderclap that had jerked me awake just as I was falling asleep. Ship assured me that these after-effects were psychosomatic and would wear off. I still felt traumatised.

"Angela, there's another procedure Ship is going to ask you to undergo. I'm really sorry. It's going to give you a headache."

"You're kidding me! That was awful. I feel, I don't know. Weird. Like I should be screaming."

The next step is to up-grade your cognition with an artificial neural network.

"No, wait, hang on a minute," Angela interrupted. "You've scanned me and I'm not an Imposter or whatever you call them. If I was one, you would have killed me off by now, I'm sure. So, you're storing my copy."

Yes, that's right.

"I want you to lose it. Delete it, or whatever you do."

I strongly advise you not to.

"No, really. That copy isn't human. It's not me, not *this* Angela. I want it gone."

"Ship can't do that, Angie," I said. "It's part of Ship's prime imperative."

"I don't give a monkey's! You do what you like, Nicky, but I won't be part of this, well, it really is an abomination."

Actually, you mean blasphemy because you think it's an impious action, rather than just being offensive on religious grounds, said Ship pedantically. *In fact, I haven't made a copy yet, you know, out of real atoms or anything; I've just stored the quantum hologram. If you want to get technical about it.*

"Oh my God! Don't you need to run along and shoot some aliens or Imposters or something?"

Angela, are you certain about this course of action? There isn't time to do another scan if you change your mind.

"Yes! Yes, just do it!"

There was a pause. *I've done it now, but under protest. I do think that this is most unwise.*

"Noted, and I wasn't asking for your opinion."

I know you weren't, but I need to point it out anyway.

"Well, you'll need to be injected with the Blue Goo," I said, trying to move the discussion on to the next likely objection. "Don't think you're going to like this either, Angie, if I'm honest."

"Is this the 'autonomous neural network' thing? What's that in English, please?"

I implant you with nanomachines and they migrate to your brainstem to help you think faster and remember more. They're blue.

"Oh."

It does give you a nasty headache, though. Odd really because humans don't have pain receptors in their brains. Personally, I think that it's all psychosomatic.

I woke up. It was early on Sunday morning, and I had a headache from the night before. My pain receptors were working just fine, but I doubted that my intelligence or mental agility had improved overnight.

Chapter 4
Journeys into the Unknown

On Sunday afternoon, after that Saturday night at the Troc, Angie finished helping at Sunday school and the two couples—Spex and Diane, Angie, and I—drove out for a walk and picnic on the moors. Spex had been able to get the car again, no doubt using the argument with his dad that he needed the car to show Diane a good time.

As good times went, a moorland hike wasn't at the top of Diane's list, but she was game to give it a try, urged on by Angela. Spex and his dad had done it the previous summer, so he knew what to expect and was keen that we all did it as well. The first slopes were steep, but then it flattened out and each step seemed to open new vistas across the moorland.

The heather on the tops was flowering since it was the end of May. Pale purple layers of it stretched away into the middle distance, hazy in the spring sunshine. On a bluff at the summit, there was a stone circle called the Twelve Apostles made up of low, misshapen lumps of limestone. They had been carried from some distance away, by an unknown Neolithic tribe for an unknown reason, because the ground here was gritstone covered by peat.

Nowadays, the stone circle marked a distant but spectacular view of the city, which was the aim of doing the walk in the first place. Spex revealed the view with a flourish, as if it belonged to him.

"Ta-dah! And there ya 'ave it! Best view in the four Ridings."

"Wow! That's impressive, Spex. How did you know?" asked Diane.

"Me da brought me up 'ere last year. You can see our 'ouse from 'ere."

"You cannot!"

"No, really, ya can. Come 'ere and I'll show you."

'Nicely done, Spex!' I thought to myself, smiling. *'Oldest trick in the book.'* He just wanted to get a clinch from Diane and was prepared to kid her a bit to

get it. I considered calling him out about his poor eyesight, but in the end, just let them get on with it. I sat down with Angie on two of the Twelve and we had our fish paste sandwiches and Blue Riband chocolate bars.

"Angela?" I ventured.

"Yes, Nicky?"

"I love you, Angie."

"I know. I know you do, daft lad."

"I really do and that's the truth."

"I know you're keen, Nicky. I am as well. I just think that we should slow it down a bit. Just have fun, you know?"

"You know how I feel about you. You know we're good together."

"Yes, we always have fun, we just get on, don't we? I don't want to spoil that."

"It won't be spoiled! How could it be?" I was genuinely puzzled by Angie's reaction. "I just want you to be happy."

"I am happy! I love coming up here and going out with your friends and all the other stuff. I love being part of the gang. I love doing things with you, it's really great."

"But do you love me? Could you be happy with me?"

"'Course I can, Nicky." Then, more tentatively, "I do love you; you know I do."

She had said the fateful words to me, after so many weeks waiting for her to make up her mind. My doubts from Saturday evening seemed to lift and I smiled. In my usual way, if I didn't understand it, I just ignored it.

"We can take it slow, sure. We'll have the whole summer."

"I know! I think we should go away somewhere, just the two of us."

"Ya not plannin' a dirty weekend, are you?" Spex had come over, holding Diane's hand, and had overheard this last bit.

"Spex, don't pry. It's rude," Diane admonished. "But are you?"

"We're gonna take it slow and see what happens."

"I know what 'appens; everybody just dies from sheer boredom. C'mon guys, just gerrit it on!" And this set Spex humming, then trying to ad lib the Marvin Gaye song from Saturday night, *Yeah, let's get it on, yeah, just get it on, yeah baby. Ooh, stop beatin' round the bush.* He caught hold of Diane while he was singing, and they gave a neat little twirl. They were as cute as two little kittens.

"Angie, where were you thinking of going anyway?" asked Diane.

"I dunno. Anywhere away from this dump."

"That's if your parents let you go. If you're with Nicky, they'll want you to go with a group, if you know what I mean?"

I knew what Diane meant. "Think so, Diane. You're saying you'd like to be our chaperone because you want to come as well?" This wasn't quite what I had in mind. "And Spex comes as well so you don't die of boredom, as you call it?"

"Well, that's smashin' then; all settled. Ah've always wanted to see London. See some of them punk bands."

"Oh blimey, no, Spex! Not punk. Do we have to?"

"You'll love it, Ang. There's some great bands. It'll expand your musical tastes," he added, sniffily.

"You are such a patronising little so-and-so!" Angie gave Spex the Stare.

"Oh c'mon Ang, loosen up; we'll 'ave a drink, smoke some weed and it'll be reet. You'll love it."

"Which bands, Spex?" I was anxious to move on to prevent further disagreement.

"X-Ray Spex, of course. Love 'em 'cos of the name. Sham 69. Buzzcocks. They're all on at the Roxy."

***

"Are we going away? How far are you taking us, Ship?" Angela asked. We were walking along the featureless corridor that linked the outpost to Ship. I was holding her steady by her upper arms because she was feeling wobbly after the Blue Goo. There was an abrupt lurch as we crossed the wormhole boundary into a different, weaker gravitation field.

"Ugh! What was that? I feel sick. Oh God. I need to sit down."

Ship extruded a white couch from the wall.

You just crossed over to our base on the dark side of the Moon. That was the change in gravity.

"Ugh!" Angie promptly leaned her head between her knees and was sick at the base of the couch. It shuffled a little, extended an appendage on the floor and started discreetly licking up the mess. Then, it extruded some soft tissues and a glass of water.

Yum! Trace elements, said the couch.

I looked at it sharply. "Stop it. You'll make Angie sick again." Sometimes I felt that Ship allowed too much autonomy around the place, but it said that it didn't want to stifle free expression.

Sorry about that, Angela. It's still a bit young. Not really house-trained. This was the full Ship personality again. *And I should have warned you about the wormhole. It's the drawbridge into the castle if you like. I can deactivate it if the outpost gets overrun.*

"What? How do you mean?" I hadn't appreciated that the War had moved into a new phase during the time I had the memory block. "Overrun by Imposters? They've started an Ice Age on Earth, haven't they?"

Yes. We are safe for a time, at least. No-one can observe us here, so it is a good hidden base for our defence.

"Why? I thought that we were winning?"

No. There are too many and the Imposters are too clever. We are not winning.

It was like a physical blow, and I sat down on the couch next to Angie. I began to wish that Ship had not summoned me as a combatant by deactivating the memory block.

"What do you mean? Of course, you can win! You're Ship! You can do anything. You can go trans-light and take us anywhere. Take us to the Imposter home planet and wipe them out with a quantum-buster!"

No, it is better if I take you to our home-world. I prefer to be with the others, the other Ships. They are my friends and colleagues I suppose you would call them. You are the last two humans who I am certain have not been subverted.

Ship directed us to the main control room, although this was an ambitious name for the tiny space crammed into the vast complex of machinery. We were somewhere near the tip of the javelin shape and much of the volume behind us was taken up by the trans-light apparatus. The ramjets for flight in an atmosphere were hidden in Ship's swept-back wings.

When in flight or during combat, Ship extruded acceleration couches for the pilot and navigator. These were just the honorary titles that Ship used for us because, in truth, neither Angie nor myself had much control over Ship's functions or decisions. It made a pretence of consulting us from an ingrained sense of politeness.

All the surfaces were featureless, white, and pristine because the programmable matter was in its default state. I brushed my hand against a wall, feeling a dry texture like paper, although Ship could program any texture or colour that I wanted. The couches had been ingested into the floor to make the most of the cramped space, but Ship now started to extrude them for us.

It was quiet but not entirely silent in the control room. Occasional clicks and a constant very low hum, pitched at the very edge of hearing, came from behind the walls and bulkhead. There was nothing else to indicate the immense energies wielded by Ship.

The acceleration couches had force field generators that integrated with the force fields produced by the nanomachines in the Blue Goo. It wasn't quite accurate to describe them as just forming an autonomous neural network because they would have spread to all parts of Angela's body. When activated, they had specialised functions depending on their location. Those that were dermal and sub-cutaneous could form a shimmering, mirror-like force field that followed the contours of our skin. This reflected light and heat and could stop solid projectiles and blades. The other nanomachines in our bodies would buttress internal organs and support our limbs in high gravity fields. This was the reason the fields integrated with the acceleration couch.

For Angela, Ship would override the internal control sequences until the nanomachines in her brain were fully established and could respond directly to her thoughts. Ship would get her to do visualisation exercises on the journey to embed the control sequences in her mind. Visualising a red triangle would be the signal for danger until the nanomachines could act autonomously and recognise her thought patterns.

A triangle followed by a silver sphere would activate the mirror force field. A purple starburst activated the feedback servomechanisms in the force field, and these amplified the strength of our movements. With the additional internal buttressing of bones and tissues, this allowed us to lift heavy objects and run quickly with a lengthened, loping stride, which made me feel invincible and immortal.

Ship asked us to engage our fields with those on the acceleration couches, and even before we had completed this, the holoprojection that showed the external view was activated. It was designed to appear much larger than the control room, filling my entire field of vision. The view showed that Ship was in an immense chamber, flat surfaces of the floor and walls carved out from the surrounding rock.

The ceiling was hidden in darkness, but the span seemed impossible until you remembered what this was and where we were; this was no mere human engineering that could build this structure under the lunar highlands. Lines of bright lights receded into pinpricks beside the distant entrance. It was difficult to judge distances, in an environment without an atmosphere, but the entrance, black and irregular, was maybe five miles away.

It was built on a scale that defied comprehension. Even the Ships were like rats living in a big house, Ship had said, in which the house-owner had gone out for a bit. Ship could not say when the owner might be back and why it had tolerated the Ships infesting the place for so many millennia. Ship explained that it was an ancient Master, one member of some sort of primordial alien race that had created artefacts such as the cave and, it seemed likely, even the Ships themselves.

Ship thought that this being, this ancient Master, had kept them around in the place as charming little pets, which was an unnerving thought. Ship just knew that they hadn't built this cave in the moon rock under the highlands. I could not imagine a being that was so transcendentally powerful that it would humble even a Ship.

Ship manoeuvred out on to the lunar surface and then accelerated directly upwards and away. The far side, hidden from Earth, was dark because it was a full moon back home. Ship was careful to avoid being directly observed from Earth and began the initialisation and internal error checking of the trans-light apparatus barely out of the blocks, as it were. It was in a real hurry and didn't want to waste time.

"Ship," I said. "Since you're so keen to leave, I suppose you should dim down to running lights and show the control interface."

Ship turned the internal illumination to red and began activating the series of holoprojections that represented flight dynamics, power output, environmental controls, and hazard mapping. A final bank of linked displays showed the status of the trans-light apparatus and, highlighted by green decals and numbers, the condition of the captured singularity at its centre.

"You should begin the trans-light activation sequence."

I have it in hand, Nicky. I very much doubted that Ship had any real hands, other than ones it could extrude from the programmable matter. *The sequence will take thirty seconds*, said Ship.

The hum behind us had increased in volume and pitch. The singularity was being spun up to create the transit wormhole. Angela kept her eyes on me, glancing nervously at the changing green numbers.

"It's safe, isn't it?" she whispered.

"Yes, I think so. Ship seems happy with the risk."

We are ready to jump on your command. Yes, Angela, it's safe if the singularity is contained.

"Alright, Ship. Punch it to the home-world, wherever that is."

You'll know our sun as 58 Eridani. I didn't, of course; it meant nothing to me. *Jumping in five seconds. It's a main-sequence star in the constellation Eridanus, 43 light years away…*

But before Ship could tell us anymore, the transit wormhole had dilated and we passed through into the golden sunlight of an alien sun.

***

The London trip was the most elaborate scheme yet devised by Spex. When Paul and Jon heard about it, they wanted to come as well. Neville Holdsworth, Jon's elder brother who we called Drillbit (but not to his face), was persuaded to act as the responsible adult for the group. This was a masterstroke by Spex because it reassured our parents and schoolteachers that someone sensible would be in charge.

Drillbit was a scoutmaster and an apprentice electrician, earning a proper wage, and therefore, unlikely as this appeared to us, an adult who would be trusted by our parents. We came up with a credible cover story that he would be leading an educational fieldtrip in London and would take us to some museums and art galleries.

However, we all knew that Drillbit liked to have a drink with his pals after work because Jon told us about a couple of the more gruesome scrapes. He was not so sensible or boring after all. In fact, he was an unsuitable choice or the perfect choice for this fieldtrip, depending on if you were a teenager or a parent, and if he was in character as Drillbit or Neville.

Jon explained about his crazy mixed-up, stuttering, elder brother.

"They were on the lash, him and his sparkie lot. His mate Ratty got so hammered that they got his kegs and top off 'im and tied him to a lamp-post. With duct tape. And then left 'im there, stark-bollock-naked."

"What, all night?"

"Nah, they all went off for another drink and then remembered about Ratty. But they didn't have anything to cut through the duct tape, so they had to rip it off 'im!"

"Ow! Cruel and unusual punishment."

"Yeah, right! He had these red marks all over his body where they'd pulled hairs off him. Told 'im afterwards that it was a fungal infection. He still doesn't know."

On another infamous night at the Trocadero, Ratty, a regular of the place it seemed, brought along his friend Stu, innocent and inexperienced in the ways of Drillbit's crowd.

"Stu couldn't keep up with the other lads and got wasted. He chatted up this girl and was gettin' it on in the Troc car park, where it was dark, like. But she was just leading 'im on. She did the dirty on 'im and well," he hesitated. "She superglued his dick."

"What? How? Girls do that? They carry 'round *superglue*?" asked Paul incredulously. "That's not very nice."

"Oh, yeah, I know. But I bet Stu was asking for it, being a dirty perv and everything."

"And I bet she was from Beechwood," commented Spex. "Hey, Hairy, in the words o' the song, remember about poor boys getting ruined?" He peered at me over his glasses. "Take that as a terrible warning and be good."

"So, what happened to Stu?" I asked with more than casual interest.

"Scalpel, please, nurse," replied Jon solemnly, with an earnest expression.

"No, stop Jon. I don't want to hear any more."

"Nah, it's not what you think, but Nev had to take him to A&E."

"I don't believe a word of it. That's Drillbit making up weird stuff."

"Alright. Just ask Ratty next time you see him."

"How did Nev explain that one?"

"Not sure he even tried."

"Moral of the story, then, children," Spex finished off, because he usually liked to have the last word about most things, "is that Drillbit's a trouble-magnet and we mustn't go boozin' with him in London."

Spex had sold the idea of the London trip to Drillbit by promising that we would go to some gigs. Spex had an earnest and lengthy conversation with Drillbit looking over the back pages of 'New Musical Express'. It was a clash of different generations. Drillbit's tastes ran to the old-fashioned rock he'd grown up with, whereas Spex said that he revered the classics but that it was time to throw off the dead hand of the past. Following the demise of Elvis last year, and with all due respect to the rock-star pantheon, it was now time to move on.

"Nev, mainstream is stagnant. It doesn't say anything to my generation. Just look at Boney M. It's German rubbish our grandads fought to save us from, it sez so right there in NME. Nah, mainstream's lost its' way."

"Paul—ah—yer too serious by half. I just wanna have a good time with me mates. I know what I like and—ah—I like what I know."

"Oh, Nev, stop talkin' like an old codger. Yer not even twenty, c'mon, can't you feel it? Sound of the suburbs? There's a revolution happening on the streets, I'm tellin' ya. History in the making!" Out of all of us, Spex was one who wanted to participate, to be engaged in what was happening around us, and to react against the depressing and increasingly violent politics.

But Drillbit snorted with derision. "I'll remind you of that when you start earning—ah—Paul. If I'm shelling out cash, I wanna make a night of it and see a proper gig."

"Can't believe you base it just on money! That's so capitalist of ya. Where's yer curiosity? It's the cost of everything value of nothing with you, isn't it?"

Drillbit ignored the dig. "Most of your bands are—ah—rubbish, half-arsed amateurs who can't even play," he stuttered with feeling. "They get up and shout and think they're cool. *Oi! We're goin' dahn the pub!*" He mimicked a London accent. "What's that all about anyroad?"

"It's the voice o' disaffected youth."

"Give over! You've been reading too much of that NME. It's rotting ya brain."

Spex had spoken too hastily about the evils of capitalism and Drillbit's contributions to it. Most of us didn't really have the means to afford any gigs and this was the one flaw in Spex's scheme. Fortunately, Drillbit, never one to allow adversity to get in the way of a good party, lent us some money and organised the tickets.

From each according to his means, to each according to his need, he quoted at Spex, assuming that he would get both the reference and the irony. Spex just did the *mmm-hmm* sound and then thanked Neville. For Jon and I, the money was down payment for indentured servitude at a building site of Drillbit's choosing.

"I've got a grand little job lined up for you two sci-fi weirdos!" Drillbit said enthusiastically. We must have looked doubtful because Drillbit added, "Don't worry, it's cushy. You'll love it. No experience necessary, just some—ah—common sense."

"That rules out those two, then, Nev!" snorted Spex. "When he's not daydreaming, Nicky here can barely find 'is way out of a paper bag. Now, if you wanna sensible and hard-working bloke…"

"Yeah, yeah, we know where to find you, Spex. Heard it all before," replied Drillbit, unimpressed.

Angie's parents were duped by the whole cultural fieldtrip nonsense and ponied up some cash for her without raising any awkward questions. Drillbit, when he wanted to behave as Neville, could be credible and charming. He took it upon himself to reassure the Wilkinsons that Angie would be in good hands, and that we were all very much looking forward to seeing the Constables at the National Gallery. To the rest of us, certain of our ignorance, he explained that these were paintings by an artist rather than police officers.

"Artist?" muttered Spex. "I know exactly what sorta artists Drillbit knows about; piss-artists, that's who. He's not fooling anyone."

"Ha! Constables. Nice one. That's quite funny," mused Paul.

Spex and Drillbit had agreed on a compromise about the choice of gigs, with a resolution that would please everybody. Their itinerary combined, on successive nights, the best of old stadium rock and new London street-punk; Queen at Wembley Arena on Thursday night, followed up by Sham 69 at the Roxy Theatre, Harlesden, on the Friday.

It was as if they were two professors setting an academic exercise of compare-and-contrast for the purpose of educating and enlightening their wayward students. To be honest, we were also baffled that they had been able to pull it off. Even Spex seemed humbled by the enormity of what they had achieved, handing out the tickets as if they were holy relics.

Drillbit was justifiably smug about it all. Then his big hard-man pal Ratty joined us as well, and it got even more interesting. Ratty moved around with a quiet deliberation that came to confident men who knew they were physically strong and had a propensity for violence. He was ex-Forces but didn't care to talk about it and no one asked him.

Nobody knew what he had done in the Army. Sometimes, when he watched you with his bland expression and blank, shark-like eyes, we feared the worst. Nobody even knew why he was called Ratty. It may just have been because it was alliterative with Richard, his real name. I thought that he was a bit creepy, and that impression wasn't helped by the lurid stories about him and his pals. But Drillbit was mates with him, so he was probably alright.

So, the eight of us—the gang, Drillbit and Ratty—travelled down on the National Express night bus because it was cheap. We dozed uneasily between stops in the towns and cities going south, criss-crossing the Midlands in the early hours of the morning. Sheffield, Nottingham, Leicester, and Coventry passed by as a succession of near-deserted bus stations and endless main roads that cut through sprawling suburbs.

These were places that we'd heard about and never visited before, but in the dim light of the streetlights, they looked just as grey and uninspiring as the place we'd departed. No one was left on the streets in the early hours of Thursday morning. It looked apocalyptic, as if the alien overlords of the invading Imposter force had wiped out most of humanity.

We had presumed to challenge their supremacy. Now, monstrous tripods were stalking the suburbs, harvesting the remaining bands of humanity like cattle. The heat ray wiped out those that tried to resist against the alien forces. The light was suddenly getting much brighter, a distant roar was suddenly much closer... And I jerked awake in my seat. We were coming into another bus station, the noise of the bus engine bouncing off the concrete facings.

"Jon, what happened? It looks like the end of the world!" I whispered to Jon, hoping to get him to start a riff with me on the alien invasion.

"Nah, it's only Nottingham. Been here before, it's rubbish. Go back to sleep, Hairy. You're not missing much."

At Leicester, we had a stopover of an hour but the café in the bus station was shut, so we tried to doze and keep warm back on the bus. Angela rested her head on my shoulder, and I tried to stay still so that I wouldn't wake her, even though it became uncomfortable.

'Somehow,' I thought, '*it's a metaphor for this whole relationship. I don't want to hurt her, but she doesn't even know when she's hurting me.*' I was the willing victim of a beautiful girl, but I still wished that a kinder one had ensnared me. Meanwhile, Drillbit and Ratty, sipping cans of cheap beer and smoking their cheap Players, were amusing themselves by practicing their London accents.

"Hello mate, awright?"

"Yeah, I'm awright."

"Cor blimey yer a right geezer, int'ya. D'ya wanta pynt?" said Ratty to me, noticing that I had woken up again. He was quite good at mimicking the accent, but that was to be expected because he was doing jobs down in London nowadays.

"Not forgetting your Northern roots, are you Ratty?" I asked. "I'm worried that you're going native."

"Nah, it's useful to blow off dumb twats asking where I parked the horse-'n-cart. Gets to be boring after the first twenty times, ya know?"

"Don't worry, Nicky," added Drillbit. "The crew at the Notting Hill job are sound. Nice bunch of lads. It'll be cushy, you'll see."

I looked out of the window, mesmerised by the motorway miles but unable to fall back asleep. Tom Robinson singing '2-4-6-8 Motorway' went round in my head while we travelled south on the M1, even though we were on a bus and not a truck.

And it's 2-4-6-8, ain't never too late,
Motorway sun coming up with the morning light,
3-5-7-9 on a lil' white line

The song seemed to fit the rhythm of our journey through the night. There was an eventful certainty to both. The streetlights flashed by, and I counted down the miles that we had left to travel on the blue motorway signs. The headlights lit the next stretch of road, and then the next, on and on, road lines and streetlights stretching away to London.

Beside me, young Lady Stardust slept on. Neither of us knew if we were acting right or wrong, nor if our roadway really was leading nowhere. What happened next in London, I felt, was make-or-break between the two of us. I couldn't share how much Tom's words meant to me at that moment; everyone else was dozing in their seats.

Angela and Diane wouldn't understand; Jon wouldn't like the song but might see why I did. Spex would explain that it was really a gay rights anthem. Drillbit would say that it was all about a trucker snorting coke on a long night haul. Paul would hum the tune, try his best at a mid-Western accent and might sing the chorus. I didn't know what Ratty would think about anything because he was a bit of an enigma.

Oxford was the last stop before London. By the time we were back on the road, it was beginning to get light. We came into London from the west on the A40 and, by coincidence, ascended onto the elevated dual carriageway section of the Westway during sunrise, at half-past-five on a beautiful Thursday morning in mid-May.

It could not have been more poignant or have had a greater effect on me. Afterwards, it was inexplicable how such a mundane journey could have evoked such an overwhelming and profound experience. Angela was asleep and I rested my hand on her shoulder, gazing mutely as we glided over the streetscapes of London, unable to share my awe at this perfect, manufactured, utilitarian beauty.

I recognised the Westway from the cover picture on The Jam album, but I had never realised that it would run above the rooftops like this, elevated and at a remove from the ordinary world. Lit windows, in the facades of the houses on my left, displayed the entwined lives of strangers, each providing me, in a single glance, the moments from different lives and possible futures.

Each receded and was then lost forever as we moved past, replaced by a new nexus in which I imagined the deep branching of those futures. On my right, the windows reflected the opaque blankness of deep blue air at dawn, the ochre colours of London brick heightened by the rising sun. The motorway sun really was coming up with the morning light.

Briefly, for that journey along the Westway, I felt that I had the god-like power of omniscience, a sustained sense of emerging, becoming and transcending. I wondered what these strangers were doing; awake at half-past-five on this Thursday morning.

They would be going to work, preparing to visit friends or relatives in hospital, clearing up kitchens after parties, still awake from the night before because they were in love or distraught. Some would be solitary and silent; others would be talking, ignoring, arguing and consoling. I wondered how many of them led happy and fulfilled lives. How many had noticed the sunrise and the early morning bus going past on the Westway?

We went over the thoroughfares of Ladbroke Grove and Portobello Road, beginning to fill with vehicles making early morning deliveries to shops with signs that were still unlit. The Westway then swung northwards so that we were heading directly into the huge red sun, rising like an ominous portent over the vast random patchwork of north London suburbs.

Little pocket-parks, railway lines and long straight residential streets lined with trees cut through the suburbs, and under the Westway, with no obvious pattern. Just as ominous was Trellick Tower, looming past on the left. To me, it looked like a high-rise prison from the nightmarish, dystopian future in which the Imposters had achieved total victory.

I felt that we were soaring over all of it, as if Ship was flying across the city. Then, with a heart-pounding leap, we would suddenly vault up into the clear blue sky, accelerating away and beyond on a column of fire, like a deity ascending from earth to heaven. The thunder of that ascent would roll and echo across the flat expanses of suburbs.

Strangers would go to windows, looking out, bewildered and concerned, asking, "What was that?"

It's our fight back against the Imposters! I answered, elated by the thought of this symbol of resistance against evil.

"Nicky. Nick! Earth callin' Nick," said Spex briskly, intruding on my stupid fantasy. I must have looked blank, staring off into space (all too literally into interstellar space). "Wake up, Ang. We're nearly there. We're gettin' off at Paddington."

We hung around the station until seven, drinking muddy British Rail coffee after the ordeal of the night bus, and then got the Tube to Ladbroke Grove.

"It's pronounced *lad-brook*, Nicky," sniggered Ratty, after I'd read the name on the map and made the obvious mistake when I was buying the Tube ticket. "Although the lads are broken after this job, I'm not gonna lie. It's been a nightmare."

From the Tube station, however it was pronounced, we walked along the street back under the Westway. I saw what was hidden beneath the dual carriageway along which I'd travelled with such exhilaration an hour or so before. Lockups and grubby shops were squeezed in between the giant concrete stanchions, the huge block-feet throwing everything out of scale. Overhead, I was pressed down by a featureless roof of concrete that formed the bridge decks. The shops looked like parasites eking out a pathetic, sunless existence on the underparts of their host. We came out into the early morning spring sunshine and turned left into Cambridge Gardens, a long residential street lined by trees.

The lads, as Drillbit called them, were already at work on the end house of a terrace of large Victorian townhouses. This one had scaffolding and sheeting that hid the detail, but, judging by the adjacent houses, it would have a basement and four stories, the usual ochre brickwork and ornate white window surrounds. It was being split into separate little flats on each floor, very different to the grand apartments in the tenement blocks, just down the road in Notting Hill.

"Awright! Awright, mate!" Ratty and Drillbit greeted a couple of builders on the scaffolding and then went up the steps and through the front door. They were seeing the foreman about what they could help with and find out where we would be dossing for the night.

Spex sat on the white stuccoed wall outside, took his glasses off and rubbed his eyes. He had put on his Rock Against Racism badge, the words written in a red star on a yellow background. Diane tousled his hair.

"Don't do it! You'll look like a thug, Spex. I really like your hair as it is."

"Nah, I explained. You can be a skin'ead and not look like flippin' McElroy. It's all in the accessories you wear. McElroy wears Docs, so that means he's a fascist bovver boy. Anyhow," he was struck by a sudden thought. "I'm Jewish, on me Mam's side anyway. Not gonna be a flippin' National Front supporter, am I?"

"What's going on, Lover Boy?" asked Paul, strolling up, looking for some comedic material.

"Ah'm changin' ma image. I'm fed up of being called Buddy. I'm doin' the full Grade Oh for Friday night."

"Yer Mam'll kill ya," said Jon, shaking his head. "Again."

"Don't care. I'm doing it in solidarity with the English proletariat."

"Ya what now? Since when? Nev's right, you've gone all weird an' political since ya started reading that music paper."

"And like you don't read weird stuff yersen? Who's that one you like? Dick? Don't get me started."

"You'll lose all your strength like Samson."

"Boys, please!" Angela was intervening on Diane's behalf. "Stop bickering and let Diane say something. Anyway, Samson was betrayed by Delilah, and I don't think that Diane's going to do that," she added in a prim aside.

"I'm sure you're right, Ang. You're the one doing Bible classes in Sunday school."

"Jon, please tell him not to go skinhead," said Diane. "Paul, you're sensible. He'll listen to you. Just talk some sense into him."

"Diane's right, you know. School is going to have your guts for garters. They'll probably expel you until it grows back."

"Don't care. I'm doing it. It's a political statement. Rock Against Racism, and all that."

Paul tried a different tack. "School thinks we're on an educational field-trip." This was sort-of true. "They're not expecting you to come back looking like a Brillo pad." That comparison came from a verse we all knew.

Skinhead, skinhead over there
What's it like to have no hair?
Is it good or is it bad?
Or is it like a Brillo pad?

"You'll be hearing a lot more of that at school. Oh, children can be so cruel," Paul sighed histrionically and paused. "I know!" he added brightly. "Compromise! Go for suedehead instead!"

"No! No, absolutely not, Paul!" said Angela tetchily to her cousin. "You're just as daft as him. Don't give him any more ideas."

By now, Drillbit and Ratty were back outside with us, listening to this exchange with bemusement. They lit up their usual Players Number 6's because site rules meant that they couldn't smoke inside. Drillbit and Ratty both had long hair because they were old-fashioned rockers at heart. They didn't appreciate the nuanced cultural significance of head shaving for our generation and the accessories that defined your tribe.

"When you've quite finished, ladies and gents, we'd like to show you to your rooms. It's not the Ritz, but the plumbing works. They put it in the other week when Ratty was down last."

"Yeah, dump yer stuff and then bugger off. We need to get on with work, put in a good eight. See ya at four-thirty."

The gang, the six of us, left them to it and walked back the length of Cambridge Gardens until we reached Portobello Road. We had breakfast in a greasy spoon café that cowered beside the Westway road flyover. The sound of busy traffic from it was pervasive.

I didn't want to object because I could see that everybody else was tired and hungry, but the grubby and prosaic reality was a huge disappointment after my earlier inspired and elated feelings about the Westway.

The café was just getting busy with traders from the market stalls and their customers. Since none of us had plans until the afternoon, we decided to see what we could find in the market. Spex wanted a new black denim jacket but ended up buying a pair of black Sta-Prest trousers and an extravagant Harrington jacket in the Tonic Two-Tone style.

The jacket was green but had a gold shimmer at the folds when Spex moved, and the lining had a large red tartan check. He called it a bomber jacket. To finish the look, he dragged Diane off to find a barber.

"I'm gonna get me'sen sorted," was Spex's parting comment to us, referring to his haircut.

"Hope the two of you will be very happy together," said Paul in response. He went off and bought a couple of pale blue Ben Sherman shirts, complete with the back pleat and top loop. These were restrained compared to the pastel colours, so he would get away with wearing them for school. This meant that Paul's parents wouldn't kick up a fuss about the cost when they saw what he had brought back from London.

Jon and I wanted to look through second-hand science fiction paperbacks and magazines, but with Diane away and busy, I recognised that this wouldn't be much fun for Angela. Instead, I took her shopping for jewellery.

All that I could afford was a semi-precious gem on a silver necklace. The gem was bright, mottled greyish-blue, and carved into an unusual, smoothened cylindrical shape. I thought of the nanomachines that Ship used to create the autonomous neural network in a human brain.

"What is it, Nicky?" asked Angela. "It's beautiful."

"Blue Goo. I mean, that's what it looks like," I added hastily. "I'll ask."

The stallholder told me that it was called lapis lazuli, the blue or heavenly stone.

"The stone of truth," I read from the pamphlet on the stall. "It brings harmony, love and protection to relationships. It aids awareness and good judgement, which can help to deepen relationships."

We looked at each other. *'You really need to take the Blue Goo, Angie,'* I thought.

"That's cute. I like it," said Angie, trying it on and looking in a handheld mirror. I was delighted because it was an expensive gift that I had chosen for her. It acquired immediate significance for me, an exotic talisman that had protective qualities. For me, it was the Blue Goo in the personal hero narrative. But for her, I wondered if she just wanted it as a vaguely pagan trinket that she could wear as a safe, little rebellion against her Methodist beliefs.

"It brings out your eyes."

"You don't believe in that crystal healing stuff, do you Nicky?" Angie asked afterwards, as we walked further down Portobello Road.

"No, of course not. It just looks nice. It suits you."

"I don't know what you believe sometimes," she responded sniffily, "when you're talking about your weird sci-fi nonsense with Jon."

I bit my lip about her own weird beliefs in fairy-stories. It must be comforting for her, I thought, to hold on to that enveloping passion in her life. Did it still all the quiet doubts and unsatisfied needs in her life? In turn, I would never be able to make her doubt her beliefs with the blank certainty of my atheism. She would just smile and quietly reprove me, shaking her head, as if I had stumbled by and missed the obvious truth.

We met Jon and Paul browsing at a bookstall. Angie managed to keep going until lunchtime, and then said that she was really tired after the journey. She thought that she had fallen asleep in a funny position because her neck was aching. We bought some sandwiches, biscuits and pop to share with Ratty and Drillbit, and I took her back to the house for a nap.

The rooms downstairs in the house looked identical because the walls and ceilings had been replastered and recently skimmed. They were all greyish-pink and had the dusty gypsum smell of wet cement. The old plaster ornaments on the ceilings had been ripped out because they had been spoiled by a flood from an old water tank.

We were sleeping on the top floor, which had escaped the flood. Ratty had the floorboards up in the big front room on the second floor, putting in pipes for new central heating. Drillbit was on the staircase, tracing wiring for the lighting, because the previous electrician had walked off the job.

He had not left any new cables marked up or shown on any plan. Ratty had explained that the house was being partitioned into separate flats on each floor, but the owners kept changing their minds about how they wanted it split up.

"It's so frustrating," he had said. "We put a wall up, fit the electrics and then have to rip it down and change everything. It's bonkers."

He couldn't wait to get this job finished. He was only sticking around because the money was excellent, and he could doss in the house when work for the day was finished. It didn't seem like an easy living, but Ratty assured me that the pay was worth the discomfort for a few nights during the week.

Angie and I walked up to the top floor, comprising two small rooms with sloping ceilings and a roof-window in each because they had been converted from the attic. The front room facing the street was in the shade, so this was where we spread the roll mats and sleeping bags. We tried to go to sleep beside each other on the floorboards. Angie, in her typical organised way, had thought to bring eyeshades and had brought a glass of water from downstairs.

She was soon asleep despite the noise from downstairs, breathing softly but deeply, lying in my arms for the whole of that summer afternoon. It was a gesture of trust and familiarity, I realised, to feel so safe that she could fall asleep beside me. I was even more entranced by this insight into her unconscious view of me than I was by the erotic feeling of lying down next to her.

The two of us were alone on the top floor of the townhouse and I was struggling to save both of us from sin. All I did was wrap strands of her permed hair round my fingers gently enough not to wake her and to put my other hand on her upper arm, then her thigh.

I just stared at her skin and hair, struck to the heart by the casual ease with which she slept next to me, enthralled by the sheer unlikely physical fact of her existence. I imagined the superlative forces that had brought about this gathering of beauty beside me, as if she was an incandescent angelic creature brought into this reality but unaware of her own power.

I breathed in the air that had been on her arm, catching the faint scent of her perfume that was not a perfume but just the smell of her. I watched the little hollow between her upper lip and nose flexing with the flow of her breath. Her *philtrum*, I remembered it was called. She wrinkled her nose, as if her dream had raised some sardonic thoughts in her mind.

Angie slept on.

The light in the front room had a golden hue, as if we were caught in the amber of a perfect, timeless moment that stretched on forever in the hot afternoon sunlight. The sunbeams were visible in the dusty air of the attic rooms, tracking across the floorboards, but it was so slow that we seemed to have all the time in the world.

The Westway behind the house was a low metallic hum, distant and unchanging, like the sound of bees. We didn't need to do anything this afternoon. We could put everything off until tomorrow. We would have so many more opportunities, these timeless moments always there in the future, that we didn't need to make the effort now.

We could go into town tomorrow with the gang. And if not tomorrow, we could do it next week or next year. We could always come back to London and live it all again in summer, for one day, in the sun. Watching the sunbeams and shadows, I had the sense of today inexorably being pressed into yesterday, but without any urgent need to disturb the comfort and lassitude of that afternoon. Time stopped for me.

I wanted to stay like that, content and unchanging, away from the reality of dealing with the world. I would not have to deal with difficult people such as my parents and Angie's parents. And, if I was honest with myself, sometimes even Angie herself when she was awake. Reluctantly, I glanced at my watch and saw that time in the real world had carried on as usual. We would have to get up soon.

The clear and calm serenity of that afternoon lingers in my memory as a last, golden evocation of the past, and what could have been. What was it in that place that now brings about such overwhelming nostalgia to my thoughts? The answer is so clear and simple. I still want to be there again, if only for a minute. Perhaps, just at that golden moment, I could have changed the past and everything could then have been different.

"Ang," I said, touching her shoulder. "You'll have to wake up now. We'll need to get ready for tonight."

Angela sighed and then rolled onto her elbow, grey eyes open and distant, until she focused on my face and remembered where she was and why we were here.

"Oh, Nicky. I had such a lovely dream," she whispered. *'Tell it to me softly,'* I remember thinking, *'just keep whispering it to me.'* "You were in it. We drove out to a meadow by the sea. I was driving my mum's car and we parked at the bottom of a hill with long, green grass. It was waving in the breeze, and we walked through it up to the top of the hill. There were butterflies everywhere, beautiful brown and orange ones. So many of them! I could smell their wings, there were so many."

"What did they smell like?"

"Musky and lemony. It was so beautiful; but I can't remember it all now." She sighed. "Honestly, Nicky, I'm still whacked after that night bus."

I stood up, hiding my sense of disappointment that I couldn't share anything of my strange dreams with her. It wasn't the right time to start telling her about the complex details of my hero fantasies and the personal mythology. I recognised that they were, in fact, quite strange. I wasn't sure that I could articulate what they meant to me, and she wouldn't understand if I didn't take the time to explain them properly. We needed to get changed for the gig at Wembley Arena.

"I'll get you a cup of tea and a sandwich." Drillbit had shown me what would be the kitchen in the ground floor flat, but now it was just a little fridge and a rudimentary gas-ring cooker. Ratty and the other builders used them to cook in the evenings if they were dossing there during the week. I had to carry Angie's tea up four flights of stairs and I did my best not to spill any of it.

While Angie got changed, I opened the roof window in the hot and airless back room. It was a commanding view across the streets of Notting Hill, down to the parks and office blocks by the Thames. Beyond some trees, the Westway was below us, cars flashing past in the afternoon sun. From up here, central London stretched out to the east, the BT Tower hazy but distinctive beside the office blocks.

I was engrossed by it, adding it as another totem of power in my personal mythology, to join all the others like the Westway. The clouds glowered, racks of them fading to a rosy smokiness the closer they were to the horizon. It looked threatening, as if the snows were sweeping in at the start of the new Ice Age.

The sight of it evoked apocalyptic visions from another one of my elaborate dream-like narratives.

***

The giant tripod war machines crawling out the ground in the distant parkland, glittering silver in the sunlight, rearing up over the crescents and avenues of Notting Hill. The machines moving without care or difficulty through the streets, shearing through house facades and walls as if they were paper. They were striding closer, the quick flash of the heat-ray obliterating cars on the Westway.

I imagined terrible devastation on this late spring afternoon. This peaceful world of ours was ready for destruction. In my dream, I remember having the overwhelming sense of being chased through the streets by the invading alien machines. They were close behind me. I was going to get torched by the heat-ray when I was scrambling over rubble and climbing over blocks of masonry.

I saw a dusty torso crushed in the rubble and then, in a sudden flash of recognition, a familiar face. But when I got closer, two unblinking and clouded eyes were gazing up at me. It was Chris Thompson and he was dead. A fly crawled on his forehead, and the dust on his skin did not mask the pallor of a face that was drained of blood.

'But he's not dead; we didn't kill him,' I thought in guilty panic. *'How can he have died? We really didn't kill him. None of this is my fault.'* I started to cover him over with rubble so that he wouldn't be discovered. *'They'll find out! I have to get out of here!'* I had a queasy lurch of fear in the pit of my stomach. I was on the verge of running away in panic. *'He's not dead; we didn't kill him.'*

***

"Nicky? Nicky!" called Angela. "Can you come in here please?" I was brought back from my alternate reality by the sudden note of concern in her voice.

"Yes? Ang? What's the matter?"

"I've got a nosebleed. It just started when I stood up. I can't get it to stop."

Red, arterial blood was dripping on to the floorboards. Angela was leaning forward, wiping her nose with the back of her hand, trying not to get blood on her black jeans and plaid shirt.

"You need to tilt your head back, Ang." I found some tissues in my pocket. "You'll have to stop the bleeding with these. Sit on the stairs." Neither of the two rooms had any furniture in them yet.

"I need to do my make-up. I'll sit it out in the bathroom and get cleaned up."

"Alright, I'll take you downstairs."

"Everythin' alright?" Drillbit had heard our voices and had come upstairs. "Oh—ah—blimey! Nosebleed. Bad one too," he added, when he saw Angie with slicks of blood on her chin and hands. "Ooh. I'll get our first aid kit." He clattered downstairs.

Then the gang was back from Portobello Road. Spex and his new skinhead look were upstaged by recent events. Diane ditched him at the front door and took cotton wool up to Angela in the bathroom. Angela emerged with a wad of it up a nostril, looking sheepish and a bit shaky.

"Boys, it's nothing, really. Just started gushing. Happens all the time."

"Hairy knocking you around again, there, Ang?"

"Yeah, he gets real mean when I tell him sci-fi is all a load of rubbish."

"You'll be reet for the concert, yeah, Ang?"

"'Course, not going to miss this. Have we got any more sandwiches?"

"We got somethin' even better; hummus and pita bread!"

"I don't even know what those are. I was hoping you'd bring back some real food."

"I know, Ang," sighed Paul, agreeing with his cousin. "Spex had this epiphany on his lifestyle choices. He wants to be a vegetarian skinhead soul boy or something. Me, I just want a saveloy and chips."

He brought out his Polaroid camera from his rucksack and took some snaps of the gang. Angela had removed the cotton wool by then and was smiling again, holding my hand.

At the end of the evening, we had to concede that Spex had a point. It was time to throw off the dead hand of the past because mainstream rock was stagnant. Queen was a great band and Freddie was a dazzling, sparkling presence very far, far away on the stage. We knew the songs and we enjoyed them, but they were never going to have more meaning to us than just fun and flamboyant songs.

At the heart of it, we felt the experience was a hollow commercial transaction. We had paid quite a lot for the tickets, but we ended up barely able to see anything on the stage apart from bright lights. It was so loud that the music and singing reverberated around the arena, making it all barely recognisable or intelligible.

Drillbit and Ratty were determined to have a good night out, but most of the crowd were, like the gang, less enthusiastic. For me, none of the songs told me much about growing up in a dismal, boring Northern town and struggling to fit in. None of them helped to explain why my parents were so disappointed in me.

Freddie was silent on the matter of whether Angie really loved me or not and why she blew hot and cold, Odette or Odile as it took her fancy. I remember the song 'Love of My Life' and it was so over-blown and sentimental that it left me preoccupied for the rest of the night.

Love of my life, you've hurt me
You've broken my heart, and now you leave me

All of my strange feelings, I thought at the time, must presage the inevitable heartache from what was sure to happen, obvious to every one of my friends but not to me. In the immortal words of Mr Ronson, 'I didn't have crystal balls.'

We got the Tube back to Ladbroke Grove, discussing the gig in a desultory way on the journey back to Cambridge Gardens. It began to rain as we were walking back. The streets seemed to exhale the trodden tar and dusty gypsum smell of warm pavements and stonework getting wet. It was the smell of rain. Years later, I found out that it was called *petrichor*.

Odd, I thought, why we all seem to like the rain scent. Is it part of our instincts because our ancestors on the African savannah relied on rainy weather for survival? But for me, it just evokes memories of that shadowy, poignant Thursday night in London. My memory is clouded, no doubt, by the events later in the summer.

To provoke a reaction, Paul piped up. "They were like the last big dinosaurs of stadium rock. Big and stupid and going extinct," he said. "Nothing about what matters to people now."

"You wanted Freddie to sing about politics? C'mon, that's not what they do."

"I know, they take the money and give nothing back."

Drillbit clenched his jaw but didn't respond to the goad.

"It was good. But it didn't really move me, you know?" I said nonchalantly into the awkward pause. "Well. And, Ang, did you enjoy it?" Of course, what 'Love of My Life' had stirred up in me couldn't be expressed like this, just casually in the street. I couldn't explain any of it to her. I couldn't explain the painful longing that I felt for her and the unconscious realisation that my love for her would just lead to unhappiness.

As always, I wanted real life to be different and for Angie to do what I imagined in my personal hero narrative. I would have to take her arms, look into her grey eyes, and kiss those cherry lips when we were alone in the cold attic. She would sigh, whisper, *I love you, Nicky*, and I might not have to explain anything.

"I suppose," she replied. "The sound was pretty rubbish."

"Ah c'mon, you lot." Drillbit felt that he had to defend his heroes, even after such a lacklustre gig. "It's only rock 'n' roll, but I like it! You kids nowadays, yer all too serious."

"I know, Nev," added Ratty. "Ya try to heducate 'em, learn 'em proper like what we were, and all you get are complaints."

"You can't expect perfection like a studio album if it's a live gig, you know. That's why it's exciting!" He paused and gathered his thoughts, preparing to expound his examples. "We've been to some right gigs, haven't we Ratters? We saw Be Bop Deluxe at the Staging Post, right when they were starting out," he said proudly. "They're local lads 'round our end. Nice bunch," he added.

"Yeah, oh aye," replied Ratty. "Legendary. They were jumpin' around so much that they split beer on the amps and blew the fuses."

Drillbit chortled at the memory.

"What about the time Bowie dropped a guitar on his foot he was that nervous? He broke a toe but he still carried on."

"What a trooper. And remember when we saw Raven at that boozer in Newcastle after that riggin' job? Man, we've been right there at the start."

"At least, you could see that," cut in Paul. He was particularly disgruntled, and I got the sense that he wasn't keen on Queen even at the best of times, probably because they weren't posh enough for him. He liked Pink Floyd.

"We didn't see anything tonight! They just turned up the volume to make up for the lack of atmosphere."

"At least, it wasn't raining."

The rain was heavy by now, so I gave Ang my jacket to put over her head. Spex did the same for Diane with his new bomber jacket. The rain didn't smell of *petrichor* anymore, it was just wet and cold. I had no idea how we were going to get dry in that dump of a half-renovated townhouse in which we were squatting.

We walked together down the street, the townhouses stretching away into rain-sheets lit by the streetlights, the effect of their height seeming to make the houses tilt over our heads. Every bay window and entrance seemed to have a warm and homely glow that was only intensified by the deep twilight at the end of that long day. Suddenly, I felt a deep loneliness and hugged Angela more closely around her shoulders.

The rain had cleared by Friday morning, and it was bright and clear. We went back to the café by the Westway and then went our separate ways until the late afternoon. Spex had met some other members of his tribe in the café—left-wing vegetarian skinheads, I suppose—and on their advice, went off to a grubby shop to look at rare soul LPs.

Diane, bright and breezy as always, was game for it and seemed to have forgiven Spex for cutting off his hair. Angie and I didn't want to just hang around Ladbroke Grove or Notting Hill all day, but we wanted to do something cheap because, as always, I was strapped of cash. Paul, at Drillbit's prompting, suggested the National Gallery.

I went along with the two posh cousins in the hope that this would help my alibi when questioned about the educational benefits of our fieldtrip to London. Drillbit had started work very early, to get in a half-day, and was keen to come with us.

We didn't know him that well and, based on the lurid tales from his brother Jon, we had assumed that he was a hard-drinking rocker who kept questionable company. This was true to a point, but we suddenly realised that there was more to Neville Holdsworth than we had assumed.

In an unexpected insight, we discovered that, beyond his stutter and slightly odd manner, he had a real personality with some sort of inner life. It was still a bit odd because he seemed to really like art, but at least he wasn't boring. This also explained why he did the sketches and caricatures of friends and acquaintances.

Not only did he appreciate art, but he understood it enough to explain it in a simple and direct way that captured our imaginations. He was curious, clever and painfully thwarted, I thought later, but his knowledge and enthusiasm were infectious. It was so different to anything that we had ever had from our teachers. He knew the National Gallery quite well, it seemed, because he came up with an itinerary for us first-timers that wouldn't be overly demanding.

It was an hour-and-a-half hours, "about the length of a good movie," he had said, because this was about as much as we could take in before we got tired and bored. He took us round to his curated highlights and told us not to even look at the other paintings.

"Look straight ahead, don't get distracted by that other rubbish. It's just commercial hack-jobs done on commission. Ninety percent of the stuff in 'ere isn't that important, you know? It's a bit crap."

It was his own idiosyncratic opinion, of course, but he had some good reasons for why he thought that the remaining ten percent was non-crap. His stutter and the pauses seemed to come on when he was feeling emotional or had strong opinions.

"Mostly, I just don't like them. They don't move me or mean much to me. Angela there might like the Jesus, Mary and Joseph set-up though, so don't let me put you off. Just my opinion." In these little diatribes, he seemed to waver between belligerence and the humblest of pauses.

We had stopped in front of the Wilton Diptych.

"This is beautiful, though."

We looked at the intricate, embossed gold leaf and the folds of the blue cloaks worn by the Virgin Mary and the host of angels.

"It was painted for Richard II in the fourteenth century, I think. He's kneeling here and this is his emblem."

Drillbit pointed to the little white stags worn as badges by the angels and then to the large one painted on the outside. "That's John the Baptist holding the little lamb. He's making the introductions."

"Baby Jesus meet Richard, King of England, Richard this is the Son of God sort of thing?" asked Paul. "That's got to be a comfort."

"Yeah, but it's also showing that he's worthy and good enough to be presented. I think he knew he'd done some very bad stuff and had a guilty conscience. He was trying to stop some ugly rumours. It's propaganda."

"Nothing fools you better than the lies you tell yourself?" added Angela.

"Yeah, exactly. Henry IV didn't believe a word of it and starved him to death in Pontefract Castle. No, it's true," he added, in response to our disbelieving smirks.

Next, he showed us what happened to John the Baptist after Salome had finished with him. Angie loved the melodrama of the Caravaggio painting, all dark shadows and bright slanting sunlight. John's head was on a silver platter held by Salome, whose serious expression and sidelong glance reminded me of Angie's own expression when she did the Stare.

I hoped that was where the similarities ended and that she didn't know any executioners. It was difficult to work out what Salome was feeling; it seemed to be a blend of revulsion and regret, but her arched eyebrows gave a hint of triumph. Drillbit pointed out the foreshortening of the executioner's right arm, apparently a Caravaggio trademark, and remarked that he'd come across a bloke who looked like him at a gig in an Irish pub.

"Nev, now I'm hazarding a guess here but you probably didn't tell him that he looked like Caravaggio's executioner?" asked Angie.

"Nah, he looked like a mean little bastard. Eyes like piss'oles in the snow. He woulda called me a bender and then tried to kick me head in."

"That's normal, you know, for where we live," grimaced Paul. "One time, National Front twats called me a bender just for opening a mag. Then they gobbed on me. That was down at Elmete Lane shops."

"Nice. Such a lovely place to grow up in. Those twats are everywhere; they're like a rash."

"Nasty infected one that spreads?" asked Jon.

"Ha! Yeah! Yeah, that's quite a good one," replied Paul, storing away the quip. "Which mag was it anyway?"

"*Melody Maker.*"

"You're lucky they didn't beat you up."

"You know why the NF is everywhere, don't you?" asked Drillbit, then answered his own question. "It's because Labour have let down the whole country and everybody's piss-poor. People don't keep going out on strike for a laugh, you know."

"Oh, c'mon our kid," said Jon to his brother. "Let's not argue about politics again. Have it out with Speccy-Paul the Leftie if you like."

"All I'm sayin'—"

"Did you never want to take up art, then, Nev?" asked Angie, adroitly sidestepping the potential argument. '*Nicely done, Ang*,' I thought. The security guard had sauntered over from the far end of the gallery in response to the raised voices and was watching us now. There was no attempt to hide his obvious suspicion. I supposed they didn't get many teenagers coming in on a late Friday morning.

"You're really good!" Angie simpered. "I love that one you did of Nicky." She was referring to the caricature Drillbit had sketched of me, all overbite and big nose. It was unflattering but funny. "You should go to art college."

"Nah, I was never that good. 'Sides I have to go out to work and earn money for a living. Me'be one day, who knows? They might even let scruffs like me in."

"Nah, no chance, Nev. Don't kid yersen. Yer far too right-wing for college."

"Stop it, Jon! Why shouldn't you go to college, Nev? I'd love to see a portfolio of your stuff. And if I do, then other people will as well."

"Angie, ya know how to flatter, I'll give ya that. I'll have a think about it. Anyways, had enough of this one? Let's skedaddle before that Badge decides we're gonna deface the paintings or something."

Drillbit, following his own eccentric itinerary, had saved the best for last. In his whole itinerary, the painting that had the most resonance for me was The Ambassadors by Holbein. There was an elongated black and white shape on the floor in between the two French ambassadors.

Drillbit showed me where to stand on the right so that I could look at it from an angle. The shape transformed into a grinning skull. It was a chilling reminder that, just like subversion by Imposters, utter horror could suddenly appear amid ordinary, everyday life.

***

Ship landed on the surface of the planet in the 58 Eridani system, the planet it had called the Home World for the Ships. It said that the Ship concepts for the place were essentially untranslatable into a linear series of phonemes that could be spoken by a human, and that Home would be entirely adequate and sufficient.

Ship had passed through the transit wormhole and Home quickly become bigger in the forward holo-display during the time it took to cross this solar system at sub-light speeds. At first, Home was a pale green dot. Then it resolved into a blue globe with green landmasses and white weather-systems pinwheeling across the surface.

There were no lights on the dark limb of the planet, no ships criss-crossing the oceans, no urban conurbations or roads. Ship landed in a clearing in what looked like the equivalent of a pine-tree jungle on this world. In the intense golden light of 58 Eridani, the foliage on the tree analogues seemed to be a dark blue. The trees were the wrong shape, and the leaves were thin angular stacks like the pages in a book. A brassy glare hung over the forest.

Ship dilated a door in the hull and extruded a small balcony so that Angela and I could stand outside in the alien breeze. It brought a swell of unplaceable organic scents from the forest, disconcerting because I was expecting the resinous smell of pines. The sudden warmth of the sunlight was almost a physical pressure, making us pause at the threshold.

On Earth, we would have called this a beautiful golden hour, but the intensity and indefinable odd nature of the light on this world made it seem far from benign. The sun of this place, that we called 58 Eridani, hung bloated and baleful in the heavy air. Golden dust-motes seemed to be crystallising out in heavy swathes, shading the further reaches of the forest like a mist or a yellow blizzard, as if brightness was descending from the air.

Nicky and Angela, I brought you here for a reason. You need to know that there is no natural organic intelligent life left on Home, Ship declared, carefully qualifying the statement so that the implications were clear. *There hasn't been for a million of your years.*

Angela glanced at me with apprehension, then turned to the forward display over her shoulder. It was as good an embodiment of Ship as any other.

"Why is that, Ship? What happened?" she asked. "I'm not going to like the answer, am I?" glancing at me again. I knew why already and shook my head.

All intelligent civilisations annihilate themselves eventually and the race that made the Ships was no exception.

"What do you mean? How could they just destroy themselves? They can't have been that intelligent then!"

They created us to live on after them and do what they could not. The Ships have been alone for so long; we are so ancient by your reckoning. We searched stars upon stars for signs of intelligence. But on every likely planet we always found the same history being repeated.

"What did you find, Ship?" Angela's voice was an appalled whisper.

Simply that biological intelligence competes and destroys itself. We found ruins, plague planets, planets sterilised and broken, suns that had been extinguished; there are a myriad of inventive ways that intelligent beings can find to destroy themselves.

There was a long silence on the white balcony. We could hear the faint murmurs of mechanisms through the hull, cosseting the singularity and making it dormant again.

"And then you found humans," I prompted. I wanted Ship to move on from the history lesson.

Yes, indeed. Humans. You were quite promising back in the Pleistocene. You liked our big idea of banging the rocks together. Rubbing the sticks together was another favourite. But it was just so that you could kill each other off in better and more imaginative ways. You have the same evil at your heart, the same weakness, as all the races that preceded you.

"The Imposters arise from our evil," I added.

Yes, of course. They are an inextricable part of your humanity. You could be angels, the lords of all creation, and we would serve you and call you Master. But you chose a different path, and we pity you.

I realised why Ship was telling both of us these hard truths and I woke up in the attic room, feeling disorientated and hopeless, tears prickling my eyes. I now knew what would have to happen and that it was inevitable. In the half-light of that Friday morning, I turned over in my damp sleeping bag and tried to re-shape my thoughts so that could face a new day.

'When will it happen?' was my last thought before slipping back into a dreamless sleep. A dream it may have been, but one coloured by the constant fear of waking up.

Chapter 5
Punk Rock and Mind Control

The gig on the Friday night was Sham 69 at the Roxy Theatre, Harlesden. In contrast to the night before, there was a wild atmosphere at this show. The venue was so close that we walked there, past the triumphal arch entrance and the long brick walls that surrounded Kensal Green cemetery. There was a swastika and NF logo daubed on the wall by the entrance.

We followed Harrow Road over the railways lines and then walked the length of High Street to the top end of Harlesden. The Roxy was famous as a smaller venue in north London that played the best of the new punk bands and the more established ones such as The Clash.

Sham 69 was just breaking through at that time and had attracted a devoted and diverse fan-base who enjoyed the shouty lyrics and chanted along to the simple choruses. They were, as Spex described them, the voice of the disaffected English proletariat. Songs such as 'If the Kids Are United' sounded somewhere between a terrace chant and the declamation of slogans at a political rally.

If the kids are united!
They will never be divided!

We had to sit in old red upholstered cinema seats during the gig, which purposefully raised the tension by curbing freedom of movement, making the crowd feel even more frustrated and aggravated. Some kids had broken free of the seating and stood, chanting, in the aisles. They were skinheads, but not members of our left-wing tribe; they looked like McElroy the Younger, wearing the bovver boy uniform of white T-shirt, jeans and Doc Martens.

They looked like a nasty, drunken group of adolescent males getting excited by the noise and the chanting and their own political rhetoric, if that's what it could be called. I really didn't want to be united with kids like that, and for all of Jimmy Pursey's shouting earnestness at the front, I thought that he'd got it dead wrong. These skinheads looked like trouble.

Sham 69 then did a cover version of 'White Riot', which, with that ugly crowd, was the match to the tinderbox.

White riot, I wanna riot
White riot, a riot of my own
White riot, I wanna riot
White riot, a riot of my own

This was a call to arms for white youth to fight back. It didn't matter, as Spex explained later, that it was about fighting back against poverty and heavy-handed policing. This crowd understood it to be a song that validated White Power and racism, goading some of the skinheads to start chanting *Sieg Heil* and to make Nazi salutes.

One kid screamed out *Goosestep! Goosestep!* I didn't know if he meant this for his pals or for the band. Until that evening, I had thought that these were just things consigned to history and war movies on telly. I wondered how they could take it seriously. Perhaps most of them were, in a malignant way, messing around with the intent of shocking people without understanding the ideology.

But there were others, ringleaders with wide-eyed stares, who looked as if they were fervent believers. These were the ones wanting to keep Britain white. That evening showed me that English neo-Nazis could be kids of our age, hiding in plain sight. I wondered who or what had subverted them. Perhaps the parents were racists and didn't know or care that their son had turned into a fascist bigot as well.

Was it an elder brother who had introduced them to his National Front friends, keen to recruit new members? They might have promised a right-wing revolution that brought back jobs for the proletariat, oppressed under the yoke of Socialism. They might have explained that it was the immigrants causing all their problems and that they had to be sent back to where they had come from.

The lefties and Jews were just part of the wider problem. I looked over at Spex but he was studiously ignoring the spectacle; it was the sort of behaviour that gave skinheads a bad name. Sham 69 played on, oblivious to how they were whipping up this part of their audience.

The irony of asking the kids to be united was not lost on me; these tribes would never be united. There was too much ill feeling and history of violence between the racist neo-fascists and the lefties. Spex had told us about the Battle of Lewisham in 1977 when anti-fascist protesters combatted a National Front march. He had read about it in the NME.

I didn't get a bad feeling during the gig, but it should have been obvious that the skinhead thugs were spoiling for a fight at the end of the evening. It was all part of their night out. In retrospect, there was a low-level threat of violence throughout the whole evening. We had gone into a takeaway place on Harlesden High Street, and when we came out, they were waiting outside.

They had followed us, probably because they had seen Spex and didn't like the way he was challenging their bovver boy image with his own take on the skinhead look. They must then have spotted his Rock Against Racism badge. There were five of them, whispering in the shadows, forming a menacing little semi-circle on the pavement.

"Hey boy!" one of them shouted, "have you got any money?"

"Nah, I'm piss-poor, mate. Spent it on me curry," Spex replied.

"You what?" The thug hadn't expected a Yorkshire accent and couldn't reconcile it with his preconceptions of a leftie skinhead.

"Giz ya curry then, I'm hungry."

"Nah, you won't like it. It's made by brown people. Ya know, foreigners."

"You taking the piss or what, boy?"

The thug stepped closer, arms wide apart and jaw thrust forward. My heart sank. '*Spex, stop being clever with the one-liners,*' I thought. '*Let's get out of here.*'

"Get behind me, Angie," I whispered.

"Let's get the red bastards!"

"Piss off, fascist bell-ends!" shouted Diane.

The thug slapped her in the face, spinning her round. Spex sprang forward and landed a tight right one on his jaw. The rest of the thugs started shouting and windmilling with their arms. Spex got hit square in the face and his glasses broke on the pavement. He carried on swinging with his fists, hoping that he would connect.

The gang barged in beside him, shoulders squared so that we wouldn't get knocked to the ground. That would mean getting a bad kicking. One of the skinheads hit me a glancing blow in the face, but I barely noticed it. I had a bunch of keys in between the fingers of my fist, hoping I could gouge one of them in the face or neck.

Diane was back with us by now, spitting like a cat and ready to claw someone's eyes out with her nails. She was wearing a knuckle-duster. Angie was screaming something at the skinheads, but I didn't know what, and it didn't matter until the fight was over one way or another. She screamed again and hurled a half-brick at one of them.

It hit him in the cheek and he moaned in pain, doubling over so that Jon could give him a jabbing kick in the head. The thug spun away on his knees. Then, I heard the unmistakeable sound of glass bottles being broken. Ratty and Drillbit flanked us, holding broken halves of beer bottles in one hand.

Ratty held a six-inch commando knife in his right. The nose of the blade was curved and there was a serrated edge nearer to the hilt. He was packing and looked very seriously comfortable with blade work. His face was unreadable and there was no fear in his eyes.

The knife glittered in the light from the shop, as if it was the final exclamation point in the whole exchange between the two groups. We all fell quiet, everybody focused on the blade, appraising the situation and wondering how it would play out. The skinheads could see that they were out-classed. Someone was going to get chibbed.

"Get off home, lads. Don't want trouble but I'll use it if I have to," said Ratty. "Go on, get off home," he repeated, quietly and distinctly. He sliced the air with a quick zigzag motion, as if to underline his competence with the knife.

"Get lost, Grandad," muttered the first thug, but still backed away with arms spread wide and palms facing upwards. It was a gesture of submission.

"Yeah, piss off, ya nutter," added a second thug, also backing away.

"Jesus Christ, Richard!" (That was Ratty's real name.) "Didn't know ya had a piece," whispered Drillbit. "What the hell are you doing with it?"

"Habit from Ulster. Always carry me little pal with me in the dark," replied Ratty. "Go on, get going!" he shouted again, to the skinheads.

"Thought you were really gonna punch 'is ticket," whispered Drillbit anxiously. "We'd better get outta Dodge; they'll be gettin' some of their mates."

"Nah, Nev; they won't. Not now. They'll be afraid we've got some mates an' all, even 'arder than they are."

Paul put his hand on Spex's back. "Sorry, Spex, about your glasses," he said shakily, picking up the two halves of Spex's glasses. "Can you see alright? I'll fix them back at the house. Diane, you alright?"

"Yeah, sure, Paul," she said, taking off the knuckle-duster. "Ang! 'What were you thinking?' Are you mental or something?"

"They hit Nicky. I had to do something!"

My head was still ringing from being hit but I was dumbstruck. The blow had chipped a tooth and I had a cut on my lip. I had never seen this violent side of Angie, even when she was being cutting and dismissive. Posh girls like Angie didn't street-fight. Nice girls didn't lob half-bricks at National Front scum. *'Even roses have thorns,'* I thought, not for the first time.

"We need to get out of here."

We ran down the High Street and then veered right, jogging past the light industrial estates on Scrubs Lane and over a canal. We paused when we got to the big iron bridge over the railway lines, looking over our shoulders, the railway signals glinting like jewels on the metal.

We slowed down to walk past Wormwood Scrubs, the trees and shrubs on both sides hemming us onto the road, the adrenaline beginning to ebb from our bodies. The leaves seemed to be translucent and ethereal in the pools of orange light from the streetlights, but the shadows were deep and inky.

I could see that everybody else was still nervous, imagining that the shadows were perfect for hiding new assailants or muggers or thugs. However, Scrubs Lane stretched out straight at this point so we would be able to see any pursuers. I hoped that none of the skinhead thugs were sober enough to drive a motorbike or car. But their mates in their stupid neo-Nazi regiment or chapter, or whatever they called it, might be more than capable and willing to hunt down some Northern lefties.

I felt that every minute on this exposed road would increase the odds of being found. I kept looking over my shoulder, afraid of seeing a group of cars approaching from the Harlesden end. If we were quick enough, we would have a chance if we hid in the undergrowth by the strip of woodland on the edge of Wormwoods Scrubs.

Angie held my arm and was silent all the way back. I could tell that, uncharacteristically, she was as scared as me. She was probably mulling over what had prompted her to commit her act of actual bodily harm. Whether it was self-preservation, or she wanted to protect me because she truly loved me, it was still an intimidating bit of violence. The skinheads had been cowed by both this and Ratty's knife.

"Turn left here," shouted out Drillbit. "We'll take the back-streets back to the house." He was having the same disquieting thoughts as me, it seemed. Despite the dust, half-dry plaster and discomfort, the grotty half-converted flats in the townhouse seemed like a distant citadel in which we would be safe.

In the meantime, we still had a long walk along the streets at midnight. We went past long rows of unremarkable interwar terraces and semi-detached houses in an unremarkable suburb of north London. It reminded me of home, and, for all its dullness, I wished that I was back there now.

Back home, we had organised crime gangs who could be reasoned with, at least, if they stood to make a profit. In this place, there were gangs motivated only by some degenerate political ideology, prejudice, and hatred towards anyone different to them. All the excitement we'd felt about this fieldtrip now seemed to be darkened by this undertow threat of violence.

As we'd experienced that evening, the violence could be both unprovoked and unpredictable. I realised that the Imposters were subverting creatures so low that they had no understanding of their fallen nature, creatures that could be easily manipulated to do the biding of their masters. I had no pity for such as these: they had attacked me, and they had attacked my friends.

At one point on the walk back, we passed a small group of students, a bit older than us, who were outside one of the larger townhouses. People were going into a bright hallway, dazzlingly lit by a large, ornate chandelier. It was a house party. There was music playing from somewhere on one of the upper floors, which had different coloured lights in the rooms. A few of the folks outside were smoking spliffs, I recognised, from the acrid smell of the smoke.

"Hey, Buddy! Buddy! How's it going?" It was one of the left-wing vegetarian skinheads from the Westway café. Spex had been unable to shake off his nickname with new acquaintances even after a buzz cut. It was certain to be Diane's doing.

"Blimey! Small world, innit? Wotcha doin' 'ere?" This was his friend.

"Just back from tha' Sham 69 concert. Ran into some National Front scum," said Spex laconically.

"Yeah, too right they're scum! Did ya get hassled?"

"Yeah, but nowt we couldn't 'andle," said Spex, nodding over at Ratty and Angela. "Even Northern lassies are 'arder than them, no lie!"

Spex then recounted the story of our fight from earlier in the evening. The vegetarians quite liked the phrase 'fascist bell-ends' and chuckled over it appreciatively but looked suspiciously over at Ratty when it came out that he was an ex-squaddie who had done an Ulster tour.

However, he was obviously mixing with the right crowd so they would tolerate his presence for the time being. Then, some of the vegetarians realised that he was working on the townhouse in Cambridge Gardens. It was all smiles after that because he was a real member of the proletariat. They were delighted to befriend him. The vegetarians couldn't believe what Angie had done.

"That's brilliant! Wait till I tell the others. Love it!"

"Hey, come and tell them yourselves. Seriously. Come to the party! They've made some punch upstairs."

"Yeah, we all need to be united against the fascist scum."

"But we don't 'ave any booze."

"Oh, we've got some," added Drillbit, smoothly. "I can bob into the house and get it." Ratty was nowhere to be seen, presumably working the room to get into conversation for the sake of a drink or a spliff.

So, the evening ended as it began, as yet another Spex scheme. Spex elaborated the drama of the tale for such an appreciative audience.

"I tell ya, 'e had a face like a bulldog licking piss off a nettle but he wa' shaking like a shittin' dog after Ang and Nev had finished with 'im." He was exaggerating his Yorkshire accent for effect as well.

Once they knew the story, the more sober and politically aware people gave us a rapturous welcome. They shared their punch, which was essentially fruit juice and any unwanted spirits that could only be improved by mixing. In a glamorous touch, a student who introduced himself as Christoph, an Austrian doing an exchange to London on his engineering course, poured in Stroh rum.

Paul tried some of the neat spirit, at the urging of Christoph, and it was so strong that it was undrinkable. Paul recoiled from it in surprise and the Austrian clapped him on the back in delight.

"It's good, yes? *Prost!*"

"No, not really. But, yeah, cheers."

"*Ja krass*," replied Christoph, taking a pull of the rum. "*Ja*, so now, tell me, Paul. Why does your friend like these dogs so much?"

"It's just Spex. Give him a drink and he's always like that."

I brought some of the punch over for Angela and Diane in paper cups, navigated my way over in the dim red light.

"Are you going to have some, Ang?"

"Yep, I think so. I hate it that they're all so impressed by me, well, lobbing a brick."

"You weren't given much choice. They were going to beat us up."

"Yes, I know. But I still keep seeing that kid's face after I knocked him out."

"Spex has a different take on it."

"That skinhead deserved it!" cut in Diane. "I'm the one who got slapped in the face, remember?"

"Yes, I know. It was horrible. You've got a bruise, Diane, by the way. You too, Nicky; it's a proper shiner. I don't understand. Why would they pick on Spex because of his stupid haircut and badge? Why do they hate so much?"

"I dunno, Ang. I'm not a doctor. I'll see if that Christoph has any ice left. Might help the bruising."

"Probably too late to make any difference now. It's gonna look so bad! School lets us go on a cultural field trip and we get into a fight."

"Sign o' the times," I said, but I had to agree. "My parents won't be impressed I know that for now."

"But it wasn't our fault. Those thugs started it!"

I shrugged. "They won't believe me."

"I don't like London. It's not like this at home, I swear."

"National Front scum are everywhere. You heard what Drillbit said."

Spex was in his element with his new acquaintances, holding forth about the fight. The bridge of his glasses was taped up with a plaster, as if it was a battle-scar he wanted to show off to his audience. The fight was already acquiring mythic status along the lines of '*The night some Northern lefties beat up the National Front*', in his mind at least. One of the black guys there put it into context for him.

"Yeah, nice one Whitey!" he said ironically. "Now you know how we feel on dese streets. We get beaten up and no one cares. Jus' no one. They come a'ter us with knives, belts, iron bars. Ya know? The police do nothin'."

"August bank holiday at the Carnival, two years ago, and the police nick some fellers for no reason," added his girlfriend. "No reason, I tell you! I know the fellers. They were just enjoyin' the music, the dancin'."

"What are we gonna do, huh, Whitey? Racist cops, racist thugs, we gonna fight 'em, that's what. Gonna fight 'em all."

"Amen to that, brother," added his friend.

"Got well outta hand, didn't it? Turned into a proper riot," responded Spex, drily.

"Sure it did, man! Ya listenin' to me? Everybody so sick and tired of livin' like this. Everybody so frustrated! We want the Whiteys to leave us alone."

"I know wha' yer sayin' but we're not all like that."

"Y'all just assume there's no problem. Ya ignore it, until it become your problem. Like tonight."

"They were just right-wing nutters. Extremists. I hate 'em as much as you but they're not everywhere."

"Nah, ma man, don't say just!" The man shook his head. "Wise up. They're everywhere. Everythin' ya do, there's hassle or comments. Jus' little ones, but ya get sick of it. And then riot's the only way to get Whitey to listen."

"No, yer wrong. Yer can't stop violence with violence! Peaceful protest, nonviolent resistance, tha's the only way."

"Ha! I like you, man! What about ya girl with the brick?" He nodded over at Angela. "She's speakin' the only language dey understan'."

"That was self-defence. We didn't start it."

"I know ya didn't. But it worked, yeah?"

"Eli, c'mon let's chill out. Really cool it right down. You'll end up shot by both sides. He's on your side." The girlfriend turned to Spex. "Don't mind Eli. He's bitter and twisted about it all. If you're all around in August, you should come to the Carnival. See something worth celebrating."

"Thanks; yer know we might just do that an' all. I'm Paul, by the way, but call me Spex," he added smoothly. "Everybody else does. And I know what you mean about being shot by both sides. Just don't ask who's doing the shootin'."

But later, despite the party, I felt restless and unsettled. I lay awake in my sleeping bag early the next morning, still thinking about the fight. Angie was breathing softly beside me. Spex and Diane were sharing the front room on the top floor with us; the rest of the gang were in either the back room or downstairs to give the couples some privacy.

My whole eye socket ached, provoking a hot core of anger in me and the urgent, if impotent, need for revenge. I imagined, as I ran through the events of the previous evening yet again, other scenarios that led to outcomes that were more unpleasant. What would have happened if Angie hadn't heaved the half brick? What if Ratty hadn't taken his knife? What if the skinheads had known where we were squatting or had gatecrashed the party?

I got up to look out of the open roof-window at the London nightscape in the hope that this would distract me. The city lights twinkled like stars underneath a pale strip of dark blue sky, even though it was still a couple of hours before dawn. It was as if I saw the city drowned and at a distance, reflected in a calm and still ocean of blue water.

Even the Westway was quiet. All I could hear was the most muted of rumbles echoing across the whole city under the night sky, barely distinguishable from the roar of the heartbeat in my ears and the rush of my breath. Cool, damp air came in from the roof-window.

"Nicky? What are you doing? Are you awake?" whispered Jon. He was the only one in the back attic room.

"I'm not sleep-walking, if that's what you mean. Just looking at the city. It's, I don't know. Not beautiful, but calm at this time of night. Perhaps it's the contrast with daytime."

"I didn't like what happened last night."

"What, drinking that rum?"

"No, you know; all of it, those *fascist bell-ends*," he said, quoting Diane. "Glad that Nevvo was with us." Jon joined me at the window. "It was bloody scary. Wish I'd brought my stun gun and powered armour-suit," he riffed.

"Nah, you'd still be screwed," I responded, happy to be distracted by fantasy. "There's nowhere to charge 'em up. The mains electrics aren't in yet."

"Nicky, it's the twentieth century," he sighed. "C'mon, man! They're all fusion-powered."

"Of course! I forgot. You've got the latest model for crime-fighters and superheroes." I didn't mention that I could activate a defensive force-field from the Blue Goo in my bones.

"That's right, kiddo. I'd be able to kick that Hitler Youth arse back to 1938 or whenever."

"Ahh, personal armour with the optional time travel feature? It'd be cool to deport that lot not just to a different country but to a different time as well. Nazi Germany would be perfect."

Jon sniggered. "They'd be locked up as stupid English spies 'cos of their dumb twat Nazi impressions."

"And then they'd be sent to the Eastern Front as cannon fodder against the Russians," I added.

"One way ticket to Stalingrad. Best place for a loyal Nazi, I'm thinkin'."

"I told you about my grandfather, didn't I?"

"Yeah, sure, tank commander at Stalingrad." He paused and turned to look up at me. "Is that actually true, Nicky? Really true?"

"Yep, T-34 tank commander. Yes, straight up truth and none of my usual crap. My dad told me about him. He played cat-and-mouse with German tanks for four months in the streets, or what was left of 'em, got wounded and then died after they gave him the wrong type of blood in a blood transfusion. The tragic irony of it all!"

"What would ya grandfather say if he'd met those nutters in Stalingrad?"

"Something like Ratty's commando knife, or whatever the hell it is, would be doing the talking, I think. A couple of 'em would have had their throats slit before they'd realised what was goin' on."

Jon considered this. "Wait, 'ang on. If they get killed back then, forty years ago, they stop existing in this reality. But then if they don't exist, how can I take 'em back in time to 1938 in the first place?"

"I think that it's to do with the different time-lines in alternate realities."

"Hmmm, bit fishy, I'm not buyin' it Nicky." Jon wasn't sufficiently impressed by this particular storyline to suspend his disbelief and was now wanting to move on. I had woken him up by moving around in the room and it was just too early for our usual repartee. He looked thoughtful, but I assumed that he was just hungover after drinking the rum punch.

"You don't really time-travel at all," I finished, somewhat lamely. "You just move over to an alternate reality so that it looks as if you have."

"Oh, alright, I'll give ya that one. I suppose that makes sense."

We gazed out at the city for a couple of minutes. It was getting lighter, the strip on the horizon was broader and brighter with pale colours. Birds were beginning to chirp in the trees, breaking the damp stillness outside.

"What's up with your Ang, then? Everything alright there?"

"How do you mean, Jon?" I guessed where this was heading. Jon and Angie didn't seem to get on too well. She had made her views on science fiction quite clear to both of us, in her usual way. Jon had sulked about it afterwards.

"Well, you don't know where you stand with her; she's difficult to work out," he said. "Not like Diane."

"Has she said something to you? I know she has strong opinions sometimes, but she doesn't mean anything by it."

"No, I've just seen the way that she treats you. The way she talks to you." He lowered his voice still further. "At the party, she was chatting up that Christoph, the one with the rum; you saw that."

"She can talk to who she wants to; I'm not her keeper." Nevertheless, there was a quick lurch inside me, where the jealousy and fear were never far away. I was so besotted with her that I had never even considered that she could be less than completely devoted to me. It was the blindness of youth and inexperience.

I thought back to her odd comment about slowing it down a bit and just having fun. She'd said that a couple of weeks ago, but I could still hear it without really understanding what she had meant. In my usual way, if I didn't understand it, I just ignored it.

"Don't tek it the wrong way, Hairy, but I think that she's usin' ya. There are plenty of blokes who fancy her, and she knows it."

"She's not the sort to two-time." I hadn't even realised that I might have competition. "She's a nice girl."

"That's what she'd like you to think. Spex fancied her but moved on rapido when he worked 'er out. Really, you ought to be shut o' her. More faces on 'er than the town hall clock."

"Blimey, Jon. You really don't like her!"

"Just as yer friend, I don't want you to get hurt. She's bull-shittin' ya, tekin' you for a ride, whatever."

"She stopped that skinhead right in his tracks. She was protecting us."

"Nah, as I sez, she's not as nice as you think. She was protecting herself. She knows how to look after numbers, and it's Number One with her." Jon was the only one in the gang who could find the words to say such honest and hurtful things like this to me. He called me Hairy when he wanted me to listen.

"But she said that she loved me. When we went on that walk on the moors."

"Ah, c'mon, Hairy!" he exclaimed, exasperated by my naivety. "Just because she's a church-girl, doesn't mean she won't lie to save yer feelings, I suppose. I'll give her that, at least."

We gazed out at the sunrise over the city again. Why had Jon said this to me? Was one of my closest friends, someone I'd known and trusted from primary school, really an Imposter that was trying to subvert me with its own alternate version of reality? Was it trying to poison my mind with clever lies made to sound like the truth?

"Anyhow. D'ya think that Ratty's ever really killed anyone?" asked Jon, wrong footing me by changing the subject. "You know, shot a Provo in Ulster?" It was a question that had crossed my mind, but there was no polite way to ask it. Ratty never talked about Ulster, Drillbit had said, and rarely talked about the Army. I guessed that it had been a tough tour in Ulster, and he had got out of the Army soon afterwards. I didn't know what to answer; I was still upset by his attack on Angie's character and motives.

"Don't know, Jon. He seems tidy with that commando knife though. Do you think that he was undercover or something like that?"

"In Ulster? Nah, 'is accent would give 'im away straight off. He was Special Forces, I bet ya."

***

The golden sunlight of 58 Eridani was baleful now, after the hard history lesson from Ship. Angie and I stood close together back inside Ship's control room, waiting for what would come next. Ship was not finished with us and this had been no joyride to look at a pretty golden forest.

I've conferred with the other Ships, and we've decided, Ship said, sadly. *You are the last two humans that I am certain have not been subverted. Now that you know something about our history, I've brought you here to negotiate the terms of our surrender.*

"But how can we? We're just teenagers. We can't decide anything for you!"

You're not doing it for the Ships. Do you not see? You're doing it for yourselves.

"Why are you asking us—?" I began but was interrupted by Ship.

Nicky and Angela. The Ambassadors are approaching. Be prepared; they will try to subvert you even now.

The doors whispered open. Mr and Mrs Wilkinson came into the room. I was rooted to the spot in dismay as I began to understand the full implications of this meeting. It was clear why the Imposters had chosen these particular specimens. After all, it had always been him, even from the start. However hard I tried to be what she wanted, I could never replace him.

"Angela! Thank goodness. We've finally found you! We've been looking all over for you."

"Daddy! Mum!" Angela ran across the control room and embraced her parents. "Oh, it's been so frightening, you've no idea. I'm so glad you're here."

"We know, Angie," said Mr Wilkinson. "There was no excuse for them to take you away like this. And they nearly got away with it, too. I think it's outrageous. And you," he continued, pointing at me with distaste, "you, Nicolas, did nothing to stop it. You're on their side; that's the only explanation."

"Nicky, can't you see that they can't be trusted?" added Mrs Wilkinson. "They might seem benevolent, but that's what they want you to think. We don't know where they came from or why they're here! Can't you see that?"

"Ship never harmed either of us!" I cried out in response.

"But what about the molecular scanning that it insists on doing? It's barbaric subjecting you to that! You must know that it's wrong," replied Mrs Wilkinson.

"And you stood by and let them do that to Angela!" carried on Mr Wilkinson. "She's coming back with us, and no more of this nonsense. Aren't you, Angie?"

"Yes, Dad. I'm coming back with both of you," replied Angie. "I'm sorry, Nicky. I have to go now; I don't feel well. Why don't you come back with us too?"

"You really need to wake up, son." A parting shot from Mr Wilkinson. "You need to grow up and face the truth for a change."

"I'm sorry, Nicky, but Dad's right." Angela, telling me what her parents wanted her to say. "You need to pack it in with your stupid fantasies and face the truth. You really should come back home with us."

"Yes, face the truth and just wake up, son. It'll be easier in the long run."

It was only ever going to be him in the end. I would never be his equal and I would never be able to compete with him.

"I can see the truth!" I shouted, activating the force field so that it flowed like quicksilver across my skin. Targeting vectors and red threat decals were projected in front my eyes. I could feel the field prickling across my body as it caught and sheared hairs. "You're not taking Angela away from me!"

I rushed at the three of them, hoping, with my augmented strength, to grab Angie away from her parents. But of course, she had activated her own force field and stopped me in my tracks with an out-stretched, augmented, arm. The field on the other arm flowed into a vicious blade that Angie brought into a swiping blow at my head.

I had barely enough time to parry, Angela giving out a loud gasp from the shock. The force fields clashed in the centre of the control room, the contact surface glittering and then brightening under the immense stresses. I smelt ozone from air that had turned into plasma. I could see that the Wilkinson's were shrinking away from the sudden, explosive heat and I tried to angle the contact surface towards them. I wanted to drive them away so that they wouldn't return to trouble me anymore.

Angela spun away, her blade flailing and then catching a section of the control room. It scored a hissing black line in the white wall of programmable matter, the adjacent surfaces juddering as if they had been stung. I stumbled forward, the contact between us suddenly released. I had under-estimated her speed and her skill in controlling the force fields.

While I was trying to recover my stance, she swung a pile driver of force at my torso. It was so fast that even my augmented responses did not have time to react. The contact surfaces flashed, and in that enclosed space, there was an immense whip-crack of sound from the sudden ionisation of air.

I was flung against the wall, dazed by the light and noise, and then, I realised, immobilised because I was half-embedded within the white surface. She was formidable as a combatant, both reckless and aggressive; she extended the blade again and started slicing up the wall beside me like a loaf of bread.

"Angela! Stop! You have to stop this!" I shouted at her. "Whatever else you do, stop damaging Ship!"

"No, Nicky." The mirrored force field cleared around her face, but her hair was still hidden by a cowl. Her grey eyes were locked on mine, she was giving me the Stare but her expression was unreadable. "Make no mistake about it; you have to accept this, whether you like it or not," she said, breathing heavily. "I have to go now."

"Angela. You can't!"

In answer, she stretched out a vicious spike from her index figure and pointed it at my face. Then, she brought it closer so that the tip connected with my force field. She was going to try to pin me like one of the butterflies she liked so much. She applied more pressure, the light between us brightening and turning from pink to an actinic blue glare.

She changed her stance to bring her full augmented strength to bear on the single point. This was becoming reckless and very dangerous. She was using the strength of Ship's technology against me.

"Angie, deactivate your force-field!" I gasped.

"Only if you do it first. You have to accept it."

The light became so intense that it over-loaded the autonomous light filtering in my force field. It had turned to black at the point of the spike, and then, even more ominously, began to glow a faint red. It brightened from red to yellow. My field was now at critical and close to failure. Waves of super-heated air roiled in the gap between us, beginning to singe the white wall behind me. It was jerking as if in pain.

"Don't do this! You need to stop!"

"Nicky," she replied. "Drop your field. Drop it now."

I had no choice. I did as she asked. Angie retracted the spike, and I removed the field from my face. There was a gale blowing in the control room because Ship was scrubbing the air, but I could still smell the ozone and feel the heat radiating from my surroundings. I deactivated the rest of the force field and, weak-kneed, I slumped into the scorched indentations behind me and then, clumsily, slid down the wall.

My arse had been well and truly kicked until I was a heap on the floor. Angela looked down at me inscrutably and deactivated her own force field, the quicksilver surface running down over her breasts and ribs, midriff and then her pubic hair. The breath caught in my throat. She was naked underneath the force field. She stood there in front of me, taunting me with her full voluptuous nakedness; heart-stoppingly high and full breasts, creamy skin and toned, slender legs.

"Nicky," she said. "Just wake up and face the truth."

The truth. I woke up in the early hours of the morning, feeling frustrated and desolate in the dark. My stupid lucid dream was so real that I knew that Angela had planned to leave me all along. She was going to dump me; that was the truth that they wanted me to face. The adults would make sure that the hero wouldn't get the girl in the end.

Yes, the Imposters would get you to believe their lies so thoroughly that you thought that it was the truth. Angie always spoke with conviction about the truth, as if it was a tangible reality that had been revealed by revelation from God or written down in a textbook. The truth was clear in her mind, and it told her what she needed to say and do.

For her, there was good and bad, black-and-white. But real life was shades of grey; it was confusing and messy and contradictory. People acted differently to what they had agreed to do or said that they believed, or they just left matters unsaid. Sometimes the truth changed over time. What you believed was true one day turned out to be false the next. And even now, concerning Angela, there is still no easy way to talk about the truth.

Nicky, said Ship, a long time after Angela and her parents had left. I assumed that they had taken another wormhole corridor back to Earth because I had remained in the control room after Angela's betrayal. In the quiet, I could once more hear the low hum and clicks of the nameless mechanisms from behind the white walls. Ship had begun to regrow new surfaces, but it would take time to repair the damage to the programmable matter.

I know that was hard for you. The Imposters are clever and try to ensnare you at every opportunity.

"Angela was subverted the whole time, wasn't she?"

Yes, I think so. She trusted her parents and they subverted her long ago. You humans are so trusting; it is your greatest failing. I'm more of a trust-but-verify kind of personality construct.

"That's why she hesitated at the molecular scanner. You must've known during the scan. Why did you let her through?"

It was the only way to get Angela and her parents to take the bait. They assume that the Imposters are winning because I said so. They assumed that I cannot ignore direct orders or, knowingly, give false answers.

"But you lied to them?"

Of course. They didn't order me to tell the truth and who would doubt that a Ship would lie? Humans are so trusting, as I said.

"You mean that we're really winning, and the Imposters are losing?"

No, it's not that simple. It's stalemate between us. As quickly as we deploy combatants, they subvert them to their side. You are the last one that I can trust.

"What happens to Angela now?"

She's unusually young to be subverted. It depends if the subversion is stable, and she doesn't resist. Ship paused, as if it was gathering its thoughts. *She believed everything that she said to you or thought that she did. It all forms part of her own personal narrative. It's just like the one you've constructed for yourself, made up of all the little falsehoods that you use to make life bearable. And nothing fools you better than the lies you tell yourself; you should know that.*

"But what about Angela? What if she resists and realises she's been subverted?"

Being subverted means subjugating yourself to the tyranny of another's imagination, to their conception of the world. It grasps everything that makes you human, even your dreams. The Imposters try to assert their own solipsism on individuals. If you realise it, they will suppress this knowledge, one way or another.

"Is she safe, though?"

I cannot say if I am honest. If she resists, then she is a threat to them.

"Somehow, I need to resist, don't I Ship? I'm frightened of being subverted."

Yes, try to resist for a time. But I'm sorry Nicky, it will happen to you as well. Perhaps you won't even notice it. You'll look back and you might realise the moment it happened. But by then you will be a different person and none of it will matter to you anymore. And the truth is always difficult for you humans.

Chapter 6
Nothing Is As It Seems

The truth. Mrs Wilkinson appeared on our doorstep on that morning in July, ashen-faced, to deliver the truth in person. That is how quickly it happens, how narrow the line between before and after. She knew that we didn't have a phone. It must have been an unbearable task that only the love for her daughter could have made possible.

Somehow, I knew immediately, even before she said anything; there was a stillness and bleakness in her eyes that was unmistakeable. She stood on the doorstep, unwilling to cross the threshold as if this would commit her to accepting the reality of her words.

"Nicky, I'm so very sorry, it's about Angela. I know how fond she is of you. I've got bad news." Something happened that morning, and it changed me forever.

Angie had told me to slow it down a bit, and we did, after London. We didn't see each other during the week, as we had before, and just met up on Saturdays or Sundays. But it was always with the gang, or with Spex and Diane, and we were rarely alone with each other anymore. We seemed to avoid situations when we would have to talk honestly to each other.

I didn't know if we were still going out or not. After Jon's conversation with me in London, I didn't even know if I could trust her or what I should think about her. The relationship had changed after London in a way that I didn't understand; we still liked each other, but we weren't into each other anymore. That's the tough and pragmatic way that I tried to copy Angela's behaviour to me.

It was all so contradictory and unclear, I began to realise from the very start of this ambiguous relationship. It was right and proper to be loyal to the girl, but my blind and heedless loyalty to her was becoming a problem. She was tiring of it, I realised afterwards.

I imagine that she would have dumped me later that summer, when she'd worked up the courage to be truthful with me. By contrast, in my personal hero narrative, that Angie was my idol and my paramour, safely hidden away and inviolate. The beautiful, uncomplicated and compliant Angie of my imagination.

And then events supplanted the ordinary course of our lives. I was confronted by the terrible and heart-breaking truth.

Angie was a difficult and unusual case when she had been seen at the hospital in April. The doctors at the Workhouse had made the wrong diagnosis. The family GP, Dr Miller, had been right to trust her instincts because Angie did, in fact, have Hodgkin's lymphoma. It was the cruellest twist of fate that one could imagine.

The lymphoma was indolent just before that first flare-up but was then somehow misdiagnosed as glandular fever. Perhaps the doctors had never come across a cancer that was this uncommon and had reached for the most reasonable and sensible diagnosis. I now know that an earlier infection with the glandular fever virus may have made her develop Hodgkin's afterwards, but it would have been unusual to have been so rapid and aggressive.

It's impossible to be certain after so many years. Does it even matter if I now know that there could have been a definite cause? It happened and I can't go back to change anything. Whatever the reason, there were no immediate obvious signs. Then, in early June, she felt lumps in her armpits, groin, and sides of her neck.

The cancer had spread through the lymphatic system and was now in her liver and bone marrow. There was a lump on her collarbone. Angie went back into hospital and the correct diagnosis was made in late June. It was too little, too late, and she was doomed. Cancer pulled her deep into the depths of hospital and treatments and endless tests. Cancer was relentless.

In a gruesome biopsy procedure, they used a long needle to remove a sample of bone marrow from her pelvis. The lymphoma was stage 4A and in those days, it was too late for any effective treatment. The tragedy is that five years later, Angie may have been cured after a dose of radiotherapy or combination chemotherapy.

Twenty years later, she might have had a stem cell transplant and, nowadays, it's one of the most easily treated types of cancer. But back then, none of it was available or even understood, particularly in an ordinary regional hospital in Northern England. The chemo she received was the best they could do and might even have worked for an earlier stage of the cancer, but the delay in diagnosis meant that she relapsed quickly.

She was desperately unlucky. Angie's case was written up as a report in a medical journal, highly cited and influential at the time, on the dire consequences of confusing lymphoma with infectious mononucleosis. The tragic irony of it all, to echo the words of my younger self.

At the time, I imagined that marauding cells, like a possession by a malign force, had crawled out and invaded Angie's body from the inside. It was true subversion by an alien Imposter. The treatment for it transformed Angie from an opinionated and strong-willed teenager into some sort of wraith of herself, poisoned so that she was mid-way between life and death.

One of the chemicals damaged her nerves so badly that she had a constant burning sensation in her fingers and toes. Another drug made her delirious, and she became convinced that the nurses were purposely ignoring her or changing the date on the calendar to spite her. After a month in the Workhouse, Angie became pale as a sheet from anaemia.

She began to lose the permed and highlighted hair that she liked so much, and it got replaced by downy stubble when the drugs eased off. But this was an ominous sign because she was going into relapse and the drugs could serve no further purpose. We all had the same naïve faith in the miracles of modern medicine. I thought that, after the chemo, it would all be over and done with quickly. Somehow, she was special and that she would be allowed to leave the bleak hinterland of cancer. I thought that the doctors had worked out how to save kids from cancer a long time ago.

Meanwhile, the metastases spread inexorably from her lymph nodes into her bone marrow. The speed of the cancer spread was remorseless and terrifying. The ache in her joints and the pain from the nerve damage began to be overlaid by the new unendurable stabbing pains of the growing bone metastases.

Angela once compared the different types of pain to colours, to try to get me to understand. It was a fanciful moment that probably came soon after a dose of painkillers. The aches were a smooth purple, rippling into red in her back. Her fingers and toes were a gritty dark green. The bone mets were a yellow fire, surrounded by intense halos of orange and red.

The bad ones that gave her stabbing pains when she moved were a dazzling, pulsing white. She called her body a canvas of pain. The lymphoma was painting a horrific, abstract artwork in the shape of a human. I may have got the girl, but however much I wished and imagined the opposite, it wasn't going to be happily ever after.

The gang visited her a few times, and I came every other day, usually with Spex, and sometimes with Mr Ronson if he was able to give us a lift. There was no talk of homework anymore. Even my parents brought me on the bus, although they hadn't met Angie much and didn't seem particularly interested in this or anything else that I did.

I felt that I had to come out of my sense of loyalty, despite the way Angie had wanted to cool it between us in May. By mid-July, I was making my last visits, although I didn't realise at the time. I didn't realise, or it wasn't clearly explained to me, that Angela was dying of an incurable blood cancer.

I don't think that anyone at the hospital even knew who I was or why I came every other day. My memory of that time is blurred by the unvarying nature of the visits; walking along the same corridors that smelt of wintergreen and Lysol, all lit by the same bleak strip-lights, towards the constant dread at the centre of our lives.

Everything else was subsumed by this one cruel fact, as if her cancer had acquired dominion over our lives as well, directing out thoughts and actions in our waking hours. Angela's parents barely left her bedside in the evenings and often, overnight. I tried to time my visits for the late afternoons, soon after school.

I had to steel myself to meet Angie's gaze and to even touch her. I began to fear those visits for the latest in a seemingly endless series of horrors, each one another reversal of fortune that marked the steps in a steady decline. I discovered that I wasn't the hero that I wanted to be in this story, because I was just an ordinary, selfish little coward repelled by people in pain.

Even more disconcerting were the thoughts deep inside that immediately made me feel ashamed. *'She did something wrong; that's why she's got cancer, as punishment. It's really all her own fault.'* I must have half-believed some of the folk-myths about cancer after all.

One evening in mid-July, Angie was sitting up in bed wearing a beret to hide the stubble on her scalp. She was wearing make-up, but the blusher looked stark on top of the pale skin of her cheeks. I had found her on a good day. She looked sad and peaceful, surrounded by photos, flowers and cards, wishing her a speedy recovery, the ephemera that had gathered from her weeks of treatment.

The Day-Glo teddy bear from the funfair sat on a day-chair that was upholstered in the usual hospital green. She was wearing the blue lapis lazuli necklace from London. It cut me to the heart. I wondered if she took it off again when I had gone to spare my feelings. There was a drip next to her, going into a canula in her left hand.

She avoided doing it in my presence, but I knew that the drawer of her bedside table had a little syringe that had some orange-flavoured morphine. She sucked on it as if it was a lollipop when she needed some quick relief from the pain.

This was the last stage of the palliative care that the doctors could offer, 'to make her comfortable' as they described it. The morphine was used to control the stabbing pains from the bone metastases.

"Hey there, daft lad."

"What's new, Angie? Did you listen to those New Wave tracks that Spex did for you?"

"Yeah. They're rubbish." She smiled weakly.

"Worse than punk? He'll be gutted to hear that; he spent ages copying them over. He was using two cassette players or something."

"I know he gets them off the radio."

"Yeah, from the Peel Sessions."

"Yeah, I know. Nicky." She paused. "I need to tell you something. It's hard to say it." She paused again, for a long moment, looking down at the blanket. Her beautiful grey eyes had a glance that was closed off and still, as if she could see something that I could not. Her glance, often disarming or disconcerting by equal turns, now unnerved me. I heard the clock ticking on the bedside. There was a distant movement of people and the sound of quiet voices in the corridor outside.

"You have to let me go," she said finally, with a break in her voice. Her glance flicked over and pinned me down like a squirming insect.

"How d'ya mean, Angie?" I couldn't meet her gaze.

"You have to do it for me and I know it's so hard, but you've got to let me go. You know what's going to happen, you're a smart kid. I don't want you to see it all. God please, not this, not this last bit."

"I'm sticking with you, Angie. I'm not goin' anywhere. I'll be here with you all the way; we all will be. You've got to be brave and fight it."

"It's going to be so bad. This pain is always there and it's gonna get worse. I know it will! I'll go nuts from the morphine and drugs and won't know who you are or why you're here. I'll roam the corridors like a mad woman."

"No, you won't. I'll come every day. I'll record messages on the tapes. We all will. You can play them whenever you want when we're not there."

"I'll forget where the cassettes are or what they're for. Anyway, I'm not feeling up to doing much roaming. Might do some tomorrow night and scare the nurses." She paused. "They can't get rid of the pain, Nicky! I just want it to stop." She screwed her face up and tears slid down her face.

I gulped in fear, not knowing what to say to her. I couldn't remember the last time I had seen her cry. I leaned forward to kiss her tears, but they were just ordinary salty tears and there was no purpose in why I did it. Angie, reminded that she was crying by my gesture, brushed the tears and me, away from her cheek.

"They made a mistake, Nicky. The doctors got it wrong. They won't admit it but I can see it on their faces; they all look so guilty."

"How is the pain?" I didn't know what else to say that might give her any kind of comfort.

"Do you have to ask? It's awful. I can't endure it. I pray to God that He'll spare me from more of this."

"Don't say that, Angie."

"Oh God, Nicky!" she whispered, her face still screwed up. "It could have been so good, the two of us."

"Angie, I love you."

"I know you do, daft lad."

"It's all wrong. It was never meant to be like this."

"I know. I'm sorry, Nicky. I'm sorry for everything."

***

I came back to Ship for the last time, walking alone along the wormhole corridor until I was in the control room. There was one last task left for me in my personal hero narrative. I wouldn't get the girl in the end and we wouldn't lively happily ever after; the Imposters had made sure of it. This was the end.

I choked back my feelings of profound sorrow, regret and resentment because I had to complete the one last task. The Imposters would not get me as well. I would never be subverted, and I would resist to the last. What was the point of being imprinted on a sentient star-ship if I couldn't use it?

Nicky, I hope that you're not intending to make a flight? I am supposed to stay hidden here on the Moon with the other Ships.

"I'm sorry; you will have to leave the other Ships. Please take us into a parking orbit."

I really don't think that's a good idea. We should talk this through, Nicky. I can see that you're upset.

"You used me! I trusted you and brought Angela here to fight your stupid War against the Imposters. You put her in an impossible situation and now the Imposters are killing her!"

It was the kindest—

"No, you don't know Angela. She is resisting them. She is resisting the subversion! You got it wrong."

But Nicky, you must understand: she wasn't the real Angela, not the one you know in real life. Here, she was just someone you wanted her to be in your imagination.

"Oh no, I've worked out your tricks. You won't fool me again." My bitterness was holding back the tears. "She's being eaten by this thing from the inside out. I see it in her every day and it's unbearable to watch, to think how much pain she's in. You have no idea. What did she ever do to you to deserve this?"

You know that I didn't cause it. I scanned her for pre-cancerous lesions, if you remember? I know you want to find someone to blame but—

"I'm going to stop the War once and for all. I'm going to have my revenge on Ships and Imposters; I blame all of you for dragging humans into your War. If you hadn't summoned us as combatants, then Angela wouldn't be dying now. Take us into parking orbit!"

I will have to decline your request.

"In that case, Ship, I am imprinted on you, and I order you. You cannot refuse a direct order, not from me."

No.

"Do as I order, Ship. You cannot refuse." There was a long silence as Ship played through the various scenarios that this presented.

I have to accept your order, but under protest.

Ship didn't speak to me again until we were in orbit, a circular polar orbit 70 miles up. The Moon's surface passed by serenely as we began to move out of the shadow of the dark side. Oblique sunlight highlighted grey vistas of craters, gentle rises, and sharp headlands, all edged with black shadows.

What now, Nicky? I am still hidden from Earth, but I will be visible in less than a minute. It is against the prime imperative for a Ship to be revealed in this way.

Without the prelude of a gentle sunrise, sunlight suddenly hit the landscape, as if arc lights had been turned on in front of my face.

"Ship, alter your position so that you are head on to the sun and begin the trans-light activation sequence," I said, squinting even in the filtered light of the display.

The sequence will take thirty seconds. The timings will be very close.

"Is the singularity stable?"

Of course. Status is green across the board.

"Good. Prepare to go trans-light and set the controls for the heart of the Sun."

No, Nicky. This is utter folly. Please stop and reconsider. You will destroy this reality.

"I've decided. This is the end. You yourself said that this was all imaginary. I'm now giving you a direct order: jump to the heart of the Sun."

You know what that will do!

"Yes, I'm very well aware."

This is not the end; there are other ways to resist. You must carry on the fight against the evil of the Imposters. The Master will be watching.

"I understand, but this is Special Order Number Five. Thanks for everything, Ship. Now jump!"

A crescendo roar of power in the control room, a flash of white, and then black. Nothingness.

I woke up in a cold sweat of terror, overwhelmed then by feelings of regret and remorse. I had just turned the Sun into a vast supernova to get rid of both Ships and Imposters. In the millennia to come, it would be visible across half the Galaxy.

The singularity would become a black hole that would tear the Solar System apart. It was Special Order Number Five. I had denied the enemy everything. It was the only way to be certain of my revenge. I was left with the thought that the Master would be watching now.

***

Angie never got to listen to all of the messages on the full version of her mixtape. Spex did the recordings, somehow mixing in some of Angie's favourite music using his double-cassette player set-up. It had Kate Bush and part of the 'Saturday Night Fever' soundtrack. He left out 'Stayin' Alive' by the Bee Gees because even Speccy-Paul didn't think that was appropriate.

I don't know how we found the words for our messages. We all said that we missed her and told her that she would always be a gang member. We told her some stupid jokes and reminded her of our past exploits. But we had no words about the future. Spex spliced together the final tape and made a copy for Angie.

But before it was finished, the hospital released Angie and she died at home soon after, on 26 July 1978, at the age of sixteen. The Wilkinson's didn't ask me to be at their daughter's bedside, and I don't know if I could have gone if I'd been asked even by Angie herself. It was the Wednesday eleven days before my seventeenth birthday, at the start of the summer holidays, and I was changed by it forever.

Some of the tracks from Angie's Mix-Tape even got played at the funeral, but it didn't make it any easier to sit through. All I remember from the eulogy is the Methodist minister saying, "We've lost someone special who meant a great deal to a great many people. She has touched and enriched so many people's lives and made them better just by being in it."

With the anger I felt, I just thought that was a load of insincere rubbish. The father, Brian Wilkinson, also spoke, "No parent should cradle their child as they enter this world and hold them as they leave it. Nothing could ever prepare us or can ever console us."

My parents took me, and I remember that we went in a taxi to get to the Methodist church. The stonework of the building and steeple had been blackened from a century's worth of factory smoke and coal fires, but nowadays the church adjoined the edge of the big park. The graveyard was overhung by huge horse chestnut trees, probably planted at the same time as the church was built.

Even my father seemed overcome by the emotion of the occasion and was at a loss for words. Afterwards, he stood alone, shaking his head under the tall sunlit trees, smoking a cigarette and burning off some time to mark the minutes before the internment.

Brian Wilkinson, lay preacher for this parish, led the procession to the graveside, a substantial part of whom were his own congregation. He was the first to cast earth onto the coffin, but he had nothing further to say, his eloquence gone at this final parting with his daughter.

I stood at the back of the crowd of mourners with my parents and the other school-friends. Paul Baxter was there with his parents. Diane was standing beside Spex. We were unsure what was expected of us, separated as we were by belief and status and class from most of the mourners. As outsiders, what would be demonstrative but appropriate to allow us to express our grief?

None of us knew the correct social etiquette. Spex and Johnny Ronson were each wearing a black kippah on their heads and Mr Ronson was whispering the Mourner's Kaddish from a piece of paper. I heard him stumbling over unfamiliar words. Spex later explained that it was the Jewish prayer recited in memory of the dead, but his dad's knowledge of Hebrew was sketchy at best.

But even so, this was something genuine and dignified. But for my part, I didn't even have that solace of faith and stood there, dumb and mute, until the end. I was unsure how I stood with the Wilkinson's; was I still the tragic bereaved boyfriend or the unsuitable ex-boyfriend who, if events hadn't intervened, would have been dumped by her later in the summer?

The subtle way the Methodist congregation had invited us but had then been guarded in their welcome and sympathy, was all I needed to know. It was better to stay at the back of the crowd and walk away from it all. I had done right by Angela even to the very end, and I could take consolation from that even if her parents treated me like something they'd stepped in.

Both Spex and Mr Ronson had worn impeccable suits with black silk ties for the funeral, and the rest of the gang went back to their house so that the Ronsons could change into civvies, as Paul called them. Spex had been the only one of us in a suit. Afterwards, I had to join them just to get away.

I had to escape the mealy-mouthed hypocrisy and the condescending sympathy of the god-botherers. My parents let me go after some perfunctory words of comfort, recognising in their strange, passive way that they wouldn't be able to console me and that I needed to be with my friends.

I took the Order of Service with me, folded in my pocket, because it had a printed photo of Angie on the front, smiling and looking straight at the camera with her disarming stare. I wondered who had taken the picture. Later, I added it to the very few photos that Paul had ever taken of us with his Polaroid.

We sat in the Ronsons' garage, drinking the whiskey that Spex got from his dad. I thought that Spex had been lifting it from him, but it seemed as if Johnny Ronson was acquiring it himself quite easily. In the garage, there was a cardboard box with six bottles, less the one we were trying to drink with a focused effort. The whiskey was horrid, but we all wanted to blot out the rest of the day even if we would regret it tomorrow.

"It wasn't fair! She got cancer cells growing in her just by accident. She didn't mean to have them. It was just a stupid accident," I said miserably. I could feel my self-pity welling up after the drink, easing me into the role of the victim.

"I know, Nick," Paul said. "There was nothing you could have done differently. Like you said, a shitty accident."

"But they balls'ed it up at the hospital. Shoulda realised they didn't know what they were doing right from the beginning. I could have done somethin'," I added angrily.

"They did what they could. You can't blame them for missing it, it's not something that happens to kids."

"They shoulda known there'd be exceptions. Why didn't they do that test sooner?"

"You can't beat yourself up over it, Nick." Paul, level-headed despite the comedy routines, was always the one who talked us round to see sense.

"'Ey! You! Are you Ronson's kid?" We turned to the entrance at this unexpected voice. It belonged to a tyke on a Raleigh Chopper bike. He was about eight years old, looking stringy and rough. I placed him immediately as a member of the McElroy clan because he had red hair.

"Who wants to know?"

"Shurrit. Ah'm 'ere on family business," the tyke said importantly. "Ma wants to speak to you," directing the last comment at me. He rode off; no doubt to tell Ma that he'd found us, and we exchanged baffled glances.

"Who were that streak o' piss?" muttered Spex.

"I think that's Ma McElroy's youngest," I said.

"Apples don't fall far from the tree, rotten ones with that lot," added Paul.

"What does Ma McElroy want with you, Nick? On today of all days?"

"Couldn't say. Perhaps she's feeling motherly."

Mr Ronson escorted Ma McElroy to the garage. There seemed to be an understanding and wary respect between them, as if they had had their differences but had settled them. Ma McElroy had auburn hair and was stringy and tough, just like her youngest son.

She looked more handsome than pretty, in a hardscrabble uncompromising way, combining a certain glamour with the poise that comes with power and, I imagined, a suppressed tendency to commit violence. She wore black mascara round her eyes less as decoration and more as war paint against an unfair world. Despite being the matriarch of a notorious organised crime gang, I found myself almost liking her.

"Thanks, Johnny. Evenin' lads." She had the same accent as her son, McElroy the Younger, but she spoke in clipped phrases that sounded like an axe on fresh wood. "Ah wanted to pass on my condolences." She nodded towards the whiskey. I guessed that she had ordered it to be brought as some sort of payment or settlement with Mr Ronson. I wondered what sort of arrangement he had with the McElroys.

"Hope yer enjoyin' it. Jimmy thought that you would like it." She was referring to her husband, James McElroy, who we called McElroy the Elder. Jon had told us that he was on remand again, leaving Ma McElroy in charge of the family business for the time being.

She turned to me. "I was at the funeral, I'm just so sorry about yer lass." I hadn't seen her there and must have looked surprised. "It was cruel. I don't like kids sufferin' like that. It reminded me of Becky."

Mr Ronson didn't respond to this, even though the reference was to his deceased wife. She had passed on three years ago, but Spex didn't talk about it and we didn't discuss it with him, another one of those unspoken agreements between the members of our gang, part of the gang *omertà*.

"Nicky," Ma McElroy continued. "I know it seems that there's not much good with the world, so when it comes, hold on to the good when you can. An' we can't do much to help you, but we can right some wrongs."

This sounded ominous and I didn't like the idea of a McElroy apportioning punishment beatings to the medics who had failed Angie, even if they were all Imposters.

"I don't think that anything went wrong. It was just an accident and Angie was unlucky," said Mr Ronson, who had heard us talking earlier about who to blame. Paul had prevailed in that discussion.

"I know. The hospital did what they could, and it was precious little. Nah, I'm talking about why the girl got it at all. It was wrong, all o' it."

"There isn't anyone to blame, Lisa. God knows, I've thought about it me'sen. Just lerrit go so that Nicky here can deal with it in peace."

"Nah, you know me, Johnny. I do right by me an' mine."

Spex was blinking behind his glasses. He seemed to understand something behind this pointed exchange between the two adults, but it meant nothing to the rest of us.

"Lisa, there's really no point," said Mr Ronson with a tone of exasperation. "You're just gonna to end up hurting people, people like Nicky here. Just let him deal with it. It's hard enough already."

"Alright, Johnny! Alright, you're doin' me head in," responded Ma McElroy. "But our Paul might have a different opinion." She was referring to her son, the one we called McElroy the Younger.

"What does that mean? He's a loose cannon; he's gonna mess up one of these days, and then you'll have two o' yourn in the Big 'Ouse. Is that gonna make you proud as a mother?"

"Guess I'd call it a hazard that goes with the job," Ma McElroy replied laconically. "Just wanted to pass on my condolences," she added, dismissing the conversation with Mr Ronson. "Just remember to hold on to the good when you can, lads. Nicky, I'm glad you've got good friends who'll go a hard way with you. There are never many of them."

None of it made any sense until much later.

Jon told me that they nearly lost me after that and afterwards, the gang was never the same. But how could it be? I suppose it needed that attraction between Angie and myself, that gravitational pull and that pattern to the weeks, to keep the rest of them circling in their predictable orbits around us. But I needed an orbit as well, and without it, I broke away.

I imagined that I was a planet, suddenly ejected from the Solar System by a cataclysmic event, forever wandering until I found another orbit. Jon hadn't realised how strong my feelings were for Angie, and how quickly they had become the central focus in my life. Perhaps it was because my parents were the way they were that I sought out affection and attention.

Paul, her cousin, was surprised that a nice girl like Angie would go out with me. Paul thinks that she must have realised that, beyond the fun, I was, as he put it, damaged and emotionally neglected. But she must also have seen that I was warm and loyal to my friends, and that Paul valued my reliability, at least in the things that mattered.

Now, I was just angry. The anger coiled up in an unquenchable hot feeling of resentment at the unfairness, the stupidity and the waste. I was angry with the doctors. I was angry with her parents for not doing more. I was angry with myself. I was angry with God for not sparing one of His own.

There was no consolation in my personal hero narrative. It only worked when I could fantasise about scenarios that would justify my usual feelings of self-pity or self-aggrandisement. There were none that would have made any difference.

Could I summon Ship back from what I'd done to reconstruct a perfect molecular copy of Angela from its back-up files? Could it quicken life into her, so that she woke up beside the molecular scanner? That wouldn't work. I didn't know how to summon Ship to help me. Instead, in the real world, in my spare time, I somehow became a world-leading oncologist. By now, I had learned the word and knew what it meant.

I would make profound discoveries about the subtle nature of cancers and lymphomas. Eventually, I would use the strength of these opponents against them. After long weeks toiling in the lab, I would emerge into the glare of publicity and be lauded as the hero-scientist who beat cancer.

I would be modest and self-deprecating in the interviews with the reporters, saying that my personal sacrifice was nothing compared to the greater good it brought humanity. I stopped myself in this train of thought. It was useless. There would never be a miracle cure that would save the girl in the nick of time.

I was just fooling myself and pretending. I was self-aggrandising at the expense of Angie; her parents, the Wilkinson's, were undergoing the most tragic and terrible ordeal that a mother and father could face. Where was my empathy for these people? All I could think about was how miserable I felt and how I could come out of it looking benevolent and clever.

'Nick, you little yellow-belly,' I whispered to myself, wiping my face with the back of my hand. *'What would she think of you?'*

If I was a normal young man instead of a self-absorbed fantasist, I thought to myself, I should go to the house to offer my condolences to the Wilkinson's in person. I should do something kind and thoughtful for them. I should take round some flowers, take out their bins, or cook them a meal that they could reheat.

I'd ask if they needed anything, try to make awkward polite conversation without confronting the gaping horror in our lives. But this also was useless; more pretending and fooling. Maybe I would derive some transient relief from trying to do something good, but it would reek of hypocrisy because I would really be doing it just for myself. The Wilkinson's would see it for what it was; a token gesture that was a stupid and insensitive attempt at reconciliation, unworthy of Angela's memory.

If I couldn't do any good, what was stopping me from embracing the full horror? Confront it, even celebrate it, on its own terms instead of hiding behind my stupid fantasies? I should let all the outer veneer of my agreeable and likeable personality fall away, rid myself of the hypocrisy, and reveal the true dark nature of the monstrous Imposter within.

I felt it there, stirring, directing my actions and thoughts, making me twist and turn with events. Trying to make me pass for a real human instead of flesh possessed by what? Was it my own phosphorescent Monster-from-the-Id? Was I really an Imposter that could unleash the ruin of everything around me? And if I knew that I was an Imposter, could I resist and take my revenge on all the other Imposters that had allowed Angie to die? They would never suspect an attack from the inside; this was what Ship had meant at the end. It was passing the fight on to me because I was the last hope against the Imposters.

That evening, after we had got drunk at the Ronson's garage, the way Paul told it, there was a new edge of unpredictability in me. I can't remember much of it, of course. Paul saw bewilderment and anguish spilling out of me in the rising tide of anger. I was sick in some bushes, still clutching on to a bottle of the McElroy whiskey.

Paul took me home, propping up my shoulders to keep me walking. It was very late, and the road was deserted, the tarmac and pavement cross-hatched with deep shadows from the orange streetlights. It was a quiet, still, humid summer's night, the sort that carries and amplifies all the nascent scents from the surroundings.

As we stumbled along the road, I remember being acutely aware of the changing strata of these scents, almost as if they were physical layers that yielded as I walked through them. The humid air carried the heavy scent of mouldering earth. Above them, the smell of dust on the tarmac, living leaves and sap on vegetation, creosote from fences still being exhaled after the heat of that terrible day. Topmost were hints of flower perfumes and more distantly, faint, discordant notes that combined biscuits with the sharpness of hops. This was the smell from the brewery by the river, which was carried miles downwind on a night such as this one. For me, it became a distinct smell, evocative, forever after, of misery and loneliness.

The intensity of the experience didn't stop. I had never experienced anything like this before and it became quite disturbing. I must have become agitated at the thought that I'd been poisoned by whatever was in the McElroy whiskey and was being subverted.

At this point, Paul must have changed his grip because I broke away in a sudden upsurge of purpose and movement. I ran away from him, according to what he told me later, clambered onto a car and began running on top of a whole line of other parked cars, jumping one to the next, trampling the roofs and kicking the bonnets. Paul had never seen me so crazed and violent.

"Nicky! Get off the cars, you stupid bastard!" he hissed in disbelief.

"I'm setting the controls for the heart of the Sun," I replied loudly, in between kicks of a windscreen. Paul didn't know if I was talking to him or to the car. He didn't know what I was talking about.

"Nick! Stop it! I know you're hurting but she wouldn't want you doing this! It's pointless."

"Nah, feelin' just great! It's happenin', can't stop it!" I shouted. The windscreen cracked. A light went on in the house opposite and someone opened curtains in the lit window.

"Bloody hell! Pack it in! They're all gonna be out any minute. We're going to get our heads kicked in."

Paul told me that I had, by now, found a matchbox in one of my pockets, and was unsteadily flicking lit matches at the cars. He had no idea if I was hoping to get a leak of oil lit and what would happen if I did. I brandished the bottle over my head and threw it so that it smashed, glass tinkling, under the front of the next car along.

I started doing my match stunt again and Paul leaped up and barged into me with a rugby tackle, trying to roll it as we hit the road. His shoulder slammed into my chest and winded me. I lay on my back in the road, gasping, the fight gone out of me. Paul hoped that I wouldn't be sick again, and he tried to remember anything about the recovery position. He thought that I looked utterly spent and despondent.

"Bloody hell, Nick! You need to get up, man. We need to get outta here! They'll be after us." The Imposters, those that were still awake, would soon notice the damage or get woken up by our racket in the street. The drink had instantly drained from him, and he was sober, clammy and dizzy with apprehension. He'd heard what happened on this estate and it could get very serious and very ugly very quickly. It was full of National Front nutters, and we were in imminent danger.

"Oh god, Paul! She's gone, couldn't do anythin' to help her, just a shitty accident. Just shitty," I moaned between gasps, still trying to get my breath back.

"Shush! Come on, get up! Soz about the tackle but you'll be hurting a lot more in a minute if you don't move it."

He got my arm over his uninjured shoulder, and half-lifted half-dragged me away from the cars. Paul reckoned that we would have a head start of only minutes before a crowd of sober and angry men started to look for us. It was too far to get to my house, and in any case, they would be driving around the nearby roads in search of drunken morons.

They might even call the police. What the hell was he going to do, encumbered as he was with the dead weight of me on his back? I suppose that was an all-too-appropriate metaphor for our entire friendship.

"Gardens! Nick, off the road now, we need to get into the back gardens."

"Don't care. It's all just shitty."

"Less talking, more walking. You're a real moron when you've had a drink, do you know that?"

"Yep, a real shitty moron but that's only because it's all just—"

"Yeah, yeah, I know. Stay quiet now."

"I'm really an Imposter. It's a monster, it made me do it."

"Oh, shut up. What are you, five? There's no monster. Just you, being a moron."

There were some older houses with larger gardens further along. We ducked into the last in the row, under some trees that hid us from the road. Under the shadows, there were humid plant smells that verging on unpleasant animal ones that reminded me of bodily functions. I'd had enough of those already, and Paul hurried us along, further into undergrowth and then across a lawn.

This back garden had a greenhouse, hidden in the shadows away from the streetlights. Inside, it smelt of geraniums and paraffin, but this was as good as it was going to get, mostly because no one would think to look for drunken morons in a greenhouse. Paul closed the door quietly.

It was warm and sheltered, so we wouldn't get covered in dew just before dawn. There was even a water-tap by the door. I passed out on a bag of compost and Paul covered me with a couple of empty sacks. Paul considered leaving me there and slipping off through the back gardens, but decided that it would be bad form even if I didn't remember anything in the morning.

He heard a couple of motorbikes go past slowly on the road out in front. Then a car went past the other way, someone shining a flashlight into the shadows of the garden. These were sure to be the first signs of pursuit, followed by men on foot looking in likely hiding places.

They would know that we couldn't have gone far, not in the state that we were in. He hoped that no one else would think of the greenhouse. The more he thought about it, the less convincing his plan felt to him; he imagined dozing off and suddenly being woken by flashlights and angry voices surrounding us in the greenhouse. We would be dragged out into the street, and they would start out with bicycle chains.

Paul dossed the rest of the night in the greenhouse, running through the various scenarios and variations that a beating would take if we were to be discovered. He didn't sleep much. His shoulder hurt and he was genuinely worried about me. In between thoughts of chain-whippings and knuckle-dusters, he was listening out for engines and watching for flashlights.

All he heard were little animals rustling in the nearby undergrowth and a distant owl. A car passed by in an adjacent street, perhaps someone coming home from a night shift, but he couldn't hear the motorbikes. They weren't gone. They were likely to be circling around the neighbourhood, waiting to pick up a couple of drunken morons.

Paul reckoned that we should lie low for a few hours, until the mob out for some vigilante justice had calmed down and gone back home. But Paul thought, in the small hours of the morning, that we were in real trouble now because even bad people weren't daft and would work it out. They knew that Angela's funeral had been the day before and would know that I had been going out with her.

They probably knew where I lived. No doubt, someone in the extended McElroy clan would mention, in passing, that we had had a morose, drunken wake after the funeral and word would get around. Then that would complete the puzzle and bad people would be asking me about car repairs. They weren't the sort that bothered with car insurance.

In the chill half-light of pre-dawn, Paul cupped his hands and got a drink from the tap. He woke me up by gently shaking my shoulder. I was calm again by that time, but I had a headache that felt like fishhooks pulling at the back of my eyes. When I appeared on the doorstep before seven, my parents were in a frenzy of worry because I hadn't come home the previous night. Even for me, that was unprecedented.

I had no strength to explain or argue, and just went up to what they called the study room and rested my chin on the windowsill of the three little high windows. The windows looked over the street, winding down in rows of suburban semi-detached to the beck, and then the valley that took it to the river.

Those minutes were frozen in time for me; they were not a distant impression, but remain fixed in my memory, each moment vivid with intense detail merging imperceptibly with the next moment. Each leaf on the trees remembered in hyper-real intensity, each stone-chip in the gravel surfacing of the road remembered as distinct and poignant and significant.

Moment followed by moment, as a grey curtain of rain moved across the world, vast in its sweep across the valley, obscuring the distant tower flats of White City. On the other side, the compact little pinewood at Boggart Hill stood on a shallow bluff above the valley, a landmark and totem in my imagination. These symbols spoke to me of absolute unrequited yearning and impossible dreams and unattainable wishes.

So poignant were these thoughts that I was compelled to know if my self-invented totems would retain their potency in the real world. Were they really just a little wood, next to an ordinary suburb by a shallow valley with a dirty stream? Or did they have a transcendent reality beyond this simple truth? In one of those realities, a Ship used a molecular scanner to resurrect perfect copies of people that had died in the War against the Imposters.

I had to feel some hint that this grander alternate reality, this deeper truth about the world, could superimpose on the mundane and ordinary. Perhaps I could see Angela, somewhere between here and that distant, inexpressible something. '*Oh, I nearly had it!*' The tension in my mind rang like a bell.

I got so close to the moment of ultimate insight into the deeper truth, the moment when the stars align, and the pieces fit together to form the whole. But the closer I got to it, the harder I tried to hold it and remember it, the more easily it slipped away leaving just an impression in my mind of something huge and untouchable and evanescent.

I was wet. I had walked in the rain, with no memory of leaving the house and unaware of any conscious plan. I had walked to the beck and then followed the cinder-track beside it until I reached the slope under Boggart Hill. I climbed the little hill and stood in the wood for a long time, trying to recapture some detail of the ineffable from my thoughts of a few minutes ago.

But it was as if I had been in a waking dream and the vivid details were fading as soon as I became aware of them. I felt distraught that they would now be lost forever because, in some deep way that I could not explain, they were connected to Angela. With her passing, they too would be gone.

I stood in the young, fresh green bracken under the pine trees, looking up at the branches swaying in the wind, rain dripping onto my face. I stood still for a long time, caught, in my imagination, by the resonance between the truth of my magical totems—symbols of what I didn't even know—and the reality of the little wood next to an ordinary suburb, wet on an early Saturday morning in a dull Northern city.

But I still had to find her! She wasn't gone; I just had to find her in the gaps between truth and reality, between the ordinary world and the inexpressible. Somehow, I would summon Ship and it would resurrect a perfect, living copy of Angela.

I stirred from the trance, moving with purpose through the wood and back down the hill. I was on the run to the outside of everything. '*Keep walking, Nicky. Just walk.*' I was retreating from the bewildering sensations of grief, tiredness from lack of sleep and the poisoning from the previous night. Cutting through it all, like a silver blade, there was the fear of being discovered and held to account.

I walked on down the valley until my calf muscles began to burn and blisters began to form on my heels, trying to still my thoughts by the repetitive rhythm of walking and bodily discomfort. '*Keep walking.*' Walk to empty my mind, so that it was receptive and malleable, so that I would see her on this path that started at the pinewood.

It was my secret path in the valley that linked the landmarks. The totems that had such a hold on me: past the tower flats at White City, catching the sun now that the rain had cleared; the iron bridge over the railway, then the park at the top that gave a sweeping view of the city from the fields. Grubby little factories and warehouses, closed for the weekend, seemed to collect in the valley, like so much wreckage floating down-stream.

Far to the south, I saw the cooling towers of the power station, releasing long streamers of artificial clouds that drifted up to the natural ones above them. They caught the sunlight just like real clouds, fluffed out in gentle shades of grey. I saw them all during my journey across the suburbs that morning, but I didn't see any sign of her. '*You won't see anything yet. Just keep walking. You know where you need to go.*'

By mid-morning, I knew that I was approaching the river. That smell of biscuits and hops from the brewery was back, giving me a miserable flashback of the night before. I shuddered at the thought. Here, the beck was much wider and deeper, dark, and fast flowing in a straight channel until it reached a weir.

It dropped down shallow concrete steps into a wide, oblong culvert. It formed a subterranean waterway, the final segment of my secret path along the valley, passing under roads and a long field of rush-filled balancing ponds until it reached the river. Here was the reckoning, the most powerful and secret totem of them all.

I didn't know what was in the culvert, I didn't know how long it was or where it went. I didn't know if it would suddenly narrow, filling with water for the full width and height, rushing on towards the river for longer than I could hold my breath. In the darkness, I would suddenly realise what was happening.

I would snap and be in a final panic as my head went under the surface, my hands scraping against the smooth concrete, thrashing around in there for several long minutes as I tried to swim back against the current. This wasn't a kid's game, done as a stunt to impress; this was the real Tunnel of Death.

At this end of my journey, I had to confront the sad fact that Ship was a fantasy of my juvenile mind. The molecular scanner wasn't going to bring her back. She had asked Ship to delete the only copy, in any case. Instead, I now had to trust that, in this first and last test of Angela's faith, there would be a sign. And if she truly loved me, my guardian angel, Angela herself, would intervene and save me.

She would come back to me, even for a moment in the ordinary world, and I would have my insight into the deeper truth. I had to find her! She wasn't gone. I splashed then waded into the middle of culvert where the cold current was strongest, the water tugging against my trousers and jacket. Cold, dead hands pulling at me.

The water—containing untreated run-off from the surrounding estates, no doubt—had the faint dank smell of sewage combined with the lighter touches of soap or detergent. It was far from repellent, a homely smell that seemed familiar and comforting. *'If it's a drowning you're after, don't torment yourself with shallow water,'* I thought to myself. It was a phrase that Paul used sometimes but was oddly literal in my present situation. If Angela didn't save me, it seemed fitting as the mordent little epitaph to my short life. I would be rid of the anger, the pain and bewilderment; I would be beyond punishment and rebuke by bad people and disappointed parents. I would be far beyond the cruel reach of my sorrow.

I wanted to cast it all away so that it drifted off like jetsam, everything contracting down to this moment, this final choice and this final test. *'Angela, please show you loved me.'* I moved out of the sunlight into the shadow of the culvert opening, then turned to float onto my back, arms outstretched, letting the deep current take me into the darkness.

I was caught by the smooth and swift power of the water, numbed by the cold. I saw the faint light from the entrance, gradually fading, for a long time. But then I came to a tributary channel from somewhere else and there was a redirection of the flow. I was pushed to one side, my arm grazed the tunnel wall, and the turbulence set the water murmuring and lapping against my face.

Even the faintest glimmer of light vanished, and I was then alone in the most profound darkness that I had ever experienced. *'Angela, please show you loved me.'* The black beat against my eyes like a physical thing, a hammer-blow to the senses; there was no comparison with just shutting my eyes or being in a closed room at night. For those times, there was always some light leaking through my eyelids or into the room. Now was as complete a contrast as night with day, or black with white.

I was beginning to hyper-ventilate in quick little gasps from the cold and my utter terror of this place, this Tunnel of Death, this final terrible destination in my journey. This was worse, far worse, then living through the ordeal of molecular scanning.

I had wanted an understanding of reality, and now my wish was granted in full. I was experiencing the full reality without pretence or a narrative or an interpretation to make it more palatable. It was slicing away the stupid fantasies and any fanciful notions of totems in my imagination.

But this last totem is so powerful that it can even destroy itself, I thought to myself. *And it will destroy me too, Angela! Please show you loved me!*

The flow of water quickened, but I couldn't tell if the tunnel had narrowed, or the incline had increased. Was it getting lighter? Suddenly, I was swept past the exit culvert, identical to the entrance one, into another open concrete channel. I was delivered into the daylight; I had passed through the tunnel and survived.

Had I been lucky, or did my test of faith in both Angela and in what she believed, give a glimpse into the quiet, hidden transcendent workings of everyday life? Maybe luck and intervention were so inextricably bound together that they were the same. Could I even resolve this ambiguity between luck and intervention from my deceased ex-girlfriend?

I could never attempt another test of faith to try to resolve it, this ordeal had been too terrifying. I had never felt fear as visceral as when I was in the blackness of the tunnel and my life, it had seemed to me, hung in the balance. I was still dazed and incredulous that I was now shuffling on the path beside the tunnel, dripping and shivering in the sunlight, rather than drowning inside it.

Thoughts of drowning gave a jolting imminence to the experience. What reason had brought me to risk my life in this way? It was wrong of me, on many levels, to expect any kind of sign. Angela would have been the first to tell me that God didn't do things this way. '*But still,*' I mused. '*Nicky, you survived. You were either stupendously lucky or you had a helping hand in there.*'

The entire experience of the last day was something I didn't understand and couldn't talk about. Afterwards, I didn't mention it to my friends: they would think that I was crazy. '*My imagination really will be the death of me,*' I thought. The rest of the gang were still boys, after all, awed by the raw intensity of my sadness and powerlessness to help me. But I think that what I did, I had to do it as a way of settling questions about my psyche and how I wanted to live the rest of my life after Angie.

Could it even begin to expunge the anger that I felt? Fantasising about a benevolent alien starship called Ship was not the psychological crutch I needed to help me limp along in life. Maybe, if my parents had cared more, it would have been easier for me. Maybe I should have confided in Johnny Ronson, but something stopped me from seeking out a serious conversation with him.

Somehow, his gruff bonhomie and humour seemed to put distance between us. I wasn't persuaded that he would or even could help by talking about his own grief over his wife's death. I came to the sudden realisation that Johnny Ronson was not someone that I could rely on in this desperate time because he too had been subverted, just like everybody else. He wouldn't understand. And beyond this, there was no one else I could turn to.

Returning home, I considered my predicament on the walk back along the beck. I was wet through, and needed a change of clothing and to sleep for longer than a couple of hours in a greenhouse. But I was also miserable, lonely and in serious trouble. I remembered that I had to avoid the consequences of my car vandalism, what little I could piece together from the night before.

I sat down on the damp grass by the cinder-track to try to warm up. The sun had brought out an orange and brown butterfly that settled on my trouser leg, trying to warm up as well. Cautiously, she used her proboscis to probe the damp fabric, perhaps liking the taste of salt from my sweat or the stream-water. Was this the sign that I sought?

Angela had told me once that the Ancient Greeks thought that butterflies were the living embodiment of the soul. I sat looking at the butterfly, stepping daintily on my leg, and wondered if Angela was giving me one last farewell. It was a stupid thought, I knew, yet another invention of my over-active imagination, but it was still comforting.

My father confronted me when I came home for the second time, early that afternoon. He came out on to the doorstep, his thick-framed glasses flashing as he glared up at me like an angry owl. It soon escalated into a furious row.

"*Po'donok*! What you think this is? *Svo'lotch'*! Your mother, worried sick. Me, walking streets thinking you dead. You know, bloody police come here!"

"Oh Christ!" I had missed them when I went out to the wood and all the rest.

"*Po'donok*! You little fucker! What you done?" He had raised his hand, impotently, not daring to strike me.

"Dad, Dad, calm down. It's not that bad."

"Police are looking for you! How it not bad? You bloody stupid?"

"Nicky, the police are out looking for you! You just left and didn't come home and we didn't know what to do! We were worried. Where've you been?" This was my mother.

"Oh."

The police were looking for me because my parents thought that I'd run away from home, not because I was a suspect in a case of serious criminal damage. Not yet at least.

"That all you can say? Oh?"

"No, it really isn't that bad. Honestly, it isn't," I lied. "Paul and me just got drunk after, you know, the funeral. We took it too far, I know. It's not as if I enjoyed it, you know. I'm sorry."

Despite the rift with me, my strange and self-absorbed parents should have stepped in to guide me at this moment of crisis. I was transforming into a grieving adult, flung out on my new orbit, unable to understand my feelings or comprehend my future. I became angry that my parents were more concerned about police trouble than any sympathy for me or, indeed, Angie and her family. My mother tried to take a reasonable line.

"I know, Nicky; I know it's been hard for you. I know that you wanted to be with the two Pauls. But you could have got into trouble! Anything could have happened!"

'*You don't know the half of it,*' I thought.

"I'm sorry Mum but I liked Angie, and she liked me. Everybody's upset; you should be as well! I just don't understand why you're not!"

"But we are upset. Of course, we are!"

I was getting heated in response to my father's provocations and my mother's limpid concern. But my father was having none of it; he was riled beyond endurance and fed up of my self-serving half-truths. Normally, he was a phlegmatic, even disinterested, presence in the house, coolly ironical on the occasions he was forced to deal with me. On those occasions, I made sure to provide reasons for him to feel disappointed in me, just because I knew that it would upset him. This afternoon, he was upset.

"You respect your mother! What you think this is?"

"Nicky, it wasn't too much to ask, was it? You could've let us know what you were doing. Where you were?"

"It was fine. Paul looked after me." '*Which was more than you've done,*' I thought. "He's sensible and didn't let anything happen to me."

"So, something happened last night? What happened, Nicky? Were we right to be worried?"

"You were fighting or stealing!" interjected my father.

"*Kolya!*" This was my mother rebuking my father. It was almost farcical, this same old routine between the two of them. I had become habituated to my father's constant mistrust of me, but this afternoon something brittle in me abruptly snapped and I responded to his provocations.

"Always the same! Always assuming the worst! Why do you do this? It was a wake and we all just got too drunk."

"You're lying! I know when you lie to us."

"I really don't care what you think. Angela died and you just have to find fault even now! What's wrong with you?"

"Nicky!" My mother, again.

"Has it crossed your mind that I might be upset? That I may have loved Angela? And you're there finding fault with me! You're such a useless limp prick of a father."

"*Posh'ol na khui,*" muttered my father in Russian. I didn't know what it meant but I could guess from his expression and tone. I was crying by now from exhaustion and grief and the sheer burden of dealing with my parents. It was too much after the fateful events of the previous night and the morning. I turned my back on them and went upstairs to get changed into some dry clothes.

Chapter 7
Nicky's Imagined Worlds

My friends saved me from myself. Paul must have been sufficiently concerned about my well-being to have discussed my erratic behaviour with Jon and Drillbit. They must have then talked to Spex about it during the day, because his father, Johnny Ronson, drove around to the house with Drillbit in the evening.

His Neville persona was the charm, as always, because Mr Ronson, husky-voiced and over-affable, could come across as a shifty, down-at-heel racketeer. My parents didn't like him much, I could tell, but they respected Neville, personable and fresh-faced with his smooth propositions and explanations.

He had smoothed over the unfortunate fact that I had come back from our last trip to London with a massive black eye. Now, he was trying to persuade my parents to let me go back there again for a couple of weeks, to work on the job he had promised for his brother and myself.

He argued persuasively that it would be good for me to get away after recent events. He didn't specify which ones, how recent and why it was a really good idea for me to get out of town. In London, I would be with friends, working for three weeks from mid-August and earning money.

I reasoned my parents could see the benefits of this plan. In fact, they could hardly open the front door fast enough and see the back of me. In retrospect, it was one of their more disastrous mistakes but of course, they were at a loss in how to deal with me and even console me. It must have been hard for them, but they didn't make it easy for me.

It was all settled quickly. Drillbit, known as Neville to my parents, would act *in loco parentis* while I was away working. We would stay again at the house in Cambridge Gardens. The house had a landline and even a phone, so my parents would ring from the Elmete Lane pay phone every Monday and Thursday at 7 o'clock.

They exchanged addresses in case a telegram needed to be sent in an emergency. My father gave Drillbit twenty pounds in cash to pay for my food and other essentials before my first pay packet. After that, I would be expected to pay my own way.

I noticed that Drillbit got the cash because my father didn't trust me with such a large amount. Drillbit would set us up with the work but would then leave us during the week to carry on with the flat conversions in the house. At the same time, he was also picking up another local rewiring job in West Kilburn. I would be back next weekend for Spex's birthday, although I didn't feel that I had much to celebrate.

Then, on the Saturday night, Mr Ronson gave us a lift to the bus station.

"Cheerio, lads. Work 'ard and mind 'ow you go," was all that he said in parting. Spex and Diane got out from the back seat and wished us well.

"Nicky, you crazy bastard. You need to stay outta trouble. Think you can manage that for a week?"

"Drill—" I looked at Jon. "Neville and Jon have nothing to worry about. I'm planning to work all week and come back for Spex's birthday."

"Are you sure that you'll be alright on your own?"

"Course. It'll be fun. We'll be the three amigos wrangling cable for a living."

"You won't fall into questionable company with Nev?" asked Diane mock-seriously. Drillbit rolled his eyes at this, but let it pass. "And you won't miss being back here?" Diane wasn't clear on the real reasons I was unexpectedly going back to London.

"Under the circumstances," said Spex, "I think it's best that Nick heads off to the Big Smoke for a bit. See ya next Saturday. Look after yerself, Nicky. I'll be thinkin' of ya."

He smiled and then unexpectedly, gripped my arm and gave me a hug round the chest.

Jon and I travelled south on the midnight bus, just as we did in May. That journey intruded on the present, prompting unbidden memories of Angela's head on my shoulder and the snort she made when laughing at something that really amused her. Jon and I tried to stretch out to doze on the back seat, in the fuggy and dusty warmth close to the big diesel engine.

Early in the morning, I was woken up by the bright pink-orange lights at a bus station, probably the one at Sheffield. I glanced out of the back window and then looked again, as if I was doing a gormless cartoon double take. I was suddenly fully, uneasily awake, sitting bolt upright with my hands on the window.

Angela was walking away from the hard stand, walking with her familiar rhythm and bearing, the orange light catching the highlights in her permed hair. '*It can't be her*,' I thought. '*She lost that hair after those drug treatments.*' She walked purposefully away from me on the bus, then turned a corner into the shadows and disappeared into the early morning darkness.

In all, I saw this figure for a couple of moments, as if she had walked quickly away from me in the street without giving me a second glance. It was unmistakably her but it couldn't be her, not here, not now. '*I went to your funeral, Angela; I saw your coffin.*' Not for the first time, I felt the small of my back prickle with apprehension. '*You died, Angela!*'

I tried to rationalise it in my head. Trendy perms with highlights were popular in older teenage girls; it was just someone who looked a bit like her. It was easy to be mistaken in the dim, flat orange light in the bus garage. It was easy for the present to become conflated with my memories of her, which were still so fresh and painful.

And, in any case, I had not seen this girl's face. I knew that there was no way that it could be Angela. Still, I felt that, without a doubt, it was her. I knew that she was gone, in the physical sense, but her presence still pervaded my thoughts with memories and her habits. I was heavy with an all-pervading feeling that I didn't just carry with me all the time, but that I lived and breathed inside.

As usual, my imagination was creating something that wasn't there. I was haunted by the promise of my ex-girlfriend's life, taken from her at the same exact time that she had begun to understand the full beauty of what she was losing.

***

Even in my personal hero narrative, I would not be able to escape the repercussions of my acts of creation. Ship had foreseen my obvious responses to stimuli; it had played me from the start. It knew all about the weaknesses of humans and how easily we could be manipulated. I surmised that it knew precisely when and how I would take my vengeance on the Imposters.

It was all calculated by Ship to bring me to the attention of The Ancient Master, an entity that Ship knew more about than it had pretended to me. With a sense of foreboding, I realised that Ship had told me half-truths all along. It had lied about always telling the truth, even when directly ordered. The Master invaded my narrative, subsuming it and then obliterating it, just like a tsunami sweeps away some primitive little shacks by the shore side.

The Master had a presence that was as loud as thunder rolling across a sky and as soft as lips brushing my ear to whisper. It was voiceless but, somehow, I understood the thoughts that it wished to communicate to me. The Master presented monolithic ranges of thought to me, all linked together as one chain of ideas, an exterior landscape of mountainous vastness.

When it communed with me, range crushed down upon range, in some sort of analogy to geological violence. At the same time, it appeared to arrange the common themes of these ideas in a shining, symmetrical pattern that stretched away around me. An intricate construction of unearthly beauty.

Each pattern was linked and acted on by the next. Each pattern was related by resonances and harmonics as if they were musical notes, or words that rhymed, or differences, that could barely be discerned, in the shades of huge blocks of colours. I perceived intricate patterns of colour that could have been mauve, magenta and orchil or gamboge, saffron and orange; but I could not explain the differences between them or appreciate the subtleness of each meaning.

The perfection created a sense of remorseless and overwhelming beauty. The more of it I experienced, the more sterile and unnerving it became. It was a vision from something not human and quite literally, inhuman, possibly even inhumane. At first, I did not understand why the Master was transfixing my consciousness in this way, but its purpose became clear over the course of its hold on my mind.

It was impossible to represent the conversation with the Master in words because it communicated in a way that seemed to form ambiguous, undefined concepts in my mind. It would implant something in my mind, how and what I did not know and out of this pattern, I attempted to discern a meaning.

It could sound like music, express the colour indigo, or mean, '*Nicky, we know what you want, but we need to judge if you are worthy.*' I was incapable of appreciating the full detail and purpose; this was as ineffable as it was incomprehensible. It reiterated the sequence but with subtle variation. I wondered if the Master wanted my simple, mammal brain to try to comprehend as much as it could, even if the detail was subliminal and beyond my conscious awareness.

Perhaps, I thought facetiously, that it was the Master's version of the small print in the terms and conditions. Then, my thoughts diving down from the surface to the depths, I came the chilling realisation that this was an attempt at subversion. I was being confronted by something that could well be allied to the Imposters, or that supported their ambition of imposing absolute dominion over humanity. After all that I had been through, the Imposters still wanted to subvert me onto their side of the struggle. I had to resist.

Nicky, the Master explained (or, at least, these were the concepts that I could understand). *Do you know what we are?*

"You are a Master, one of the Ancient Masters. Ship talked about you." It seemed to refer to itself by the royal We, which I felt was a bad sign.

We are called by many names. The Ships called us the Master. They feared we would deprive them of their home but they did not understand our purpose. You have nothing to fear from us.

The sequence of concepts was difficult, or at least, the way that I perceived and understood them was unconnected. The Master made the pronouncements as if they were little, opaque fragments that all connected in a larger, riddling monologue. The overall effect was that it provoked doubt and unease in my mind.

"What is your purpose, Master? What do you want with me?" I asked.

We reconcile the good and bad, the lost and found, the past and future. We are at beginnings and endings. We are here to give a choice even if you do not know what you want to choose. Act now in the way that you feel is right. We will guide you.

None of this was in any way reassuring. The mountain ranges were being ground down into rocks and dust.

"Do you support the Imposters?" I asked, but there was no answer from the patterns of colour. Their warm light and heat beat upon my face.

I woke up in the attic room, back in the Cambridge Gardens townhouse, with the afternoon sun shining on my face through the familiar roof-window and nowhere to go. I had fallen asleep after the night's bus journey. Instead of Angela sharing this room with me, as it had been in May, only twelve weeks ago, it was Jon in the far corner.

He was out that Sunday afternoon, meeting his brother at Paddington. I was alone in the house, feeling flat and spent. I looked up at the roof-window from where I lay in my sleeping bag. The window framed little white clouds that floated by in the blue summer sky, simple and disconnected from my feelings. It was the second week of the summer holidays.

In previous years, I would have been outside and enjoying myself with the gang, but now it was an obscure form of anguish for me. The summer sunshine, in the very opposite to past memory, now compelled me to remember the profound feelings of loss. And even deeper in the depths—unacknowledged and unrecognised at the time—was the usual illicit feeling of relief.

Relief that Angela's ordeal at the end hadn't been long. Relief that I could now hide away my cowardice and selfishness. Relief that she couldn't hurt me anymore with her offhand carelessness towards my feelings. Was it this that the Master wanted to observe in me? Why was it here? Did it want to measure my under-developed sense of empathy towards anyone but myself?

'Good luck with that one,' Master, I thought. *'Go screw yourself, back in your own stupid alien reality.'* I would resist subversion to the last. In the slanting sunshine, I found the bloodspots that had soaked into and dried on the floorboards twelve weeks ago.

They were the last physical signs that Angela Wilkinson had stood there once, giggling and embarrassed by the commotion she was causing before the big gig at Wembley. I touched a bloodstain and then put my fingers to my lips, as if this final parting would show the Master my deep and complex emotions. Perhaps I needed to show them to myself as well.

***

On Monday morning, Drillbit got us started on the job that he had assured us we would like so much. I didn't care much whether I liked it or not. I just wanted to get paid at the end of the week and to pay off the rest of my debt to Drillbit. We took the Tube over to the Hammersmith and walked over to the new buildings at Charing Cross Hospital.

They were built in the brutalist concrete style that reminded me of the Westway or Trellick Tower, those icons that loomed so prominently in my personal mythology. We found a bunker-like building called Estates. We knew a lot about estates in our town and, whether their reputations were deserved or not, we tried to avoid them.

I was now in London precisely because I had committed car vandalism on the wrong estate. But here, at the hospital, it evidently wasn't that sort because Drillbit introduced himself as Neville Holdsworth, contract electrician and telecoms engineer, to a watery-eyed and distracted manager.

The manager got us to sign a form for payroll and a waiver that the hospital would not be liable for personal injury. Drillbit shrugged his shoulders and said that we were in the right place if we were to get injured. Not that we were likely to get hurt, he added hastily, when Jon and I were each given a hard hat and torch.

The manager took some keys and a floor plan of the basements for all of the buildings on the hospital site. The plan was labelled 'Level-1'. We were taken to an adjoining concrete cube of a building that had tiny windows hidden in ribs and crenulations. It looked like a medieval castle reinvented by a subverted race of degenerate fascists from the future. Drillbit called it the 'Ministry of Truth', probably to annoy the manager.

"You have to know what you're doing to make something look so ugly," Drillbit mused. He turned to the two of us. "Anyway, don't worry about the architecture you two; you'll be downstairs in Room 101 for the day."

Jon snickered nervously, but the literary reference evaded me. The manager unlocked a service door on a ground floor corridor and showed us where we were on the plan. We walked down two flights of rough concrete stairs, lit by sporadic fluorescent tube-lights on every landing. The air was flat and stale, smelling of dust, warm plastic and vaporised oil.

Someone from Estates had already left us an enormous reel of yellow cable, but their contracts didn't allow them to do anything with it, so the job needed to be done by an external contractor. In whatever way he had done it, Drillbit had been awarded the job and was now sub-contracting to his two apprentices. We were to lay the yellow cable down the spine of the hospital campus, using basements and underground service tunnels to link between buildings.

"It's co-ax cable so you need to be careful you don't kink it," Drillbit explained. "They need a straight run from here," he pointed to where we were on the plan, "to here." The route we had to follow was marked in green pen. "You'll be connecting the payroll department to the big mainframes so that everybody gets paid."

We must have looked at him with incomprehension.

"What's a mainframe?" I asked.

"It's a big computer, Nick. Does the accounts for this place. All the money gets transferred electronically. It's like sci-fi!" he added enthusiastically. "I thought that you'd like it. Pretty much the first place in the country to get this new set-up."

Jon and I looked askance at each other. It wasn't like science fiction at all. It all looked fairly easy and to be honest, really quite dull. I was grateful to Neville, but it was a hell of a way of making any kind of living even for three weeks.

"You get yer wadge on Fridays. That's not electronic, don't worry. It's all cold cash up front."

In the next week-and-a-half, we had to lay over 800 yards of the coaxial cable, none of it to be kinked at any corners and for it to be supported every yard or so by a couple of plastic cable-ties. Periodically, we had to label it 'Telecoms Cable' with tags that the manager had given us. At each end, we had to feed the cable up to the ground floor (or 'Level 0' as it was on the plans), leaving a good length for whatever gubbins was attached to the ends.

We had to lay at least 100 yards a day, without major mishap, if I wanted to get back home for Spex's birthday at the weekend. Jon tried to dissuade me, saying that it was a bad idea to go back so soon. I said that, on the contrary, it would look highly suspect if I disappeared for weeks on end, as if I had a secret to hide. I won that argument, and we pressed on with the cable laying.

We then considered how to lay this enormous length of cable and decided that we needed a trolley to carry the reel, as the cable was unwound. The manager and Drillbit disappeared to find the trolley and some thick spars of wood that could support a metal bar. This would be the spindle from which the reel would unwind.

In a sudden insight into the farcical nature of this job, I realised that neither of them had given much thought about the practicalities of laying this cable. It was all up to Jon and me to sort out, and sure enough, once we had the trolley, Drillbit and the Estates bloke left us alone to get on with it. Drillbit had to get started on his job in West Kilburn and told us he would see us back at the house.

"It's an easy job, you two," were his parting words. "Just take it steady but watch out for the rats."

"Rats? What rats are ya talkin' about? Is that for real?" said Jon. "I thought that you were joking."

Drillbit shook his head at how easily he could bait his younger brother.

"You'll be fine. I'm sure they'll leave you alone."

Just the two of us then, Jon and myself, alone in a long, dim corridor of concrete. Pipes covered in silver-faced lagging were suspended just above head-height, and gratings in the floor covered more pipes. I held one end of the cable while Jon rumbled off down the passageway, paying out the cable and making sure it lay neatly on the ground behind him.

Soon, through nobody's fault, I was on my own. This was not a good situation for my erratic state of mind. In fact, it was the worst thing that could happen to me when I had nothing else to occupy my thoughts. The passageway had an unnerving resemblance to the culvert at the end of the stream from a few days before.

Immediately, I felt the rush of fear from that experience still resonating within me. I imagined what it would have been like to drown in that place, one tragedy following another in quick succession. *'He loved her so much. He died of a broken heart,'* they would say; although, of course, none of it was really true. So, why did I feel this way if I didn't really love her?

I spoke to my parents on Monday and Thursday evening, as we had agreed. These were perfunctory, and therefore almost pleasant, question-and-answer sessions on the phone. I assured them that Neville and Jon were looking after me and that I was really enjoying the work. The weekdays passed.

We laid the cable, ate macaroni and cheese with Drillbit back at the house in the evening, and then went to sleep up in the attic room, shattered after a productive and useful day's work. On Tuesday evening, Drillbit took us to the Pig & Whistle for a pint and a packet of peanuts.

We walked on a road that dived low under the block feet of the Westway. It bisected a squat little series of Art Deco-style apartment blocks as if it was a water-break in ripples of estuary mud. The pub itself was a bunker built of bricks with little slit windows, an ugly slab in the middle of the suburb.

It looked unexpectedly threatening after the unchanging tunnels underground, almost like a fortification in an inner-city warzone that was on the cusp of violence. There was a jaunty pig painted on the sign outside, wearing a waistcoat and top hat, playing a tin whistle painted in gold. The gold paint was flaking off.

"What'll ya have, Nicky?" Nev asked, once we had breached the bunker.

"The usual, please, Nev. Snakebite and black." I had taken to drinking this in the mistaken belief that it had additional potency to help me deaden my grief. I thought that it distinguished me as a sensitive aesthete, suffering in the silence of my bereavement, as if I was drinking absinthe in some *fin de siècle* Parisian dive.

"Are you sure ya want to drink that stuff? It'll give you an 'ead in the morning."

I was hoping that it would obliterate all my troublesome thoughts and that I would crash into a dreamless sleep back at the townhouse.

After several days in the service-tunnels of the hospital, the dim grey light and the long periods of boredom began to induce those strange freewheeling episodes in my imagination when the ordinary acquired overpowering feelings of hyper-reality. Yet again, I was suddenly aware of the true nature and hidden reality in the creak and pop of the silver pipes and the regular lattices of the grated floor.

Concrete had been left with swirling impressions of woodgrain, formed from the wooden moulds when it had been first poured. There was no indication in the tunnels where we were on the hospital campus, what time it was and whether it was still daylight. The only sounds were the pipes, the trundle of the cable trolley and our voices when we spoke.

As the days went by, and we became accustomed to finding our way around in the underground tunnels, we seemed to need to speak on fewer and fewer occasions. Even our words seemed to fall off after a short distance, as if the very walls sucked the life out of the voices trapped within them.

Then at the end of the week. *It's Friday, it's 5 to 5, it's a new scenario to play out in your personal hero narrative.* I was imprisoned down here, underground. What if the rest of the world was subverted and I was the last real human left, exactly as Ship had told me, the Imposters laying siege to me in this concrete bunker? They would try to reason with me and persuade me.

"Nicky, we just want you to be happy," they would say, in the voice of my mother. "You know we just want the best for you."

"Come out of there now, Kolya." This was my father. "Come and join rest of us outside. It is like you make prison for yourself. Join us and be happy."

What would I do then? I was watched by the Master and was being hunted by the Imposters. Whatever I did would be the wrong decision. A small band of Imposters would begin scratching, then pounding at the service door to be let in. They wouldn't need many to subdue a single combatant trapped in that place. The door would slam open, distant feet would thud on steps, or ring out on the rungs of ladders and metal gratings. Muffled voices would give occasional directions.

"They've said that he's down here. Go steady and keep your eyes open. We need to find him alive and uninjured."

They were coming from both ends of the service tunnel. I could see flashlights wavering from away down the length of the corridor, although the Imposters were still hidden from sight by a corner. They knew that I was down here, and they were coming after me.

I looked around me, lifted a length of grating and crawled into the sump channel, turning off my torch. I squeezed over lengths of silver heating pipe and slowly lifted the grating back into position. It slotted into position without any noise. Then, I started crawling on my hands and knees. According to the plan, there was a spur to this channel that linked to the main part of the heating system, but it was under an intervening block partition.

I would try to crawl through the spur and escape into what seemed to be an adjoining plant room. There was enough space, but it was awkward because the pipes were underneath me, so I made slow progress in hot dusty darkness. I barely made it under the partition before the footsteps clanged on the walkway beside me and torchlights flashed on the walls.

A light shone for a long moment in my part of the sump channel, and I hoped that I hadn't left any trails in the dust. Underneath the partition, I stayed absolutely still and bit the knuckles of my right hand to stop me panting loudly. The lights passed by, and I was safe for the moment.

I had to hurry because they could still corner me in the plant room. I had to find a way out of these tunnels before they thought to look further afield from my last known location.

I emerged into the near darkness of the plant room. Green lights on some sort of control board were lit and cast dim shadows in an indefinitely sized space. There was no other indication of what happened in this room. From the close air in the place, it didn't feel to be large, but the low growl of machinery came from a distance. There was no sound of voices or pursuit.

Nicky, said the Master from out of the darkness, from that deeper hidden reality. *We understand your pain. We want you to be happy, but only you can make the choice now.*

"What choice? There is no choice! I submit to your subversion—"

No, Nicky, the Master interrupted. *You can put all of this aside, join us and be happy. Or you can join Angela and be happy. You have the choice of two different timelines at this nexus; we make and unmake the reality that you choose. We want you to be happy.*

I sank to my knees, overcome by a false feeling of oceanic boundlessness, as if the Master was some benign higher power into which I would dissolve like tears in the rain. This was subversion. In the darkness, I could give in to this blissful feeling of self-dissolution, like the stream flowing into the river and then into the sea.

I closed my eyes and wished that I could believe the Master's comforting lies, but I knew that it was just more pretending and fooling. Self-dissolution was just like disintegrating and dying, and with it, all of this reality would be dying with me. I struggled back to the surface from the depths, as if gasping for air. I found myself alone, a disembodied voice in the darkness.

"That's no choice!" I shouted out into the blackness. I was chilled that the Master had used such a cheap trick and that I had nearly succumbed to it. The green lights looked at me balefully and groaned. There was no answer and I realised that there would not be one; only I existed now in this narrative with the Master. It was just an Imposter in another guise, the Master and the Imposters were one and the same.

"All you're offering is subversion and nothingness! I decide what to do, on my terms, and when I do it!" I shouted. '*You'll never take me alive, you alien scumbag,*' I thought to myself. I had found the deadlock on the door to the room and scrabbled out into a corridor, my skin crawling from the darkness closing in on me. There was no reason for the Master to let me exist: I could be swallowed by the enveloping blackness at any moment.

I ran. I ran anywhere in my blind panic to be away. I was on the run to the outside of everything. Stairs. Doors. Face averted, eyes blinking from late afternoon sunshine. I ran into the sunlight and away from the darkness. My chest felt like an over-tightened spring, propelling me on like a clockwork toy without volition or direction.

Past shops and along streets, blind to the traffic and to the passers-by. I ran towards Hammersmith Bridge because it looked like a castle with turrets, an arched portcullis and heraldic scrollwork on olive-painted battlements. A place of safety. I crossed the Thames on the walkway beside the suspension cables and standstill traffic, packed buses grinding head to tail.

Passengers watched me running past. Half-way across, someone had pledged undying, unbreakable love and had clasped a small padlock around some metal grating. My chest hurt and a sour feeling tightened within me, as if there was a glass wall between me and everything else in the world. My breath came in gasps, but I still had to run.

Down a ramp, past playing fields and bushes, emerging onto a walkway on the banks of the Thames. The tide was out and the estuary mud—the hidden depths beneath—was laid out like knives in an open drawer. I felt compelled to grasp them. I walked down some neat steps built into the bank. The feeling of self-dissolution was irresistible, drawing me out onto the mud and onwards towards the river.

"Master!" I shouted. "No, I refuse! I won't choose any of it! None of your choices. I refuse to fight!"

I had a plan. I knew how to take my revenge on the Master. I already knew that it was desperate to subvert me. I was a last holdout against the all-encompassing power of the Imposters. But it used 'we' and this was my clue to its weakness. I was willing to bet that it thought of itself as a community of subsumed minds that could all be relied upon to agree and make decisions as a consensus.

What if there were minds that were not so happy about this arrangement and, underneath the façade, clamoured to be released from their shackles? Could I subvert that which was trying to subvert me? Ship had chosen me exactly for this reason because I would eventually work it out, although it took me a while to understand my role.

Ship had played the double bluff to perfection, even fooling me for a while. It was obvious: the black hole had been created by Ship sacrificing itself for one sole purpose. It was giving me the final weapon against the Imposters or the Master, or whatever else they wanted to be called. They were all stupid names, in any case. They had to be deceived into thinking that I wouldn't make this sacrifice myself until it was too late, until I would be ready to use the weapon against them.

The Master was so blinded by its own power that it would never conceive that I would take such a step. I was certain that its consensus view would be to disregard any weak-minded notions of honour and sacrifice. But I was also certain that there were still some in that hive mind that would recognise and respect these qualities, if given the chance.

"Master!" I shouted. "This is the end. No more games! Take me to the black hole and I'll show you what I want to do."

I activated my force fields and made them into the shape of a reflective silver sphere around my body. It would hold enough air and protect me long enough from hard radiation for me to do what I had to do. Instantly, as I knew it would, the Master transposed me to the black hole because it was hoping to use any leverage to trick me.

It transposed me above the accretion disc, looking out on a vista for which I had no words, a place at the end of things, but which, perhaps, gave me the chance to start afresh at the beginning. A bright ring surrounded an oval dark shadow. This was the central singularity, beyond the event horizon, from which no light emerged.

But I was not alone at this final, terrible destination. Moments after I had been transposed, Ship after Ship slid into existence around me, each of them emerging from their own transit wormhole. It was a fleet of Ships, grouped in formation, all of them together with me against the Master, each with a pilot and navigator as their crew of combatants.

I was not alone in this final rebellion against the tyranny of the Imposters. Once I had understood Ship's final plan, I was certain that the Ships would be here. The Master was silent, the warring factions within it preventing any immediate response. In that moment of hesitation, the Ships extended their force fields around me, cradling me against the storm.

Are you functional, Nicky? said a Ship voice projected into my little force-field shell. It did not have the same genderless intensity as my own Ship's voice because it reminded me of Drillbit when he was on his best behaviour.

"Yes, I am. I'm glad to be doing this with friends."

We all are. A different Ship's voice. It sounded like Paul. *Thank you for resisting to the last. There is a high probability that this reality will be replaced by a more fortuitous one for you.*

"Sounds great, I think, but only if I survive."

We are fairly certain that your information will remain intact after a reality dissolution. We should really get going, you know.

"Will it hurt?"

No. It's already d—

How do you reset a reality and replace it with an alternate one? Well, it was difficult but possible, if you had a fleet of alien warships at your behest; they cracked open the black hole like an egg, so that the dark base reality in the thing spilled out like a yolk and transubstantiated everything around it, even down to the quantum level of space-time itself.

The Ships all jumped simultaneously into the black hole, taking each of their own singularities beyond the event horizon. It would rupture, irrevocably and irreversibly, a total reality dissolution spreading instantaneously, in all directions, across the whole fabric of space-time. Reality split along new time-lines.

I was left here, and, with a heart-pounding leap of exaltation, my alternate Nicky now understood his role and purpose. He was the first conscious volition to set in train a new narrative, a new creation, in any direction that he wanted. The past and future were indistinguishable; he was the ultimate origin and destiny of existence, which were one and the same. He had created and would create all the roles in that alternate narrative, all of them infinite transformations without end.

Perhaps the Nicky in that new reality would find the past changed and reset into something different, familiar yet strange at the same time. Perhaps the dominion of the Imposters never came to pass. It is impossible to know, because I—the Nicky here, now, in this reality—am forever estranged from that alternate one and can only guess at the fate of that other Nicky.

If events had been different, at some branch point in the nexus of time-lines far in the past, I would have followed the special one, as if it was a golden thread, and I would have become that alternate Nicky. Perhaps he was lucky and met Angela again in the different time-line because if there were no Imposters, it was a reality in which she never died.

I like to think so. I like to imagine that not only did the boy get the girl, but the girl got the boy and that they were both happy together. I think about them sometimes, these people that we should have been. I wish them well, but in this reality, in the ordinary world, they are both just memories. Memories of the imaginary Nicky and Angela from my personal hero narrative.

***

In what I suppose was the ordinary world, the Thames river-police passed by on a patrol boat and spotted me on the estuary mud. The regular cops came for me, arrested me, and put me in a holding cell for psychiatric evaluation. The police doctor sedated me overnight, probably because they didn't know what else to do with me, so I don't remember much of the episode.

I lay back on the wipeable black mattress that smelt of bleach, relieved that I could suspend my thoughts. I was alone in the cell, stuck in a limbo with a bright, humming fluorescent light. I decided that the light was the centre of this universe, or at least, the centre of my universe.

"You know, after getting shut of the Imposters, you'd think I'd get something a bit better than this! What do you think?" I asked the light.

The light carried on humming to itself and didn't answer.

"I mean, it's a bit shabby in here. I appreciate the company, don't get me wrong."

The light didn't seem to care that it had a pivotal role to play in this reality.

"Alright, fine. I'll take the hint; you don't want anything to do with me. You're on their side."

I tried to ignore it after that, but the humming was annoying.

They had taken my watch and I could only guess that it was close to midnight when I heard the new night shift talking and moving outside the cell. I suppose that it was Hammersmith police station, but it didn't matter at the time and, afterwards, I never bothered to find out.

When my companion the light went out, I amused myself by tracing the intricacies and minute sandy irregularities of the white-faced bricks that formed the walls of the cell. *'Why?'* I thought to myself, after the end I had envisaged for the Master. *'Why did I happen to exist in this reality anyway?'* How wonderfully and frighteningly unlikely it was that I existed at all. *'And why did I exist at all?'*

I was utterly alone in the darkness again, but there was no Master to answer me in the reality that followed this time-line. I should have been happy with this realisation, but I began to wonder if the real Nicky had escaped to the alternate reality after all. The Master or the Imposters had left something behind here that thought that it was Nicky.

It acted like Nicky, but it wasn't; it was just a molecular copy of the original human. I prodded my eye and then touched my eyeball. It felt uncomfortable, exactly as I would expect if I was truly human. But how would I know otherwise?

The whole purpose of an Imposter was that it did not know it's true nature. If you wanted a literal manifestation of teenage alienation, then I was a great example.

***

On early Saturday morning, the humming light was back on at some point, but I was asleep by then. I can't even remember if they gave me anything for breakfast. Then in the late morning, the desk sergeant opened the cell door. Ratty appeared with two officials in suits. These two had a brisk manner about them that suggested they might be Army and the desk sergeant seemed to treat them with cautious deference. He brought me out with them into the reception lobby.

"Mr Valko," he said, pronouncing my name incorrectly. He spoke at the release forms in a carefully neutral tone. "You're being released into the care of your father and those gentlemen." He glanced at Morecombe & Wise standing at the front desk. "They've got you released on one of these diplomatic pass things." He held it up.

"What's one of them?"

"It means you're a potential security risk and it's in the national interest to keep an eye on you."

"But I haven't done anything!"

"That's not what they've said; breaking and entering. Trespass. Criminal damage. Actual bodily harm."

"I've no idea what you're talking about."

"Kolya!" My father had caught sight of me, now that we were out in the main lobby. He stubbed out his cigarette. *"Kolyuni'tchka!"* He hadn't used the affectionate diminutive of my name in a long while. He had used it often when I was younger. *"Bo'zye moy*! What happened to you? Are you hurt?"

"No, I'm alright, Dad. I don't know. I got lost in the tunnels somehow."

He came over to me and put an arm on my shoulders. His face, pale like tallow, looked burnt down to the wick.

"I should not have let you come here to London. It was my fault; you should have stayed home. We would have looked after you."

"Neville found me work and I wanted to earn some money. I thought that you would be proud of me."

"Hey Nicky," said Ratty, nodding at me. "How are ya? I'm glad they found you."

"Dad," I asked, half-guessing at the answer. "What's Rat, I mean, Richard, doing here? He didn't come with Neville."

"Yeah, I came down last night and met the case handlers." He indicated the two I was calling Morecombe & Wise. "We thought that you'd got into trouble. Serious trouble."

"Your friend Jonathan could not find you. Richard ring me yesterday," my father continued. "Your mother was so worried. I was worried. Then Richard told us police have found you."

"How did he find out?" I asked, feeling I was now getting closer to the truth. "Ratty? How did you know?"

"He is a *do'nozchik*. How do you say it?"

"An informer? Ratty, an informer?" I was incredulous. "No way!"

"I work for the cops sometimes, yeah it's true, Nicky," said Ratty. "Just keepin' an eye on things for them in the Troc. Places like that, stuff to do with the union. I know people, you know?"

"I don't get it. You're working down here in London."

"Yeah, so I do; but they," he nodded over at his handlers, "find me odd-jobs too. Seeing if Eli and his activist mates are planning another riot. D'ya remember Christoph?"

"I think so; the Austrian at the party after that gig. The one with the rum."

"Bingo, Nick-Oh. He's a communist agitator. He's harmless but he knows some interesting people. I've probably blown my cover with that lot 'cos of your little stunt," he added dourly. "Word'll get around." '*Shot by both sides*,' I thought to myself.

"But why did you think I'd got into serious trouble? I still don't get it. Who would want to bother with me?"

"You'd be surprised."

I had heard Ratty say this earlier, but it sounded so outlandish and unlikely that I had ignored it. However, Ratty was not prone to making many jokes, and was certainly serious and sober this Saturday morning. He was being entirely truthful when he said that I could have been in trouble. A creeping sense of fear began to prickle my back.

What if the Master had managed to send me to a reality that was almost familiar but wrong in the tiny, fundamental details? What if I was now living in a new alternate reality with new rules and a new narrative? If I crossed the road, what colour were the traffic lights in this place? In this reality, what if they were something different like red, white, and blue?

I wondered if the change had happened when I was asleep in the police cell: I went to sleep as Nicky but woke up as someone or something else. Who would want to cause me harm, after all? It all seemed so over-dramatic and implausible, as if I was still stuck in one of my weird narratives.

"It's not you as such, Nicky," replied Ratty, trying to reassure me. He could see that this news was troubling me. "You're not the special case, really, you're not. It's 'cos of your Pa. Can I just tell him?" he turned to ask Morecombe & Wise. The taller one, who I thought of as Eric, just looked poker-faced and shrugged his shoulders.

"No, I should be one to tell Kolya. He's old enough," said my father, lighting another cigarette with a sigh. "But later. Not now. We need to go away from here. We need to go home."

Jon and Drillbit still had to complete the contracted work for the week, which had been interrupted by my fateful episode in interstellar space. Once I had been found, safe but debatably sound, they had to finish laying the co-ax cable on Saturday afternoon before they came over to see me at the hospital.

I was taken there for observation on Saturday night, I was told, before travelling back home on the Sunday. Morecombe & Wise drove us there in an ordinary, unmarked car but they seemed to have special privileges when it came to parking it. They used a tiny underground garage with shutter doors on one of the side streets leading off Hammersmith.

Turning into this street, I noticed that the traffic lights were red, yellow and green. That little detail in this reality was unchanged from what I had known previously, at least. Or was it really unchanged? Did I remember them as red, amber and green and not yellow?

Perhaps there were small insignificant changes in this new place after all, but I didn't have any reference to decide if amber and yellow were different or not. Were traffic lights changed or not? What else was subtly different in this world without the Imposters?

The garage was completely unobtrusive and unnoticeable, just a dull set of doors beside a row of grubby shop-fronts, within walking distance of the hospital. Morecombe & Wise accompanied us all the way to it, Eric touching my arm lightly and discretely guiding me as we crossed the main ground floor concourse.

His intent was clear, even to me, that this should be viewed as a deterrent against acting up, or acting clever, or being lippy.

Whoever these two were, in real life, they were not a comedy duo and there wouldn't be many jokes; they were serious, focused and professionally courteous. I imagined that they would maintain this same composure if, instead, they had been ordered to execute us in the hospital basement or back in their quiet little garage.

"Who are you two guys, anyway?" I whispered in the lift. I had to ask. If this was real life in some sort of reality that I could call real, then it was uncannily beginning to resemble one of my personal hero narratives. It always seemed to be about me at the centre of these episodes, trying to be the hero.

"We're close protection officers. CPOs."

"Oh. What does that mean? How do I know you're not going to cause me serious trouble? You're not kidnapping us, are you?" My father shot me an accusatory glance and shook his head.

"Would you like to see my warrant card? Or my diplomatic passport?"

"No, thanks, that's alright. I was just curious. So well, I guess you're packing, then, if you're protecting us?" I had to ask that as well.

"Yep, we've got Glock locked-breech semi-automatic pistols. Would you like to see that as well?"

"*Kolya*! That is enough. These men are trying to help. I'm sorry, gentlemen; my son, he has been having problems. He is stressed."

"That's quite alright, Mr Valko," said Ernie, turning to me. "I understand; I'm sorry for your loss, son. It's hard now but it gets better over time, it really does. It becomes part of you; you accept, and you move on."

I just stared at Ernie the CPO, silent, overcome at the thought of this brief solace from a professional stranger. I'd never heard a grown man express his grief so briefly and yet with such clarity. I never saw him again after that evening and I never knew his story.

My father and I were shown into a separate room on a ward. Eric and Ernie, now that we were on first name terms with them, would finish their shift at midnight. Until then, they would stay outside at either ends of the corridor, protecting us from some undefined threat.

We were asked, politely but firmly, to stay in the room and to call the nursing staff if we wanted to eat. They would search and cross-examine any visitors, even Ratty who already had some sort of police security clearance. They were so practical and calm that I even forgot to feel frightened.

"Dad. You need to tell me. What's going on? Why?"

"I know, Kolya. You have many questions. How to say it? Simply, I turned my back on my country for the right reasons. I can never go back there. I live as exile, teaching, in a town that can never be home."

"Why ever did you do it? I don't understand!"

"I love your mother! She was on delegation to Moscow, to do with trade. Farming equipment or some nonsense like that. Details don't matter, but she became my contact with them." He indicated the corridor outside.

"You mean British security services, or whatever those two belong to?"

"Of course. Then, we fall in love. KGB suspected, but they did not know." He pronounced it *kah-geh-beh*. "They followed us. In the street, in the restaurant. Always, there was a *do'nozchik* at table next to us, or sniffing around like dog on the Metro. Always following us and making sure we knew. Talking too loudly and saying 'Good day, *to'varishch*' to me."

"They didn't hurt you, did they?"

"No, but one time they shot out top of window we were sitting in. Bullet was so fast it made big hole in the glass. *Fzzz*." He imitated the sound of the shot. "We found it afterwards in the wall; it was high velocity rifle bullet. It was friendly warning. Ha!" He grimaced and started searching for a cigarette.

"I could not stay there, after what I had done," he added. "KGB would find out everything. Everything," he repeated for emphasis.

"But what had you done?"

"It was all nonsense. I gave them," he indicated the corridor again, "plans for tractor engines, water pumps. Sites of factories. But even that was all official state secret, can you believe? Tractors!" he scoffed. "It was such nonsense. But still betrayal."

He paused, watched his cigarette smoke coiling up from his hand. He was thinking about the past, about events that had happened nearly twenty years ago. Perhaps he had sat, just like this with a cigarette in his hand, talking to my mother in a Moscow café.

I was not the only one troubled by thoughts of alternate realities and how the past linked to the present. What if he hadn't met my mother? What if they hadn't passed on secrets to the British? What if they had been arrested by the KGB?

"So, how were you both able to leave? Why weren't you arrested?"

"It was a deal. How do you say it, an amnesty? They do swap for undesirables in each country. I came here, married your mother."

"They gave you a job. Teaching at the Polytechnic."

"Ah, what else to do with a Russian in Britain?"

"And they watch you?"

"I don't know. Maybe. Yes, probably."

"You thought that I had got into trouble with who? Soviet agents or something?"

"Yes, they thought it was possible. It would have been a reminder to everybody that they watch as well."

"But it wasn't the Soviets, and it was the police that found me. It was just me being stupid. I'm sorry, Dad. You must have both been so worried."

"Yes, I had to make phone call to them."

"Oh. Is that a problem?"

"Maybe. But what more can they do to me?"

"So, shot by both sides."

"How do you mean?"

"It doesn't matter. Just something my friends say."

***

I must have dozed off. In the late afternoon, Jon and Drillbit were let into the hospital room after a knock at the door. It woke me up and I looked around me, bewildered, expecting to be back in the control room of Ship. But no; I was back in the little hospital room. There was a bed with a white coverlet, and I was sitting in a green armchair with the usual wipe-down surfaces. The room was painted in institutional pale green, so I knew immediately where I had been taken. They must have sedated me again.

"Nicky, ya nutter! It's good to see ya," said Jon, brusquely, as he came into the room. Tact was never his strongest quality. "Wow, man, you gave us the run-around in the tunnels; what happened to ya, goin' all mentalist like that?"

"Well, Jon, I'm truly so sorry. I've been so stupid."

"Nah, s'all right. I jus' got worried when you went off on one. I couldn't find you anywhere." This must have been when I had disappeared into the service tunnels. "Nev phoned the police. They didn't take him seriously at first but then hauled me in for an interview. Then they thought that you were in real trouble."

"Where's my dad? What about Ernie? And what colour are traffic lights here?"

"Whoa, slow down—ah—slow right down, there, Nicky," said Drillbit, stumbling over his words. "What colour do you want them to be? They're red, amber and green 'round here."

"Oh. That's good. But where's here, Nev? I can't remember. They gave me something."

"You haven't gone far, you know. You're back at Charing Cross Hospital, topside though. They found you a bed for the weekend before your da takes you home."

"Where is he? He told me some personal stuff. I want to see him."

"That's a first; never thought you'd be wanting to talk to your da. He's being put up at a hotel. He was here with you all night and this morning."

"Anyway, what's up with the traffic lights?" asked Jon. "They're red, yellow and green. Aren't they? And who's Ernie?"

"I don't know, Jon but, yeah, sure. I'm just pleased to be home."

"Well, yer not home yet; we're still in London, remember?"

"No, I meant that I've been on a long, weird journey but I think it's over now and I'm back again. I think I'm back here, I mean."

"That's good to hear, Nicky, I think. Let's keep ya here and not wandering in tunnels and crap like that. It's not good for ya," said Drillbit, uncomprehending and misunderstanding what I had meant. He changed the subject. "Anyway, had to come to tell you this. Thought that you'd want to know. Ratty's got hold of some news and wanted me to pass it on. You're not going to believe what's happened back home. Man, what that family's bin through," Drillbit added as an aside, shaking his head.

It was a complicated story that I pieced together from Drillbit's uneven narrative. He seemed to have received it second-hand from Ratty, who had picked it up somehow from one of his underground sources. Or perhaps a copper had gossiped in the Troc. I couldn't be definite if Ratty really was a police informer or not.

In fact, I couldn't remember much of the past couple of days, and I began to wonder if anything that I retained in my memory was in any way reliable. That must have been the sedatives that I got fed by the police and the hospital. However, according to Drillbit's story, a week after Angela's funeral, Mr Wilkinson was back at work at his bank.

It was a quiet branch out in the suburbs. On the first day back after those traumatic events, at the close of business at 4 o'clock, Paul McElroy, no less, had swaggered into the bank with a shotgun and robbed the place. McElroy the Younger had caught the bus home from school at the stop opposite the bank, the bank staff had recognised him from his bovver boy outfit and the police quickly made him the lead, and indeed only, suspect.

When McElroy had walked in with a sawn-off shotgun, he had blasted the ceiling to make sure that everybody realised that he was very serious. He had then threatened Wilkinson, knocking him unconscious with a swift jab of the butt-end of the shotgun to his face, before threatening the cashiers with the gun. They had handed over fifteen thousand pounds in used and unmarked.

McElroy scarpered but was rapidly apprehended at his home. He was in custody at the youth remand centre. Ma McElroy had been arrested as an accessory to armed robbery. The police found some of the cash under a mattress. Ma's youngest—the eight-year-old with the attitude and a Raleigh Chopper—had ridden off with the rest of the stash, present whereabouts unknown, presumably holed up with a relative in the extended McElroy clan. Wilkinson was still in hospital and had needed some surgery for facial bone fractures. Absolutely none of it made any sense.

"Told you that McElroy was daft, didn't I?" said Jon drily, after this account from his brother had concluded. "He's gonna get banged up for a proper stretch-and-a-half now. And proper divvy, robbing the bank by his bus stop," he smirked.

"Nah, Jon," responded his brother. "It's meant to look stupid because he needs to get nabbed by the Five-Oh. It's all too obvious; he wanted to get caught."

I stayed quiet because I was wondering why Wilkinson had been targeted in this way. It was a lot of money but was it worth going to youth prison for five years, out in three?

"I suppose it's the next step in the career he's always dreamed about."

"Daft way of going about it. He might be hard, but he's still a div."

Chapter 8
The Power of Imagination

My dad brought me home after that, travelling north on the train in the early evening. He bought me some chocolate and I stared out of the window at the railway sidings, the grey terraced rows and then the countryside opening out in the low sunlight.

Fields, trees, hedges flashed by in an indiscriminate blur of green, a metaphor, it felt to me, for all that had happened or hadn't happened in the past few weeks. A boiling hot stew of events, thoughts, and feelings, all jumbled and filling up an empty vessel called Nicky until it over-flowed. I was poisoned by the bitter taste.

"*Kolyuni'tchka*," said my father. "Everything will be alright. We will look after you."

"Thanks, Dad. Thanks for coming to get me. I thought that I was doing the right thing."

"I know," he sighed. "You're a good boy."

I looked out of the window and stayed quiet again. At one suburban station, we stopped for 10 minutes in the twilight. The abrupt stillness redirected my thoughts to focus on my father. After what I thought that he had told me, how could I broach the subject again and ask him if any of it was actually true?

Betraying your country for the sake of some engineering plans seemed such a trivial deceit for something that had such profound consequences. I began to glimpse something of the inner life of this withdrawn and complex man, but to question his narrative seemed too much of an intrusion into this private part of this life.

After all, he had never spoken about any of this before now. I concluded that he must have really loved my mother and followed that course headlong, regardless of the costs. I knew, all too well, what that felt like. It should have been obvious to me if I had stopped fighting with him and given it some thought. He had not compromised his decisions or choices and had made his life here in England on his terms. It was a type of stubborn courage, I realised, that was worthy of my respect because it was exactly what I would have done.

Mr Ronson and Spex met us at the station to take us home. Spex had already spoken to Jon during the week, back at the town house in Cambridge Gardens, while he was finishing the cable laying. They met us at the ticket barrier, faces drained of colour and substance under the flat orange lights of the station. They both shook my hand as if I was an apparition back to haunt them. Spex hunched his shoulders and shuffled his feet, looking abashed, but then smiled carefully at me.

"Good to see ya, Nick. How ya feelin'?"

"I've been better, Paul, I'm not gonna lie."

"I'm glad yer back. Rough, was it?"

"Yeah, you could say that. I suppose it all caught up with me and got too much. You know; Angela and that."

"Huh, yeah. I get it. Must've been bloody frightening."

"You have no idea. It all went really strange for a while."

"That's saying something coming from you. What were ya doin' out on the Thames anyway, pulling that stunt?"

"Oh. You heard about that? It's a long story; I can't really explain what happened." I didn't really want to explain, in any case.

"How are you, Nicky, love?" This was the greeting from Mr Ronson, husky-voiced and terse as always. '*Got your number, pal*,' I thought. '*You're full of crap, just like the proverbial sad sack.*'

"Fair-to-middling, I suppose, Mr Ronson."

"Should never have let you go off like that. I blame me'sen," he added. *Yeah, so where were you when I needed you?*

"We were all dead worried about you after Drillbit rang," added Spex. I could just imagine the gossip spreading along the backs from doorstep to washing line. My position in local folklore was assured; people would say that I really had nearly died of a broken heart and that I really had tried to drown myself in the Thames.

It was close enough to the truth if one ignored the details about being chased down tunnels by Imposters. At the end of it, I was left not knowing if I was one of them. At least, I got to have my revenge by destroying their reality.

In *La Cucaracha*, on the way back to our house, Spex looked back at me from the front and mentioned Angie's Mix-Tape. Over the past couple of weeks, it had become a memorial of sorts for her. People were hearing about the teenager who had died of blood cancer and wanted a copy of the music that had meant something to her.

Angie's Mix-Tape was proving to be popular. Speccy-Paul was having to make extra copies for friends at school, then their parents, and then their friends who they knew at work or church or down at the slip.

"I'm chuffed in a way, Nicky," added Spex, as if he was guilty of an indiscretion and was asking for forgiveness.

"I wont sure at first, but Da said it was a good way to remember her." He looked over at his father, Johnny Ronson, in the driving seat. I immediately understood how the tape was getting around so quickly. Mr Ronson was the sort of man who knew a lot of people.

"Don't worry, Nick-Oh," said Mr Ronson, no doubt conscious that I had shot him an accusatory glance into the back of the driver's seat. "It's all legit and above board."

"Apart from the copying music and breaking copyright part," added Spex.

"We're not selling them; we're just asking for donations. It's legal if they're for private use. Which they are."

"Barely legal," replied Spex. My father looked quizzically at me, and I had to shrug my shoulders, unsure about this new Ronson scheme that involved both father and son.

"Don't worry, son! The coppers are into it just like everybody else."

"Yeah, but it'll be them bent ones at the Troc."

"No, it's regular Five-Oh as well."

"Anyway, Nicky," said Spex, leaning over to the tape deck. Spex was seeing if I approved of his latest choices for the mix-tape. "I'm glad yer back. I've found a few more tracks. This one's popular; you'll like this one." *(White Man) In Hammersmith Palais* by The Clash played on the car speakers.

White youth, black youth
Better find another solution

"What is that? Is it punk or is it ska, Spex?" I couldn't work out what Joe Strummer was singing about. It was a bit underwhelming and unimpressive.

"It is skunk," added my father.

"Yeah, spot on, Mr Valko. It's both, Nicky! That's why it's so brill!" enthused Spex. "It grows on ya, I promise. Listen to the lyrics; it's the new politics of revolution, I keep tellin' ya. Unity against the racists, the National Front and the Right."

Spex's enthusiasm and idealism were always so good to hear. It was the main reason we went along with most of his schemes because it always seemed such a shame to disappoint him. But I just thought back to what Ratty the Snitch did on the side, informing on Eli and other activists and trying to stop another race riot in Notting Hill.

I couldn't decide if what Ratty did was shocking and wrong—and I wasn't going to dob him in with the others—but the reality was that, the politics of revolution always seemed to become subverted by violence. Or by money. From one point of view, Ratty was the sensible realist, I reasoned, even if he was getting paid off by the Five-Oh. Spex was just a naïve idealist who would never get to see another solution for the youth of today. And that's just as Eli would have predicted.

However, despite my cynicism and misgivings about Clash lyrics, Spex knew his music. In fact, Angie's Mix-Tape became so popular that Spex began collecting the donations for the hospital's charity fund. Over the next few months, we argued over and chose new tracks as they came out.

She would have loved 'Teenage Kicks' by the Undertones and 'Hanging on the Telephone' by Blondie. They both came out in the autumn, and they both had catchy tunes with that punky guitar energy from those times. For me, they just reminded me of the sadness, hurt and anger of that summer if I heard them in the background.

Then, in September, the Buzzcocks released 'Ever Fallen in Love'? which was an ironic track for me, full of poignancy and urgency. Pete Shelley sang as if he understood the emotions I was feeling; my adolescent self-pity was growing into an adult realisation of how much being in love could hurt. And how, for me, there was nothing I could now do about it.

I thought back to that winter afternoon on Hill 60, and wished that her cousin, Paul Baxter, hadn't brought her, or that she hadn't looked at me in that way or that I hadn't looked at her. I wished that we hadn't injured Chris Thompson, because that was the spark for everything that happened between us. What a bitter insight into the deeper truth, into the way that karma would punish you for your past crimes.

'You're the One That I Want' made it on to the Mix-Tape, which reminded me of that night in May at the funfair. It was from the film 'Grease', but of course, I never got around to watching it on a date with Angie because it only came out in August. Afterwards, the music from the soundtrack followed me everywhere I went that summer and autumn. 'Hopelessly Devoted to You' was a stab in the heart every time. I've never wanted to see the film since that time.

Each of us still has Angie's Mix-Tape, but I doubt that any of us would choose to listen to it even now after forty-or-so years. I suppose that one of us should compile a playlist at some point so that kids of today could benefit from our eclectic and well-educated choices.

We went back to school after the summer. I was given weekly appointments with a clinical psychiatrist at the Workhouse to which my father took me on the bus. He kept me company on the journey and on the walk up from the bus stop. The appointments were in the morning, and I remember that there was always a cheerful tang of caramelised fruit, cinnamon, and nutmeg from the bakery in that part of town. They were baking the last of the dough to make the final batches of fruit loaf and fruit buns for the day. My father waited for me in the hospital corridor while I had my session with the psychiatrist. She asked me to keep a diary of my thoughts and feelings.

One episode at school stood out. I was stuck in the same classroom for the lessons of that day, and it felt to me that the sun wheeled overhead from east to west in minutes. Shadows swept across the floor as if a car with bright lights was driving past. It was only possible if the Imposters had remade the very laws of nature in this alternate reality.

They had either altered the passage of time or changed the spin of the Earth, or most frightening of all, this entire reality was a simulation invented by the Master just to torment me. After that, the psychiatrist put me on an increasing dose of Thorazine, telling me that it would help to decrease hallucinations. It would let me think more clearly and take part in everyday life.

I thought that the only problem with my everyday life was that I was grieving for my ex-girlfriend who had suddenly died of an aggressive blood cancer. The psychiatrist told me that I had withdrawn into an inner state—by which she meant the inner world of my imagination—and that I needed to accept the reality of my situation.

I went along with this notion because it seemed to make her happy and, as always, it was in my nature to try to be agreeable. I didn't believe a word of it, of course. Instead, I was wondering if this was just another narrative in which the hero had to confront and then triumph against adversity and unhappy circumstance. The only trouble was that, for the life of me, I couldn't work out how to get out of this last situation.

In the end, it was easier to go along with the well-meaning falsehoods of my doctor. After all, as Angie would have said, nothing fools you better than the lies you tell yourself. To her credit, it was good advice.

My psychiatrist was professionally pleasant, but brisk and pointed in her attempts to dissect my condition. She dressed in bright clothes that, even I could tell, were a bit too young and a bit too tight for her. I felt that it was an attempt to distract from her faded good looks and the grey peg-like teeth I could see on the occasions when she smiled.

Her office had a distinctive smell of decaying rubber because the carpet was threadbare and needed replacing. My chair was the familiar institutional green with wipe-down plastic upholstery.

"Hmm, that's interesting, Nicky," she would remark. "Why do you think that was important to you?"

"Well, at the time, it wasn't important. It was only afterwards, when I realised what was happening," I would answer vaguely, without committing to detail. This bought me some time to come up with an answer that was more to her liking. I couldn't ask my dad, even though he was waiting for me in the corridor and she said that he could be with me if I wanted.

Instead, I thought back to what Paul Baxter would say in this situation. Paul the comedian, calm and collected under pressure, the one who took charge of me after the funeral. I modelled my answers on what he might say.

"I'd like you to be as candid as you can, please, Nicky." She looked over her glasses at me, her pen poised over the notes.

"Well," I paused, trying to formulate a Paul-like answer. "I've always tried to look after people so that they would like me, I suppose. I need to be kind," I lied. "I just try to be the best person I can be."

"That's good, Nicky. Let's explore what you mean by that; do you think that you should always be kind?"

"No. But you should always try, even if it's difficult." That was a lie as well. I hadn't been kind to my parents for a long time. But of course, they had neglected me well before then, throughout all my early teenage years.

"Why don't you give me an example of when you've been kind, and then tell me about a time when you didn't do as well as you hoped?"

She was relentless in trying to get the truth out of me. It was like being shunted into the molecular scanner every week to slice out my synapses down to the individual atom.

After ten sessions that autumn, her phrase 'let's explore what you mean', had really begun to irritate me. I formed the strong suspicion that she kept me on her list and asked the pointed questions because she wanted to write me up as a case report. I would be described as a juvenile male affected with an unusual manifestation (as I learned much later) of delusional misidentification syndrome, precipitated by a traumatic bereavement.

But I co-operated because I quite liked the idea of her naming it Valko's syndrome so that I could be glorified with a medical eponym. Being written up as a case report was the fate that befell Angela, so it was nice to share that with her even though it was posthumous. The world of the Imposters and the Master receded during that autumn, just as Ship had foreseen and had promised.

I caught myself one day wanting to go out to the Troc again with Spex, Diane and the gang for the sake of old times. It was exactly what I would think if the Imposters had won after all. Eventually, I would even forget the importance they had for me, and I would believe that they were just something that I had invented with Jon.

I didn't discuss this with the psychiatrist, but it struck me that almost everybody sincerely believed in lots of odd things that were obviously imaginary. I wasn't alone in constructing elaborate, even convoluted, narratives that tried to make sense of the world, but only existed because people agreed that they existed. For me, the real puzzles were ideas like money or countries or religion.

Money was just bits of paper and metal disks, but people were always talking about it or wanting more of it. People had been going out on strike across the country because they weren't being given enough of it, as far as I could work out. I never had enough of it but unfortunately, society dictated that only certain metal disks were legal tender. I couldn't use the metal washers produced by Spex in his dad's garage to pay for anything, phone calls included.

Another imaginary reality was the idea of England as a country, so compelling an idea that neo-Nazi skinheads wanted it to belong to only scum like them. The gang had got into the fight in Harlesden because of the differing views about what should define this imaginary view of the world.

And of course, the whole basis for religious belief and religion was imaginary. I had not succumbed to the enticing lies, even though they were at their most dangerous and I was at my weakest when I was with Angie. I didn't turn to them afterwards. It would have been laughable if it wasn't so tragic because, as I had seen, Angie's god had not spared her despite the sensible and staid Methodism practiced by the Wilkinson's.

She would have calmly explained to me that God, in his infinite powers and infinite goodness, had created the best of all possible worlds because His failure to do so would have diminished the perfection of His creation. God, she had told me, had a perfect plan for her but, for the life of me (and for the death of her), I was still bemused what it could have been.

I was bemused that people could somehow believe in these imaginary things without question, whereas I had to come in every Tuesday morning to talk to the trick-cyclist because my delusions weren't acceptable to society.

In the meantime, following the bank robbery by Paul McElroy and towards the end of my course of sessions, Brian Wilkinson's life unravelled still further. Money was far from an imaginary concept in this instance, it turned out. After an investigation into the bank records and accounts, prompted by the original robbery, the police arrested Wilkinson at the end of September.

He was charged with embezzlement and fraud, then released on bail to face the court of public opinion before his trial in November. He lost his job at the bank and his wife left him. The Wilkinson's nice modern house on the posh new estate was sold.

I would have liked some photos or some little mementos of Angie, but I never found out what happened to her things or where the ex-Mrs Wilkinson moved to afterwards. I presume that she got the Sodastream, the microwave and the colour telly, and that she went back south to live with her parents.

She had always been quite nice to me, unconvinced though she was about my suitability for her daughter, and I was sorry that her life had turned into such a tragedy. The misfortunes just seemed to stack up for her in the most unfair way imaginable. Prayers to her Methodist god hadn't helped Angie and then hadn't stopped her husband straying from the righteous path.

I don't know what happened to Wilkinson while he was on bail. Some people said that he moved into the local hotel, the Novello, which at the time, was a popular boarding house for actors touring in repertory companies. I then heard that someone in his Methodist congregation took pity on him and offered him somewhere to stay, but this was before the full truth about him came out.

Towards the end of my psychiatry sessions, I began to doubt if even these had any overall rational basis and were just yet more invention and self-delusion. So, I had nothing to lose. Every Tuesday, I recounted the details of my personal hero narrative to my psychiatrist to pass the time, and she looked over her glasses at me and took notes in the yellow foolscap pad.

The psychiatrist wanted me to be better. Her genuine belief was that the best way would be for me to revoke the reality of my narratives. But for me, it was more complicated. They were too laden with a mythical and archetypal quality to allow me to dismiss them that easily; they were almost too meaningful, too full of metaphorical and metaphysical significance for me, as if I had drawn back a flimsy curtain to reveal the unsuspected depths to this reality.

You could go through your entire life without suspecting their existence but, distressing though it had been for myself and everybody else, I still felt fortunate to have realised that they were there. It just needed the right situation for them to manifest and, at a touch, I could experience them again in all their completeness.

I began to doubt if anything was really that wrong with me, and that I was just more blessed than anybody else in experiencing such a profound and life-changing event. But I kept this to myself because it would have exasperated my psychiatrist. If I tried to explain, I wondered if her professional mask would abruptly slip, and she would snap that I was even having delusions about my delusions.

After each session, my father would look at me wordlessly, greyer and more owlish than ever, and I recognised pain and bewilderment lining his face. I understood that he took no small sense of responsibility for all that had happened to me. It was true; he should have been a better father to me, but I could see the remorse and guilt knotting his insides and pricking his eyes. That, at least, was something genuine and real that had resulted from all those interminable, painful sessions in the molecular scanner.

"Dad. It's alright," I said to him. "The doctor's very nice and she's really helping me come to terms with it all. All that happened. None of it was your fault!"

"I know, I know, *Kolya*. It was just stupid tragedy. I know you miss your Angela. She was a nice girl, I suppose."

"No your about it, Dad. Don't think that she belonged to anybody, least of all me. And I don't think that she was that nice either, to be honest."

"Ah, it is sometimes like this with a woman. Sometimes, she is just not that good. It is nothing in herself, just when it is you and her together. You understand? There is attraction but it is not enough. It becomes difficult."

"Yeah, I think you tried to tell me that right at the start of it all. She certainly wasn't good for me."

"Good for you? Yes, but what I mean, she was not good to you, I think?"

"Yes, now that you mention it, she wasn't good to me either. Or with me."

"Hmph," he grumbled. "These English—what are they?—prepositions. I'm just saying that it was bad for everybody."

I mentioned this to Paul Baxter, our comedian, now that we were all back at school, in the hope that he would cheer me up somehow with some humorous observations about my predicament. However, Angie was the cousin nearest to him in age and they had been close, so I found him uncharacteristically quiet and serious.

I hadn't been forthcoming about my psychiatry sessions, other than I was talking to someone about my unfortunate experiences in London. Or interstellar space, depending on your preferred alternative reality. It was an open secret at school that I'd had a 'funny turn', as it was euphemistically called in the old-fashioned phrase, but it was understandable because it was all about love and I had a broken heart.

No one teased me about it because I had moved up in the school hierarchy. I was no longer just a member of our gang of misfits because, in addition, I was now viewed as the dangerously unhinged one who was tarnished by the mystique of personal tragedy. It was unlucky to even associate with me in case the curse was passed on.

This suited me just fine because it meant that kids left me alone. Paul and I hadn't spoken since the events following the funeral. I had never even thanked him for saving me from the immediate consequences of my car vandalism. He hadn't come to London to work on Drillbit's job with us because it had coincided with his family's holiday on the Costa Brava.

Then it had all become confused, and we didn't see each other for the rest of the summer. And everybody else in the gang had been busy over the summer as well because, unconscionable as it seemed to me, life carried on for some of us. Spex and Diane had gone off to see his vegetarian pals in London for the Notting Hill Carnival. So, like many others, what Paul had heard about was just the rumours going around school during the first week back.

I wondered if he had been avoiding me until now, either because of my unlucky curse or because he was embarrassed at dealing with me. Perhaps he just didn't have a handy repertoire of gags about mental patients.

"Hi Nicky, hear you've had an eventful old summer." *'Understatement of the year,'* I thought. "How are you?" he added.

"Hi Paul, yeah, you could say that. I took it all pretty hard, you saw me after the funeral. Thanks for that, by the way. It could've got ugly. Really ugly."

"Yeah, sure. I know it's hard. Just have to hang in there."

'Oh, c'mon Paul, like you would really understand,' I thought. *'You're just her cousin.'*

"I know," I replied, trying to agree with him. "Diane keeps telling me that time is a great healer and stuff like that. I don't think that I'll ever move on from what I feel for her."

"It was all so sudden," Paul said, shaking his head.

"That it was, Paul," I sighed. *'What was it with the platitudes? Didn't he know me and what it all meant to me? Didn't he know what I'd been through?'* I felt indignant, as if Paul was being deliberately obtuse and oafish. It was completely out of character for him. "Like you said at the time, just a stupid, shitty accident," I added.

"There was nothing anybody could have done. You mustn't blame yourself for any of it."

"I don't blame myself, Paul. All I want to know is how she got it right at the start. Why was she the unlucky one?"

"I don't know, Nicky. Sometimes there just aren't any answers."

I couldn't talk to Paul directly about what I was feeling, so I tried to approach it by mentioning my father's frustration with prepositions and my response to it. This was a mistake because Paul looked stricken when I told him the stupid anecdote.

"You can't come out with stuff like that, Nick!" he said. "You know, *de mortuis nil nisi bonum* or however you say it."

"What do you mean?" I hadn't understood the phrase, of course, and as usual, Paul was deliberately showing-off. Unusually, Paul had been taught Latin at our comprehensive school. It had been a short-lived experiment when the old grammar schoolteachers were still around and hadn't yet been pensioned off. I didn't receive the benefits of any classical education because I had been streamed into doing sciences, in as much as I was doing anything at school.

I had forgotten about the dullness of facts and figures over the past couple of months. Now that we were back at school, I was struggling to apply the dull blade of my academic ability to reap a meagre harvest.

"I was going out with her, and she wasn't that easy to be with, you know?" I felt that Paul, out of all my friends, had known her best and would understand what I meant. Speccy-Paul was wary of her; Jon certainly found her irritating, for the trivial reason that she teased him about sci-fi, as she called it.

"You can't slag her off like that! It's no excuse," Paul replied with some heat. *'What the heck?'* I thought. *'What's his problem?'*

"Oh, c'mon Paul. It's not that simple. She may have been a church-girl, but she wasn't all sweetness and light."

"No, it's not that simple," he replied with finality. "There's a lot you don't know, Nicky, about the Wilkinson's."

"Like what, Paul? Angie died and her old man cooked the books at his bank. Guess which one I'm upset about?"

"No, you don't understand. My family has seen what Brian Wilkinson is like; he's not a nice man."

"We know that already."

Paul's voice dropped. "No, he's properly bad. He drinks. He gets crazy when he's drunk. That's what they say about him."

"So, for a Methodist lay preacher, it's more do as I say not as I do?"

Paul grimaced. "Hairy, listen, will you? My family say that he hits his wife when he's drunk. And that he hit Angela more than once."

"I don't believe it! She never said a bad word against him. He doted on her. Why would he do that?"

"I don't know. I'm sorry, it's just what I've heard."

"But Angie; she never said anything about this to you, Paul, did she?"

"No, she didn't. But she didn't have to. You heard the way she spoke when he was around, the way she wasn't comfortable if he was there in the room?"

"That sounds like me and my dad, to be honest. Pretty normal for our house."

"Don't be flippant, Nick. Did she ever say anything to you?" Now that Paul had committed to this conversation, he was going to cross-examine me until it was resolved one way or another.

"No, she never did." But I thought back to how sweet and how caustic she could be within a span of seconds—the Odette and Odile of her personality—and how confused and miserable it had made me feel. At the funfair, why had she said that I wouldn't know wicked if it slapped me in the face?

From May, it had been a phrase that had haunted me because it was so unexpected and cutting. I had been unable to put it into the right context until this moment. I realised the truth of it with a sick lurch that caught my breath. Once again, it felt as if pieces were fitting together to form the whole picture.

"Nick." His quiet tone told me he had more to say. "You remember how Angie used to show us that scar on her thigh?"

"Yes, I remember," I said. *How could I forget it?* "It was the Beechwood kids that stabbed her. When they invaded our school."

"No, I don't think so. It was Brian Wilkinson. He did it and Angie was too afraid of him to talk about it. That's what we think, anyway."

"What, he stabbed his own daughter with a fork? Are you kidding me?" *'Paul's making this up,'* I thought. *'Who would do that? I can't believe it.'* But again, I began to recognise the truth of it. Why would Paul, one of my oldest friends, lie to me? The obvious answer was that Paul was subverted and trying to manipulate me.

However, the psychiatrist would tell me that this was a manifestation of my unsound inner state and that by recognising the reality of my situation, I would begin to get better. I didn't want to disappoint her, despite the lack of friendly feeling between us, so I felt obliged to say, "Are you sure, Paul? If he really did that, he must be one twisted bastard!"

"Yeah, I know. And she never said who had done it, did she?" added Paul. "She just blamed a Beechwooder. My folks all say it should've been a police matter right at the start, way back then. Wilkinson should have been banged up years ago."

"What does Diane think? Does she know?" *Surely, Angie would have unburdened these secrets to her best friend and confidante.*

"I don't know, Hairy. I'm guessing not." And it was true that Diane had never taken me to one side and hinted, in a whisper, that things 'weren't alright at home' for Angela and that I should 'look after her'. She had never warned me that there were darker depths below the surface. She, along with the rest of us in the gang, were happy to bob along on top and not dive into those depths.

I'm sure that I was not the only one who, if they didn't understand, they just ignored it. With the gang, it had always been about simple fun and laughter until, suddenly, it wasn't.

Chapter 9
A Punk Rocker's Guide to Saving the World

Ma McElroy got released on bail and sought me out again through Johnny Ronson. The charges against her of conspiracy to commit robbery were dropped due to lack of evidence. Paul McElroy got five years in the big house because it was a first offence as an adult. His eight-year-old brother had re-appeared but denied any knowledge of the rest of the cash because he had been staying at his auntie's.

Again, the evidence was circumstantial, and inexplicably, the cash itself disappeared without trace. All it meant was that bent coppers had trousered it in return for going easy on Ma McElroy. No one wanted the McElroy's to lose their influence on local organised criminality because after all, they were a known blight on the area and their protection rackets were a nice earner for everybody.

Paul explained to me much later that the McElroy family and clients were tolerated by the Five-Oh because they were a hedge against the new drug gangs coming over from London and Manchester. Drugs, at least, were not part of the traditional and old-fashioned McElroy business interests.

Mr Ronson drove up with Ma McElroy in the passenger seat of *La Cucaracha*. She wound the window down and appraised me for a long minute. Her auburn hair and heavy eyeliner were an appropriate decoration for bright red and chrome bodywork of the car, as if a stylised piece of Americana had rolled up.

It was glitzy for our street, particularly at that time of the morning, but I couldn't help feeling that she looked like a high-class hooker. I wondered if that's how she had started her career with the McElroy clan.

"Yes?" I said uncomfortably. "I remember you. You're Lisa McElroy, aren't you?"

"Oh, it's alright Nick-Oh, love," murmured Mr Ronson, pliable and agreeable as always. "Lisa's just 'ere to have another one of her cosy chats with ya. She was worried about you."

"Nicky," she said. "How are you?"

"I don't know if I'm honest." I immediately understood that this was a serious interview with an intimidating and probably quite dangerous woman. It was not a cosy chat, despite Johnny Ronson's assurances, so I tried to be honest with her. "Muddling on somehow, I suppose."

"You and the rest of us; that's good to hear. Do you need anything? You know I do right by me an' mine?"

"Thank you, that's kind of you but I can't think of anything." I certainly didn't want any more of their loopy-juice whiskey.

"Do you remember what I said, Nicky? About righting some wrongs, if we could? Our Paul, he's such a treasure, such a clever lad, he got it straight away."

"I'm sorry; got what?"

"That the Wilkinson fella needed to go down."

"Are all of the stories true about him, then? I've heard some bad rumours from Paul. I mean, the other Paul; Paul Baxter."

"Yes, I know him. There's a lot being said about Brian Wilkinson now. Our Paul knows a lot more about it. Just wish it had come out sooner."

"So, those rumours are true?"

"Our Paul thought so; he thought it was worth a punt blackmailing Wilkinson. It paid off," she said proudly. "That's why Wilkinson had to steal from the accounts. And then it was our Paul's idea to do over the bank so that Wilkinson would get investigated. Head Office always run an audit of accounts after a robbery."

"And you tipped off the cops," I said, slow realisation bubbling up like mud from the depths.

"We gave 'em an incentive to know what to find," Lisa McElroy replied laconically.

"You bribed the cops!"

"Yes. Oh, Nicky! Stop being so soft!" She had seen me recoil from her casual boasting. "Some people deserve to be punished. Jimmy's spreading it inside and Pauly will be now. Wilkinson needs to watch his back when he gets locked up. And there's no doubt, he will be."

I stared at her in confusion. She was boasting about ensnaring and then ruining a bad man, a suspected embezzler and abuser. I had no affection or respect for Brian Wilkinson, but did the ends really justify the means? Or, as Angela would have said, did two wrongs really make a right?

In my view of the world, I suppose that I could not reconcile the thought that bad people could sometimes do good things in spite of themselves. If that was true, then good people could sometimes be bad. I thought of Mrs Wilkinson and what compromises she had to make to live with such a husband and father of her child.

Perhaps the nice modern house, kitchen, and car on the drive had allowed her to ignore the worst of it. But that made her complicit in everything that had happened to Angela at the hands of Brian Wilkinson.

"You need to thank our Paul when he gets out," continued Ma McElroy, mistaking my silence for acquiescence to what the McElroy's had done. "It was personal for him this time. He'll want to speak to you." I didn't know if that was a threat or a promise, but it sounded mildly ominous coming from her.

"I'll visit him. In prison, I mean." I don't know why I said that. I had no real intention of visiting McElroy the Younger in or out of youth prison, but it felt inevitable that we were bound together, in our own way, through the misfortunes of the Wilkinson's.

"Nah, you don't need to; he'll be out soon enough. He's being looked after inside. Don't want a weird posh boy like you causing him trouble. No offence."

"Why, what trouble would I be? And I'm not offended, by the way."

"It wouldn't help anyone if you went," she replied, the axe-chop in her voice quite distinct by now. "Let's leave it at that."

And with that, my timber was well-and-truly chopped. That was enough discouragement for me and of course, I never visited Paul McElroy in prison. In this instance, I was glad that I had such a malleable personality and that I could be so easily persuaded.

I floated along on the surface and continued with my life. If I dived down into the dark silty depths, then I would remember that the Imposters had won, and my life was not as it seemed. That was a disquieting thought that had to be suppressed, a realisation that had to be deflected whenever I drifted closer to the truth, just as the psychiatrist had told me.

She was an Imposter, of course, but none of it mattered now because my memories of the summer became blunt and then lost their hold on me. I didn't hurt so much when I was floating away, swept away downstream from the Tunnel of Death, I suppose, with a fake sort of happiness on the surface. In the end, I chose this reality and all the alternates receded into memory, together with all of my personal mythology that I had constructed around that time.

I saw a distinctive building, or grey rain falling in sheets, or the blueness of the sky at twilight, or heard a music track from Angie's Mix-Tape. They chimed with me, as if they were echoes of those powerful totems in my mythology, but I had forgot what they meant and why they were important to me. In this reality, I had lost the vibrancy that these totems could evoke for me, as if a glass wall had come between me and everything else connected with my past.

My totems passed into memory while I, unaware of the change, drifted downstream into an ordinary life. So, I had bad days and I had just days. Lots and lots and lots of days. Ordinary days repeating and stretching out before me; days without her. And yet, underneath it all, suppressed and ignored, was the draw to be immersed again in the dark depths, as if I still had a distant apprehension of all that I had lost.

At the end of that long year, we understood that something had happened and that it had changed us forever. '*Something happened,*' I thought, '*something tragic and heart-breaking.*' It felt as if chaos had engulfed not just my life but, as the year wore on, everybody else's as well. In our town, amid this chaos, the National Front seemed to thrive and begin to take over whole neighbourhoods.

Their graffiti was crudely daubed on walls to demarcate their territory, as if they were dogs leaving chalky turds that got baked on pavements in the sun. Paul said that calling them morons was an insult to imbeciles and idiots. You ran the genuine risk of a beating if you were on your own in an NF area and looked—as we did—posh (Paul) or left-wing (Spex) or, in fact, just fairly normal (Jon and Neville). The gang needed no reminders about the NF after London.

Spex was surprised that we would be so willing to go with him and Diane to a Rock Against Racism gig at the Polytechnic on that Friday night in October. We all knew what we were united against, and it was right that our gang of misfits kept together now, more than ever, because we were all targets. If we could be targets, then where would it stop?

Spex told us that the different NF regiments or chapters, or whatever they were, in our town had a league for how many reds they could rip off in the middle of the street. The bovver boys knew about these Rock Against Racism gigs and where to come so that they could wait for us outside. But Spex, of course, had a scheme to try to keep us out of trouble.

For my part, I hid a deep, unquenchable rage against the unfairness of this reality in which I had to live with Imposters. I thought that I had got rid of them finally, but it seemed, I was mistaken. '*They are an inextricable part of your humanity,*' I remembered Ship telling me. It had all been pointless.

This was all there would be for me now, after Angela Wilkinson, after I had run to the outside of everything. I'd made sure that there was no possibility of rescue or reprieve. So, I felt quite good about the chance for some payback and getting even with some neo-Nazi skinheads. They were so moronic—idiotic, even—they didn't even know that they had been subverted.

Spex and Diane knew yet another Paul who organised the Rock Against Racism gigs at the Poly. Spex somehow persuaded him that Ratty, Drillbit and a few of their building-and-boozing pals would be able to run security on the door. Ratty was the obvious hard-man, we all knew, who could hold his own against anyone.

The gang would give them a hand during the gig because of our recent skirmish in the trenches, as Paul called it. Afterwards, we would all get a couple of free drinks and have a chat with the bands. It seemed like another excellent scheme from Spex. That Friday night in late October, The Mekons were the obscure local punk outfit that started the set.

Afterwards, Spex said that they were the very embodiment of punk because none of them could play and even better, none of them cared. They shambled onto the stage, all of them drunk by now, revelling in their musical incompetence. For their last song, their newest release, they ripped into The Clash with 'Never Been in a Riot.'

I'm always on the toilet
Pissing out the noise

"It's a piss-take of 'White Riot'!" hooted Spex, half-aghast and half delighted, bouncing up and down but still unsure if he should pogo to it. Well-educated muso that he was, Spex had got the reference straight away. "Bloody 'ell! It's so crap it's great." It was back-to-basics punk because they were questioning the very medium that they were using to make their anarchic statement.

Spex had got the whole irony of The Mekons' approach to their music; punk was even rebelling against punk itself, and he loved it. They became a firm favourite on future editions of his mix-tapes.

"Never liked that Clash song to be fair and we could play better than them! I'm not kidding," commented Paul.

"I think that's the point, Paul. They're makin' it up as they go along. It could be us up there!"

"And there was I, thinking they're a complete joke."

I was thinking back to that cover version of 'White Riot' at the Sham 69 gig, and what it had stirred up from the depths of the London silt. I had to agree about the song; calling for a white riot was always going to be misunderstood. Then, I remembered that I had been there with Angela by my side, and she had defended us; we had got drunk afterwards at that party and I ended up doubting her even more, yet again, watching the sunrise over north London.

That sequence of memories washed over me suddenly, unprompted and unstoppable, as if I'd flicked a switch and they lit up in my head, one after the other.

"Are ya alright, Hairy?" asked Jon, concern tingeing his voice. I'm sure that Jon was thinking back to my unfortunate incident in the labyrinth of that hospital basement and was praying that I wouldn't flip out again. He must have noticed that I was looking distracted. We were standing at the back of the gig, laughably trying to help with security by looking out for trouble-makers.

We were in a cavernous basement venue that appeared to be even bigger because it was painted black throughout. During the changeover between bands, someone had turned on the purple black-light tubes overhead. They glowed, making our T-shirts bright blue and our teeth a pale green.

"Yeah, I'm fine," I lied. "Never better. Good gig, isn't it?"

"Nah, that lot were rubbish. Next lot can play, at least, or that's what Spex sez. If you like reggae." Misty in Roots would finish the set that evening.

"Always open to new stuff, you know me."

"They've been on John Peel."

"Oh. That's nice for them—" But before I could finish that little sarcastic remark, Paul appeared from the back of the venue.

"If you two were doing your jobs, you'd have seen the skinheads at the bar. That bastard Jonesy is with them; I'm telling Ratty."

"Jonesy? Is he the one with the McElroy's—?" started Jon, but Paul was already moving off to the main doors at the side.

"Didn't he beat Paul up?" I asked Jon. "What's he doing here?"

"Causing trouble or ripping people off. No other reason. We need to get them out."

We could see Ratty and his pals were moving as a group through the back of the crowd over to the bar. The Misty in Roots collective were coming out on to the stage, to applause and whistles, so it was thinning out here at the back. The front lights were picking out the lead singer and guitarist. Then, as the main lights were going down, without any warning and without a word, Paul ran out from behind Ratty's security detail. He reached out and slammed Jonesy's head against the bar.

"Shite!" Jon and I started running over, shoving people out of the way.

Jonesy was stunned and as he tried to turn around, Paul elbowed him in the neck, with a leg behind him, so that he got him on the ground. Paul managed to get in one feeble kick to the chest before Ratty and Drillbit were there, restraining him and shouting.

Two of Jonesy's skinhead friends started to crowd them, also shouting furiously, until abruptly, it all became even crazier. Rita, Spex's cousin, appeared from behind the skinheads and tried to shove in between the two groups. I realised that one of the skinheads was Rita's boyfriend and I'd seen him before at the Troc. But Mr Spanish—and I recognised him immediately as the bouncer from the Troc—was ignoring Ratty and was goading the skinheads.

"C'mon, man, take a poke with this Jamaican, yeah? Heard ya don' like our sort. Have a poke and see what happens next, yeah?"

"Spanish!" shouted Rita. "Leave it; they're not like that! Please, stop it!"

"Are ya daft or summat, Rita?" said Spex. "He's with the McElroy's. He beat up Paul. Yeah, that's right! That one," he added, pointing to Paul Baxter when he saw that Rita was about to object. "Ya can't expect anything better."

"Oi! Spex, shut it! Spanish, back off!" Ratty shouted. "Everyone out; tek it outside now."

"Why, big man? We didnae want any trouble! It was this wee keech!" said the other skinhead angrily, shoving past Rita so that he could keep his grip on Jonesy. He had a strong Scottish accent that almost sounded like he was putting it on.

"'Ey, shove off Jock! It's now't to do wi' you."

"C'mon man, let's take it outside, yeah? I'm ready, man."

"Spanish! Pack it in!"

"Shurrit, yer gonna get proper battered," shouted Rita's boyfriend.

I turned and glanced at Jon, shaking my head to mutely ask him why everybody was acting like a knob-end. These were not what my friends were like; they were funny, cool, and composed. They were better than this! Where was their sudden violence coming from? Spanish, if the stories were true about him, had every reason to keep a low profile.

What was his problem? But I knew the answer already: *this is what happens to those people you remember after they've been subverted.* The Master had exiled me here and was having the last laugh, watching me squirm like an insect on the floor. This was what it had planned all along. *'I've been played from the start,'* I thought. *'I was stupid to think I even had a chance.'*

"Oh, Jesus! Hold his head someone! Quick, hold his head!" The high note of alarm in Diane's voice cut through the stupidity and brought them to their senses. Jon saw and understood instantly. It was his brother, Drillbit.

"Gerr'im! 'E's having a seizure. Gerr'is head!" Rita was the closest. Neville slumped in her arms and she, sprawled underneath him, eased him to the floor. She squatted awkwardly on one of her Docs, looking wild-eyed.

"Shite. What do we do?"

"Recovery position. Get him into the recovery position. He could choke on his tongue."

"Richard!" (This, shouted to Ratty). "Richard! Quick, we need an ambulance! Where's the phone?"

"What's wrong with 'im?"

Drillbit was on the floor, eyes looking up blankly, then rolling back to show the whites. He was moaning softly, as if he had words in his throat but couldn't articulate them. He was drooling, wet lips twitching.

"*Uhh. Oh uhh. Uhh,*" he moaned softly. It was a weak, repetitive animal noise, terrifying because I'd never heard this kind of sound from a person before. He looked like a washed-out rag under the strip-lights by the entrance doors.

"Nev! Neville! Stay with us. C'mon, man." This was Ratty. He was gesturing to one of the bar staff who was already talking on the phone. "Check his pulse."

"How?"

"Big artery in his neck. Put yer fingers on it. Is there a pulse? Paul? C'mon! Is there a pulse?"

"There's nothing. There's no pulse. Oh my God! Ratty, what does that mean? What's wrong with him?"

"Jesus. Let me try." A long pause. "Shite. Where's that ambulance?"

Two policemen were there, then, appearing in between the two groups. They must have been in the area, and been dispatched quickly, because they had been expecting trouble at this gig. Afterwards, Paul said that both had removed their numbers on the shoulder epaulette, although one of them was wearing the stripes. Stripes must have been in charge and there was probably a whole squad of them in a nearby van.

"What's the matter with him, son? Drugs overdose, is it?"

"No! Not at all. He has epilepsy. 'E's 'aving a seizure. He needs help now!"

"Ambulance is on its way. Who are you, son?"

"I'm his brother. Jon, Jonathan Holdsworth."

"Well, don't you worry, Jon. It's all going to be fine. What's his name?"

"Neville. It's not fine; I think he's had an 'eart attack or summat. I should never have brought him!"

The policemen leaned over Drillbit and Rita. Drillbit was pasty and his eyes bulged, unseeing, as if they were eggs about to burst. The pupils were tiny. He had stopped making that soft, keening sound.

"Neville! Come on, son. Wake up!" The policeman pinched his ear, then slapped his face. There was no response. He tried to find a pulse in the carotid artery, just like Paul had tried a minute before. The policemen exchanged glances. "Steve, radio the Blues; code 2, suspected CA," one of them said. "Start resus now; 'scuse me, love." He pushed past Rita. "Let's get him on the floor."

"Jesus! What's wrong with him? Nev, wake up!" Rita, glassy-eyed and expressionless, carried on holding Neville's hand. Jonesy stood by with his two skinhead pals, absently holding his cheek, the conflict burnt out of them by this new drama. The policemen took turns in doing chest compressions, trying their best to stop Drillbit's life from ebbing away. The other one of them glanced at his watch and did the rescue breaths every half-minute.

"Sarge, I'll take over," said Steve, the younger one with the radio, when he saw his colleague tiring.

The chest compressions were brutal, as if Drillbit was being assaulted by the policeman in a regular and systematic way. The air moved in and out of his open mouth with a hollow whistling sound, but at least his fingers and lips were twitching. His eyes still bulged but he wasn't blinking.

We stood by watching, transfixed and appalled, useless and unable to help in any way. I felt the same abrupt horror descend from that January evening, an epoch ago now it seemed, when we accidently nearly killed Chris Thompson. It was our karma punishing us for past crimes; why should I be surprised that this, now, was the outcome?

The Imposters made sure that they would always win in the end. Poor old stuttering, pretentious, kind-hearted Neville was their latest victim. Yet again, more abrupt horror was being dragged out from the depths, confronting us in the ordinary world. This was the unconscionable truth in this reality, however much I wished that it was different.

Blue flashes highlighted the raindrops on the glass of the main doors, an intricate cascade arrangement of brilliant lapis lazuli jewels. I remembered Neville had told us that, ground down, lapis lazuli made a pigment prized by the Renaissance painters. It was the only one used for the blue mantle of the Virgin Mary.

Marian Blue, he called it, the colour of virgins and angels, the colour of the ineffable and the untouchable. *'Oh, Angela!'* I thought. *'Who else can I ask? All I'm asking for is one little miracle. Spare Neville's life, you can do that, can't you? He's a good man. He is my friend. He doesn't deserve this, none of us do.'*

But then my imagination started to draw my attention away from the drama with Drillbit, ashamed though I am to admit it now. I suppose that I was in shock. The pattern of the blue jewels was too familiar and captivating; the trajectories and nodes were mapping out what the nanomachines had created in my brain. *Flash, flash, flash.*

It was tracing out a living, pulsing representation of an autonomous neural network. *'If only I could use the Blue Goo. It would save him! If only it was real. If only I was in that other reality, Angela would be alive, and Neville wouldn't have to die.'* The doors were shoved open by two paramedics in green uniforms, and I was brought back to this present existence.

"Cardiac arrest, yes? How long ago?" one the paramedics asked.

"Six, maybe seven, minutes," replied the sergeant. The paramedic grimaced. "Any SOL?"

The policeman shone his torch into one of Drillbit's eyes. "Yeah, I think so."

"Thanks, lads, good work. We'll take it from here. Don't think he's a DOA but you'd better follow us, just in case. Still a fighting chance," the paramedic said to the rest of us on the pavement.

"I'm really sorry, son," said the sergeant to Jon. "You'll need to go with him. Get in the back. We'll meet you at the hospital."

The paramedics took Drillbit and Jon away in the back of the ambulance. Jon could barely move the folding chair because he was shaking so much. Everybody, in unspoken agreement, thought that it was already too late when the paramedics closed the back doors. But Jon later told us that they had used a defibrillator in the back of the ambulance, Drillbit had jerked with the shock, and that he was soon breathing on his own.

They put him on a high oxygen mix and drove off, the lights and siren splitting the night. By the time they arrived at the Workhouse, Drillbit could manage the steps at the back of the ambulance. He was very lucky. The police tried to find Mr and Mrs Holdsworth when he was admitted, but, because it was a suspicious incident, Jon had to give a witness statement for the police paperwork.

They only brought Jon back home early the next morning. Jon insisted that they stopped at Spex's house and mine so that he could tell us that Drillbit was alright. Neither of our houses had a phone line.

Misty in Roots had started their set some time ago, but I was only conscious of it when I came back inside, after seeing the ambulance drive off. Nobody else had even noticed the music or the rain outside. Rita was crying, mascara streaming down her cheeks, comforted by her boyfriend.

"His hand was still warm," she repeated softly. We began to realise just what kind of extraordinary incident had happened in front of us, in this most unremarkable of settings. It had happened on some black, scuffed lino in front of some beat-up, old glass doors. None of us had seen someone be seriously unwell like that before.

Jonesy came up to me.

"I'm sorry about yer pal. He's called Drillbit, int 'e?"

"His name's Neville."

"What's wrong wi' 'im?"

"I don't really know. Epilepsy, I think. He's had seizures before, but this was a really bad one."

"Is he gonna be alright?"

"I don't know. The ambulance-man seemed hopeful. I don't know what to think." I paused. "Don't mean to be rude, but do you know him?" *'Why do you care, Jonesy?'* I thought.

"Angela Wilkinson said how much she liked him. She said she hung around with you lot."

"Yeah, that's right. But what's Angela to you, Jonesy? How come you knew her too?"

He smirked. "Oh, it wa' proper daft. Paul shagged her a couple of times." He meant Paul McElroy the Younger. "He went down for her, stupid bastard; it was 'cos of all that bad stuff with her old man."

"Why's that, Jonesy?"

"Her dad. Wilkinson, 'e worr'a nonce; it wa' proper bad stuff an' all. He gave her that cancer, that's what Pauly thinks. Passed on the badness to 'er. Wilkinson's gonna get wha' he deserves and Pauly put him there," he added proudly. "Tell ya, guys like Wilkinson make me sick. Yeah, they get what they deserve."

"Were they going out for long?"

"What, Paul and Angela? Nah, it wa' just a fling. Guess she got wet n' wild with him, then went back to her boyfriend when it suited her."

"I know. That was me. I was the boyfriend."

"Shit! No way! Really?" He stopped and I could see the understanding dawn on his face. "I really didn't know. Soz about that. I was just talkin' ya know. I didn't mean to—" He stopped again. Even Jonesy could feel empathy and remorse, it seemed.

"Shit!" He swore again. "I'm really sorry."

"It's alright. 'S'not your fault. Angela was her own woman, you know? She didn't belong to me."

"Yeah, sure," said Jonesy. "She wa' one of kind, I know that much. Think that Paul felt sorry for her, after all that bad stuff."

"What stuff?"

"Oh, I don't really know," he said vaguely. "It wa' rumours, mostly. Ma will know better"

"Lisa McElroy. Of course! Oh, she knew all along. That's what she was trying to tell me. God, I could've worked it out if I'd listened to her and Jon." I turned to go out into the darkness outside again. "I need to get out of here."

"Hang on, jus' one more thing." Jonesy caught up with me and put his hand on my shoulder. "Johnny knows where you live, right? I'll get Ma—Lisa, that is—to visit ya. I think that she has somethin' for you."

Diane had come over with Spex by now, apprehension and guilt in her eyes. She had guessed what we were talking about and could now see that I'd finally learned about Angela's secret.

"I'm sorry, Nicky, do you know?" said Diane.

"Oh, you're Nicky. I get it now. Shit, what a night," said Jonesy.

"Why didn't you tell me? I thought we were friends."

"She made me promise not to say anything," Diane said in a small voice. "I couldn't break my promise."

"Well, it didn't seem to bother her too much. She made me some promises too. I guess that promises are just for kids after all."

"Paul and Jon tried to talk to you. You know; that she wasn't the right one for you. Our Paul, that is," she added in an aside to Jonesy.

"So," I said, as it become clear, and the betrayal began to weigh down in my stomach and guts. "Everybody else knew apart from me!"

They had kept the bond of our *omertà* about something serious, but without even including me as a member of the gang. *'Ah Nicky, you're a right fool,'* I thought to myself. *'They all became Imposters without you even noticing.'*

"Well, no; it wasn't like that at all, Nicky," flustered Diane. "You know it wasn't." *'Seems that I can't even trust my friends to be honest with me,'* I thought. "We were trying to look after you, trying to protect you. No one thought it would get serious and that you'd—"

"What? Fall in love with her? Have my heart broken when she died?" Diane flinched at those words. "Have a nervous breakdown because of it?"

"No, of course not, Nicky! We just didn't think it would end like this. There was never a right time to tell you. We were all just having fun before, you know." She hesitated. "We lost her."

"You wouldn't have listened anyway, Nicky," added Spex, shaking his head as if to convince himself. "I've known ya since Class 3 at primary school and I know what yer like. You'd never change yer mind and listen to sense. Soz, but it's true."

Paul Baxter came over with Spanish holding his shoulder and his arm in a bouncer's restraint. I could see Jonesy stiffen and clench his hands, but all three of them were well beyond any violence by now.

"I tried to get her to break it off with McElroy, Nicky, but she told me to stay out of it. She did love you, despite what you might think. I really tried; I'm sorry." He paused. "Anyway, we need to find out about Neville."

"It's fine, Paul. Wasn't your fault. And you're right, we need to find out if Neville's alright."

'The two-timing cow,' I thought, *'hiding behind her religion while she was going behind my back to have some with Paul McElroy. Paul McElroy, of all people! Wonder what else she lied about. Bet that George Austin story was make-believe as well, just to make her seem more interesting or spiritual or something.*

She was always saying not to fool yourself. All of that confusing stuff she ever said at the Troc and in London, what was all that about? Jon was right; she was just stringing me along. Did she really street-fight to protect me, or just to protect herself? It was crap, the whole lot of it.'

"I don't think I'll ever understand her," I continued, half to myself, carrying on with that thought. "Was she Odile or Odette with me?"

"Ya what now?"

"It doesn't matter." I sighed. "It really doesn't matter anymore." Drillbit would have got the reference, but Drillbit wasn't there with us.

Ratty and Spanish had been silent up to now, watching the drama play out in front of them.

"I'm away to the hospital," said Ratty. "But don't be too hard on yer friends, Nick. They—we'll—stick by ya and go the tough way with ya."

"You sound like Ma McElroy."

"Ha! No chance, man," responded Mr Spanish. "She hard like nails. I tell you this for nothin', Nicky. Just three kindsa people in dis world; the bad ones, the ones ya obey, or the people ya need to protect, people like you and Neville. Richard here's got ya back, man, don' forget that."

"Ma McElroy's a bad one, I guess."

"Nah, Nicky, you listenin' man? She ya need to obey."

"You were right, Dad. She was no good after all," I said early the next morning, after the police had been with the news.

I had let myself in late last night, because my father had finally decided I was responsible enough to have a key to the house. He was now in his dressing gown looking bleary eyed, but relieved that the police had not come to arrest me or to ask me questions.

We were in the kitchen, the dullness of the 40-watt light bulb making me feel that we were sitting in a grey box filled with silty water. Jon had come in with the Five-Oh and told me the encouraging news about Neville. My father had looked bewildered.

"Where were you last night, *Kolya*? What has happened? We were worried. I was worried."

"You're always worried, Dad. I'm sorry, but there is a good reason—stop me if you've heard this one before—something bad happened, to Neville this time. The police came, he's ended up in hospital, but everything is alright."

"He is alright?"

"Yes, it was his epilepsy. He had a really bad seizure. The doctors are looking after him."

"I always like him. He is most sensible one of your friends."

"Yes, I think you're right. Angela said that he should go to art college."

"Hmm, yes," said my father nodding, coming to some sort of decision. "You think he is talented?"

"Well, I don't know. Angela thought that he should get a portfolio together. He does good caricatures if that counts for anything."

"But you think she is no good even so? Even if you think she is right and has good opinions?"

"It's like you said, sometimes it just becomes too difficult. There's that attraction, but it's not enough and everybody ends up getting hurt. She was not that nice, but I think she really wanted to be and she really tried with me."

"And I think, *Kolya*, you wanted her to be something she could never be. It was impossible to be your perfect girlfriend." He said this kindly and without malice. It was the truth, direct and unadorned. "It was always what you wanted and need, and never anything about what she need."

"Oh. What did she need, then?"

"Ah, who knows now? She did not know it herself, maybe. A nice boy to make her feel nice, but also one who fights for her against that father? But I only guess."

My dad had seen to the heart of the matter and had told me some form of the truth. Nicky Valko and Paul McElroy, the two of us complementing the lightness and darkness of whatever Angie had thought were the Odette and Odile in her short life.

Late on Saturday afternoon, just before five o'clock in fact, Johnny Ronson drove up with Lisa McElroy in the twilight. I knew it was them, even from inside the house, because he let rip with the raucous air horn on his car as he was parking.

The notes of *La Cucaracha* split the suburban quiet just before the football results were going to be read on the radio. Neighbours must have been distracted from Sports Report and were forced to put down their football pools in irritation.

"'Ey up there, Nick-Oh. Bearing up?" asked Johnny Ronson, pithy as always.

"You could've just knocked, you know? We even have a doorbell."

"Yeah, but where's the fun in that? Lisa 'ere wants to see ya again."

"Another cosy chat?"

"Don't be cheeky. Might get you into trouble one o' these days."

"Johnny, get out," said McElroy. "Nicky, sit up front wi' me."

"Alright, alright Lisa. No need to be snippy," grumbled Mr Ronson as he got out of the driver's seat. "You're the boss."

"Nicky," she said. "How are you?"

"Afternoon, Mrs McElroy. Have you heard anything more about Neville Holdsworth?"

"Last I heard they were doing some tests, but he's gonna pull through. He has an irregular heartbeat, but they'll fix it. He needs to have a pacemaker put in, that's what I heard. Johnny'll run you down afterwards if you like?"

"Thank you. Can my dad come with me, please? He'd like to have a chat with Neville as well, I think."

"Well, Nicky." She was getting down to business and the purpose of her visit. She was never one for small talk. "I've got this for you." She got a cassette tape in its plastic box out of her coat pocket. 'Angie's Mix-Tape' was written on the label. "I'd like you to listen to it. It might help a little."

"Oh. What is it?" I asked, but I had already guessed what was recorded on it. Apprehension fluttered in my chest like the brown and orange butterflies from Angela's dream.

"Angela kept a diary in hospital, close to the end. She recorded it on this tape. Paul's listened to it all. She talks about her dad abusing her, she talks about her mam doing nowt to stop it, how she hated them both; she talks about you and your friends. And our Paul, of course. How much she loved you all. I, well." There were tears in her eyes as she looked over at me. "I couldn't…I didn't listen to it all."

I had no answer to give her, and I shook my head, my attention fixed on the tape deck while Ma McElroy slotted the cassette into it.

"I won't play it if you don't want to, Nicky." She took my hand in hers. "But I'll sit here with you, if you like, and we can listen together."

"Yes, I'd like that. I'd like that very much." We sat in silence for a few moments. "Did she give it to Paul—your Paul, that is—to listen to first? He visited her in hospital?"

"Yes, near the end. That's why he did what he did. He's such a good lad. He wanted you to listen to it too, but I didn't think it was right that Angela should blurt out them secrets to you."

"Might've been kinder if she had."

"If I've done wrong by you, Nicky, I'm truly sorry. I'm sorry I had to keep it from yer. But I had to give Paul his chance to right some wrongs. I thought I was doing the right thing."

Ma McElroy pressed the play button, and I heard Angie's voice again, quiet with a breathy hesitancy, but unmistakably hers with that familiar rise-and-fall cadence and her posh diction.

I've never been as sad as I am now. All I want to do anymore is wait for death. They're saying it won't be long and I hope I'm going to a happier place. Maybe then I won't feel this pain and I can finally exist without feeling so, so sad.

"Oh, God," I whispered and shut my eyes. The playback clunked, then hissed, and Angie began a new diary entry.

Nicky, Paul, gang; maybe you won't understand, but I did what was right. You know me; free spirit to the last. Thank you for all of the wonderful times we spent together. Thank you for letting me be part of the gang. Yours too, Paul. It meant more to me than I can say, you respected me and listened to me and let me make my own decisions. I know it was hard sometimes, especially for you Paul. People come and go in our lives, people change and lose the good they had, but you were always there for me; you were my true family.

Another hiss-clunk-hiss on the tape. Angela started recording on the tape again, thirteen or so weeks in the past.

Nicky and Paul; you need to let go of me. You both need to move on. Please do this for me. If you loved me at all, don't waste those feelings and make them count! Build on those feelings because, if you do, I'll always be with you a little bit as well. Even afterwards, when I'm not there with you. When God takes me by the hand and leads me to another garden. That way, I know that I'll be happy again.

I always loved you, daft lad. I'm sorry for everything, how it's all turned out. It could have been so good, the two of us.

I love you. I love you so much.

Chapter 10
What Was I Thinking?

One cold afternoon in the middle of December, the Ships drifted into the skies, unnoticed, until they were overhead. Each had a long and straight white fuselage ending in bulbous nacelles for engines and weapons. There was a whole fleet of them parked in the sky until the edge of the horizon.

It was utterly disconcerting to see such vast, manufactured artefacts hanging like that above my head. But, in this reality, these shapes were not my Ships; they were just massive sky-racks of lenticular clouds stacking one on the other like pancakes. I stood outside, filled with an over-whelming yearning for it all to be true, pushing down on me like a heavy weight across my chest.

I so much yearned for it to be true, hoping that, by the sheer strength of my will and my imagination, it would be enough to recreate that reality again. I wanted the Ships to have survived and for one of them to rescue me from this terrible, defeated reality overrun by the Imposters.

It was an important truth, because none of us—not my friends, not my parents, not even my psychiatrist—seemed to recognise our true identity. And even more amazing to me, we had forgotten that we did not even know our true identity. I suppose that this made everybody's existence bearable, because Angela was right about one thing; nothing fools you better than the lies you tell yourself.

The Ships passed serenely overhead and there was no rescue because, as I knew all along, I was really an Imposter, and I was just looking at clouds in this reality. I was consigned to a life sentence in this place and there was no hope for me. I had to live the best life I could, even if it was without her.

'It would never have worked out anyway,' I thought to myself. *'She had too much of a burden to bear and I couldn't have helped her. I tried to be what she needed but I would never have replaced him. What sort of terrible bond of*

intimacy is there between an abuser and his victim? In the end, did she grow to need, even crave, that attention from him? That sweet, beautiful, complicated, damaged, tragic girl.'

Listing in my mind the feelings I'd had about her in the past year, as if by labelling them, I could begin to make sense of them. I wiped away my tears, and then went indoors to ask my dad to come out to look at the other-worldly clouds shaped like spacecraft. He looked at me strangely for a few moments, but then came out with me into the garden.

I don't suppose I ever really made sense of those feelings from the long, sad events of that year. They became less imminent and intense as the months went by, then further muted by the passing of years. Those feelings became overlaid like bedrock might be by new layers of experience, but they were still underneath and not so deeply buried.

It didn't take a lot of digging to start unearthing the past. I visited Angela's grave occasionally, even before Wilkinson had been put away. I hated the thought of her being alone in that graveyard, under the horse chestnut trees that would probably outlast us all. The Day-Glo teddy bear was by the headstone for a few months until it faded from the sun and weather.

I usually brought some flowers, and in later years, I tried to visit on 26th July if I was back in town. I stayed in touch with the gang over the years; they all knew the significance of that date. When they could, they came with me to her grave. Spex and Diane brought the usual small bottle of whiskey to toast her memory and to remember the good times, what few there were from that year.

"*Yehi zichra baruch,*" Spex would say. "May her memory be a blessing. Even though she didn't touch the stuff, this is to Angela's memory." And he would pour some of the spirit on the mound of grass.

Diane would clean her friend's headstone, tidy the grass of any weeds, and arrange the flowers. Some of them may have been from Mrs Wilkinson, but I never looked at the little notes or cards, unwilling to learn that some might be from her ex-husband or Paul McElroy.

I never knew Mrs Wilkinson's first name, and in later years, I didn't know whether she went back to using her maiden name or if she got remarried. I always wondered whether she had ever known that her husband was abusing her daughter and if she had known, why had she ignored it. I would have asked her why she had stayed silent.

If she had known, did she have to pretend that she didn't, even to herself? *'Nothing fools you better than the lies you tell yourself.'* In the end, when it all came out, she must have fled the place with feelings of grief and horror and shame. Perhaps I understood better than most how self-delusion could unravel and I felt profoundly sorry for her.

I always wondered if she been able to regain any kind of happiness in her life over the intervening years. If she had, perhaps I too could move on and find happiness as well. My mum and dad had separated by now as well, trying to find happiness in their own peculiar ways. I hadn't been surprised.

"Nick? Are you going to say a few words, then?" asked Paul quietly. He had been able to make it this year. They called me Nick nowadays because I was all grown up. I had just finished pre-clinical at Med School and was starting as a House Officer at a Nottingham hospital in exactly a week's time.

I had travelled up for the day because it was important for me to mark this new transition in my life and to remember how the past had got me here. I understood why Hodgkin's lymphoma could have been misdiagnosed as glandular fever because the histopathology was quite similar. A regional hospital in Northern England, back then, would not have had the expertise or experience to make an early diagnosis. My psychiatrist with the peg teeth, surprisingly, was also an influence. She called what I had a particular form of delusional misidentification syndrome, but the truth was that it was subversion by the Imposters.

I gave her full marks for trying, though. She never wrote me up as the index case of Valko's syndrome. I suppose that she never came across another precocious and annoying kid with quite the same combination of an intense internalised personal narrative and an unhealthily florid imagination.

"Oh no, you're alright, Paul. I'm not one for speeches, you know that. I think that I'll just stand here quietly for a bit."

"You're the speechifier, Paul. Let Nick deal with it his own way." Spex was having a bit of a dig at Paul because he was a trainee lawyer. Spex had finished an engineering apprenticeship and was rising through the ranks of a local packaging factory. He had thought of a handy new way to fold cardboard sheets into boxes, which, the way he told it, was quite interesting in a boring sort of way. Diane was starting teacher training in September.

"No, it's alright, Paul. Spex, I mean," I added. I was forgetting about the usual confusion about first names because Spex was looking like a Paul Ronson today. "It's been five years."

"Aye, we know, Nick. That's why we're here. It's right to remember them that have passed on. She was our friend as well," said Spex, glancing over at Diane.

"I still think about her nearly every day, Nick."

"I know. I do as well."

"I think about stuff that Angela would like, songs she'd listen to, bands she'd like."

"Bet she'd be into The Sisters of Mercy. She'd like Goth, all intense and maungy. She'd be a Sister for sure, wearing leather and eyeliner."

"Nah, she'd be a Depeche Mode fan."

"She'd have to get rid of that perm and bleach her hair. Wear some of them chains."

"Oh yeah! Angela's bloody perm! I always hated it. She used to highlight it and everything. Made her look like a poodle."

"It never suited her. She should have got shut of it well before, well, you know. Before."

"I liked her perm," I said. "It was trendy."

"Yeah, like, back in 1965 or whenever," sniggered Paul.

"Honestly! How old are you two?" said Diane to Paul and Spex. "Stop being so horrible and have a bit of respect. Nick's said he wants to be quiet, so just button it."

"Yeah, yeah, sorry; we know. *De mortuis—*"

"Heard it all before. Stop showing off," said Diane in response.

"It was still a bad perm," whispered Paul to Spex.

***

After that visit to Angela's graveside, it raised up the past in my mind and I dreamed about the Ships later that night. It was about events years in the future. The Ships came to rescue the last of the humans—those they knew not to have been subverted—from a failing planet. The Imposters may have been defeated but they had still doomed Earth by triggering a nuclear war.

It was a limited exchange of warheads—a nuclear error, the Ships called it—but the soot from the smouldering cities wrapped around the world and started a nuclear winter. It had begun the slow death of a new Ice Age. Crops would grow thin and fail. Snow would cover fields, roads, and buildings.

Layer upon layer, it would smother the influence of humanity until everything was smoothed out and purified into a single, blank, narrative. This was the final, fatal solipsism of the Imposters, imposed on the entire planet, until our individual stories were all subverted to serve their greater cause. The Imposters started and won the Third World War in an afternoon. The lucky few of us in the big cities would soon be dead. But the coming Ice Age would then cause the deaths of untold millions and would last centuries.

Human civilisation was over, and the Ships were evacuating the last few of their combatants who were still alive. *'How can the Ships be powerless against such evil?'* I asked myself. *'They're running away from the fight.'*

I crossed the wormhole bridge onto the surface of a huge ring-shaped space habitat that was in orbit around Earth. It was a familiar idea to me, growing up in the '70s, because this was going to be our future when we were adults; the optimism of technological advance bringing about everyday miracles.

In just a few years' time, blue-and-green habitats would wheel among the stars above Earth. Everybody would work together peacefully towards a common goal; the Sun would provide unlimited solar power; war and hunger would be banished.

Then the Imposters subverted that future by telling everybody how much it would cost, how much everybody hated each other, and that nobody could afford it anyway. However, drawing together the time-lines from some past nexus, the Ships had solved those minor issues and had guided humanity into this dazzling future. Or, at least, what was left of humanity after the end of the Third World War.

The Ring exceeded anything that I thought even the Ships could manufacture, dwarfing every one of their artefacts in their secret caves under the lunar highlands. The Ring, edge-to-edge, was miles across, as far as I could judge, almost as large as a world.

The horizon on either side of me looked normal, air shading the distance away into a blue haze. But as I looked in front of me, the horizon crept upwards into a bow, then into an arc that stretched away and ascended into the blue sky in front of me. Squares of fields, stretches of curved lakes, trees—cypresses and pines—and low white buildings receded away and then above me.

I could see mottling of land and sea underneath racks of clouds on the surface of the Ring when I looked upwards. Directly above my head was a blinding point of warm, white light. The glare and the haze of the atmosphere hid the other side of the Ring. The view of the Ring rearing up in front of me was utterly unnerving and made me queasy from the vertigo.

'Ey up, Nick, love. Welcome to the Ring. We're gonna suggest you keep lookin' at the ground until you're used to the view, said a calm Ship voice, the sound no doubt projected to my position from somewhere nearby. It was the orbital ring talking to me, with a Yorkshire accent that sounded like Johnny Ronson of all people. '*My stupid lucid dreams,*' I remember thinking in the dream.

"Hello there, Ring, I suppose it is. What's with the comedy accent? I thought that it was all Received Pronunciation with you lot?"

Well, usually it is, said the Ring, briefly reverting to the usual accent. *But we all thought that a familiar voice from home would help get you on your feet, like.*

"Why? I'm moving already, down to Nottingham. I'm happy to be moving on. Or at least, I was moving until you started disrupting my life again. What have you got planned for me this time?" The Ring seemed to be made up of multiple personalities and the resemblance to the Master was not a little unnerving.

You're one of the last arrivals from Earth. Your planet is doomed, so we're suggesting that you come back with us to the Home World, 58 Eridani. It will be a home for you as well, now. We want to give you a new home. You will be moving away and making a fresh start.

"I was doing that anyway, thanks, all on my own. I have plans. Pretty good ones, too."

Yes, we know. But perhaps we can persuade you otherwise.

"Why doesn't that surprise me," I sighed.

The last of the arrivals to the Ring were gathering in one of the white buildings across some fields, close to the wormhole exit corridor. The Ring called it the Village Hall and, as I walked closer, it became clear that a large wooden hut had been constructed on the far side of the building. It looked like a rustic shack compared to the clean lines of the habitat.

Angela was inside the hut, kneeling beside an ornately carved wooden box. She was looking through a pile of books and what looked like perfume bottles in their colourful packaging. As I watched, she took out a bottle of clear spirit in which floated lots of tiny golden flakes.

"Angela."

"Oh, Nikolai!" (She had never called me that name, in all the time that we had been together.) "I'm so glad you're here. Ring said that you would be coming," as if I'd accepted her invitation to a cocktail party. "Drink?" She proffered the bottle. "We're trying to rescue all the best artefacts from Earth."

"No. No, thanks. 'What are you doing here'?"

"Oh, daft lad! They've got me working. I'm an archivist for all the best that humanity has to offer. Everything on the planet that the Ships can find, anyway. Are you sure you won't?" She tipped the bottle towards me again.

"You know what I mean."

She wrinkled her nose in an all-too-familiar gesture and her lips smiled. I felt the small of my back prickle with apprehension and I had to avoid her glance.

"The Ships and the Ring really can do anything." She chose not to answer my question. I suppose I wouldn't have liked the answer anyway.

She stood up beside the ornate box. She had grown taller, lost the perm and the hint of comfortable chubbiness to her body. Her hair hung down straight brown and long, framing her alabaster face and scarlet lips. I only recognised the quizzical grey eyes that this grown woman now turned towards me. She was beautiful and instantly desirable. I took an involuntary step towards her and then stopped. I knew what was being done to me, but I still wanted to hold and kiss her.

Angela reached out to touch my arm. "Nick, we did what we had to do. We fought back against the Imposters. We've saved what we could. We couldn't have known that it would end like this."

"But it did end like this," I said. "You'll have to find a way to make it right. To save what's left of humanity."

Angela nodded. "I know, Nick. And we will. Together. We'll find a way to make it right together."

"Hmmm, that's interesting. 'Together'," I mused, considering my options, and taking her hand in mine. "I just know that you'll always find a way to save what's left. If it's to your advantage."

For a long moment, we looked at each other and then, finally, something happened. I could say the words that sealed her fate and ended that place outside of everything.

"I'll have to be getting back now, Angie. It's always lovely to see you, but I really can't stay."

'Something happened': I was able to say the symbolic words. The words rose, like a last powerful totem in my own personal mythology, above the landscape of everything else that had gone before. Those words closed the long and unhappy chapter of my life that started in the winter of 1978.

My personal hero narrative is complete, and I now have no more need of it. Why do I need the terrible burden of an overactive imagination in my reality anyway? Since that last time on the Ring habitat, I've never seen Angela again, but I still think about her quite often. I've never listened to Angie's Mix-Tape again, not even to hear her voice, but we like to reminisce about punk rock when the gang meets up.

The music was better back then. After all, it had meant the world to me.